SEAL TEAM SIX: HUNT THE FOX

SEAL TEAM SIX:

HUNT THE FOX

DON MANN
WITH
RALPH PEZZULLO

MULHOLLAND
BOOKS
HODDER

First published in Great Britain in 2015 by Mulholland Books
An imprint of Hodder & Stoughton
An Hachette UK company

First published in paperback in 2016

1

A CIP catalogue record for this title is available from the British Library

Paperback ISBN 978 1 473 60314 1
eBook ISBN 978 1 473 60315 8

Printed and bound by Clays Ltd, St Ives plc

Hodder & Stoughton policy is to use papers that are natural, renewable
and recyclable products and made from wood grown in sustainable forests.
The logging and manufacturing processes are expected to conform
to the environmental regulations of the country of origin.

Hodder & Stoughton Ltd
Carmelite House
50 Victoria Embankment
London EC47 0DZ

www.hodder.co.uk

"Greater love has no one than this: that a man lay down his life for his friends."

—John 15:13

To the brave men and women who have sacrificed so much to protect our freedoms

SEAL TEAM SIX: HUNT THE FOX

CHAPTER ONE

Either I conquer Istanbul, or Istanbul conquers me.
—Fatih Sultan Mehmet

THEY SAT on red-striped sofas in the Meşale Café in the Arasta Bazaar, just steps from Istanbul's majestic Blue Mosque. Hundreds, men mostly, were shuffling out after morning prayers in groups of twos and threes, some whispering to one another, others lost in thought.

The crowd seemed dense and foreign to Crocker as he looked out the horizontal window and then across the table at the young CIA operative who called himself Jared. Under thirty, raised in Oregon, Jared had a father who worked in the logging industry. Minus the foot-long beard he could pass for a frat member at a midwestern university. Except, as far as Crocker knew, most U.S. grad students didn't speak fluent Arabic, Urdu, and Persian. Nor had they spent the past two weeks in Syria huddling with leaders of the various anti-Assad rebel groups. According to Jared, the rebel groups were now too numerous to count—a polyglot of Sunnis, jihadists, former members of the Syrian Armed Forces, and young Syrians who hated President Bashar al-Assad and his family. Opposing them were Assad's army and supporters, the Iranians, and the Iranian-backed terrorist group Hezbollah.

Crocker had a hunch that Syria was where he and his men were headed, though he didn't know the how, when, or why. What he did know was that this was their first mission overseas since the op in Mexico last fall that had resulted in all kinds of mayhem and trauma—including serious injuries to several members of his team. He himself had suffered a gunshot wound to his thigh, which had healed very nicely though he experienced tightness around it now.

What he also realized was that Jared's jitteriness was adding to his own feeling of anxiety. Why, he wasn't sure.

When a bell rang at the Hagia Sophia farther up the hill, the sharp sound raised the hairs on the back of his neck.

"Fascinating city," Jared announced.

"Yeah." Crocker had been intrigued by it since he'd seen *From Russia with Love*, his favorite Bond movie, at eight years old. Since his arrival yesterday morning, he had noticed how seamlessly past and present mingled here. Istanbul wasn't a museum like, say, Florence. It was an active city bustling with tourists, merchants, peddlers, students, lovers, Islamic fundamentalists, secularist libertarians, anarchists, historians, and dreamers.

It had been at the nexus of a massive amount of world history. Nearby were streets and alleys where Romans, Byzantines, and Ottomans had marched, where the blood of Armenians, Greeks, Georgians, and Gypsies had flowed. It was Europe's largest city at fifteen million, twice the size of London, and technically the only metropolitan area to span two continents, Europe and Asia.

As Jared smoked, his eyes scanned the faces in the café—mostly tourists and middle-aged men. Then he checked his cell phone and bit his nails. Frowning at the bitter taste of the black tea, he announced, "War is fucking hell, Crocker. Make no mistake about that."

"I don't." Crocker shook his head and smoothed his salt-and-pepper mustache. Last night after a dinner of grilled sardines and *zeytinyağli dolma* (grape leaves stuffed with rice) Jared had shown him photos he had taken in Aleppo—blocks upon blocks of middle-class apartments, schools, and stores reduced to rubble, burnt-out cars and buses, refuse piled in the broken streets.

Crocker had followed news of the Syrian civil war like other Americans, mostly on CNN. But what seemed distant and abstract to most people was more real to him. He had the experience to fill in the smells of death, the feelings of hopelessness and dislocation. He'd seen firsthand other societies coming apart at the seams in places like Bosnia, Somalia, and Iraq. What war did to the psyches of children, he could only imagine.

"First time I went in was the summer of 2012," Jared said with a bitter edge in his voice. "Since then I've watched civilian deaths go from five to over a hundred thousand and the number of refugees rocket into the millions. It's appalling."

What he liked about Jared was that the kid had balls. He also had a conscience. You saw a wrong or a problem, and you tried to do what you could to help solve it. He also understood that being in a war zone added a special incandescence to life that you couldn't find anywhere else.

The trick was to get close enough to feel the sparkle, but not come back brain-dead or worse.

"It haunts me constantly," Jared continued. "We could have done

5

something to stop it back in 2012, but we sat on our hands for political reasons."

"Sad," said Crocker. He'd heard about the various UN diplomatic efforts to put pressure on the Assad regime to either step down or reach some kind of settlement. None of them had been successful. Didn't people in the administration know that a strongman like Assad had to be backed into a corner and have a gun pointed at his head before he conceded? Sometimes Crocker wondered whether the people who made foreign policy were so removed from on-the-ground experience that they didn't understand the nuts and bolts of human psychology—especially of people in power.

"The truth is that nobody really cares about what happens there," Jared continued, "because there's no possible upside financially."

"You mean Syria has no oil like Libya and Iraq."

Jared leaned on the little table and nodded. "Yeah."

Crocker didn't feel qualified to judge.

"Don't you feel sometimes that we're really mercenaries hired to protect the interests of Wall Street and the corporations?" Jared continued. "Like they're the ones really calling the shots?"

"Maybe."

"And they don't give a shit about the plight of people in a place like Syria, normal families?"

"Could be," Crocker answered. "But I can't think like that and do my job." It was the main reason he avoided politics, which was a messy, cynical business as far as he was concerned and rarely resulted in good solutions to real problems. He remained, in the end, a practical-minded man who focused on the specific missions he had to perform.

Maybe, as his wife claimed, it resulted in his not seeing the bigger picture.

"Hey, you want a real drink?" Jared asked, leaning forward on the cushioned seat. "I could use a scotch."

"You're not gonna get one here," Crocker responded, pointing to the sign in English, French, and Arabic on the wall behind them: "Our apologies. No alcohol served because of the proximity of the mosque."

"Maybe we can order a narghile and ask the waiter to mix in some hashish," he said with a mischievous grin.

Crocker laughed. "I thought you guys weren't allowed to smoke that stuff," he responded, reaching for the Turkish coffee, which was sweet and thick on his tongue.

"You're right. Yeah. I'd have to bribe the polygraph dude. Ha ha. Won't be the first time." Jared was referring to the Agency practice of periodically and unexpectedly administering lie detector tests to its case and ops officers. The CIA did this to keep tabs on questionable sexual liaisons, the money the officers handled, and their use of illegal drugs.

As the leader of Black Cell, which was a special unit of SEAL Team Six (a.k.a. DEVGRU) assigned to the CIA, Crocker was subject to Agency protocol himself. The last time he'd been polygraphed, which was three weeks ago, he'd been questioned about breaking into an apartment in Fairfax, Virginia, which he didn't deny. The circumstances were complicated and involved a woman who was squeezing money out of his elderly father. Despite the fact that he'd caught her smoking meth with a Fairfax County police officer, he knew he'd probably be facing charges when he returned to the States.

Maybe the judge would cut him some slack because of what he did for a living. Maybe he wouldn't. Crocker wasn't going to worry about it now.

"They've got dervishes here at night," Jared announced as he stubbed out his cigarette and checked his cell again.

"What'd you say?" Crocker asked, sensing that they were being watched.

"You know, the dudes in the white peaked caps who spin. I was watching 'em one night when I met this cute Turkish girl named Zeliha. Real warm, with toffee-colored eyes. She explained the meaning of the whole ritual to me." His voice trailed off.

"Yeah?"

"Great girl. I wanted to keep seeing her, but I had to disappear for two weeks for work. When I got back, I found out she had taken up with an old boyfriend she'd told me she wasn't crazy about."

"Sounds complicated." It reminded Crocker of his own problems with women, including his wife, Holly, who had threatened to leave him if he went overseas again.

Here he was.

She wanted him around, but she needed space. She wanted stability, until she got bored and craved adventure. She wanted a family that included Crocker's daughter from his first marriage, but now she was asking for more independence.

He loved her completely and knew that she'd been through hell—including almost being killed by cartel hit men and losing everything when they had torched their home. He and she had even attended several sessions of marriage and grief counseling together, which he'd found somewhat helpful. He wasn't sure that she had, though, he thought, as he scanned the café again.

Jared's burner cell phone pinged. He read the coded message and said, "That's us."

"When?"

"A-SAP."

"Where are we meeting?" Crocker asked.

"The Sultanhan Hotel. Room 732. It's about a seven-minute cab ride from here, or a fifteen-minute walk."

"If we have time, let's hump it. I could use the exercise."

"You got it, friend," Jared answered. "I'll exit first. I'm gonna walk down to Torun, turn right, continue to the opposite corner, cross the street, buy a magazine at the newsstand, and turn back. Watch my back and let me know if I'm being followed. I'll meet you on the corner of Torun Sokak and Mehmet Ağa."

He was proposing that they run a routine SDR (surveillance detection route), which was standard in clandestine operations on foreign soil. The kid wasn't sloppy. Crocker liked that.

"Torun Sokak and Mehmet," he repeated. "Copy."

"Torun's that narrow, busy street that runs parallel to the Kabasakal."

"I remember. They tell you who we're going to meet at the hotel?" asked Crocker.

"I'll fill you in on the people as we walk. You ready?"

"Yeah. You go ahead. I'll pay the check."

Jared stood, smiled quickly, and hurried off. He was slight and about five nine with an awkward bounce in his step, the result of an injury sustained from an IED attack near the Afghan-Pakistani border. According to what Crocker had heard, he had been through a lot. Assignments in Afghanistan, Pakistan, and Syria, one after the other. A nervous breakdown after a rough op in Pakistan. The pressures on clandestine officers like Jared were intense.

Crocker's eyes followed him through the windows down the pedestrian walkway in front of the bazaar to the corner. He tossed sixty Turkish liras on the table, exited onto the pedestrian Kabasakal, and saw Jared standing on the corner lighting a cigarette.

Nothing unusual so far. Catching sight of Crocker, he zipped up his blue jacket, which was their prearranged signal that all was clear. Then he hung a right.

Both he and Jared were devoid of marks—in other words, anything that might cause them to stand out in a crowd, like long hair, jewelry, or unusual facial hair. With his beard, Jared could easily pass for a Turkish student on his way to the nearby Istanbul International University, and Crocker looked like a very fit tourist—black pants, black polo, black jacket, black Nikes.

The streets and alleys were jammed with people of all ages and ethnicities, merging and parting like a stream.

As Jared disappeared past the far end of the bazaar, two young men emerged from a jewelry stall and followed him. One of them carried a black motorcycle helmet under his arm. He looked determined and focused.

"Trouble," Crocker muttered under his breath, then reached for his burner cell and texted *87, which meant "surveillance detected." He thought he had seen one of the young men—the one not carrying the helmet; short and wiry with the pillar of dark curly hair—pass through the café when he and Jared were there.

Had Jared expected this? He didn't know.

Aware that unfriendly eyes might be watching him, too, Crocker pushed through a group of German tourists to the opening of the bazaar near the perpendicular street, Mehmet Ağa, and turned right. The minarets of the Blue Mosque glistened beyond his shoulder. No way to know if this was routine surveillance by Turkish MiT (their intelligence service) or something more ominous. Istanbul was considered a hot site—active with foreign agents of various affiliations.

He paused among shoppers, worshippers, and tourists to scan the crowd for Jared, who wore a white oxford shirt and a blue zip-up jacket, and to check in the reflection of the glass entrance to a luggage shop to see if anyone was following him. A one-eyed man pushed in front of him, offering to sell cigarettes.

Crocker shook his head, remembering not to make eye contact with a possible pursuer.

"American and French brands, sir. Very gud price."

"No thanks."

As Crocker juked around him, he heard a screech of tires from the direction of Torun Sokak, the shout of a driver, followed by a woman's shrill shout. A burst of pigeons tore into the air. His senses focused even tighter on sounds and movement.

What was that?

Considered a major thoroughfare, Torun Sokak consisted of two narrow lanes, both of which were clogged with traffic. Cars were honking. Drivers and pedestrians were hurrying away from the middle of the street and frantically dialing their cell phones. He caught a glimpse of someone crossing between the cars.

Where's Jared?

Crocker continued right along the constricted sidewalk to where a group had gathered. A man shouted something in Arabic. An older man pointed at a gray van stopped along the curb. He turned.

Through the open side door he saw two men grappling inside. One of them wore a blue jacket. Jared! He quickly intuited that someone had pushed the young CIA officer into the open door of the van to try to abduct him, and he was resisting.

Without calling for help, Crocker slammed into action. Ducking inside the van, he saw a huge man with a black beard and a spider tattoo on his neck squeezing Jared in a headlock, while a man in the driver's seat tried to hold something over his mouth. Without saying a word Crocker rammed his fist into the back of the big man's neck, causing him to grunt and gasp for breath. He punched the man again in the face, and this time the man let go of Jared, who scrambled into the front seat and swung at the driver.

Meanwhile, the big dude turned to reach for a backpack on the metal floor of the van. Fearing that he was about to detonate an explosive device, Crocker grabbed a fistful of his hair, planted his knee in the small of the man's back, and ripped back his right arm until it popped out of the shoulder socket and the man screamed bloody murder.

The noise filled the tight, hot space and hurt Crocker's ears. He silenced him with a swift forearm to the temple, which sent the assailant sprawling over the floor and rendered him unconscious, his eyes staring at the ceiling. Taking two hard, quick breaths, he saw Jared with blood streaming down his face from a cut on his forehead. Heads bleed a lot. As a corpsman, he knew that.

Enraged that the attackers had drawn blood, he elbowed the driver hard in the Adam's apple and heard a crack. The man fell back against the passenger-side door with a bang.

As he leaned over the big man to check to see whether he was armed and Jared took a moment to wipe the blood away from his eyes, the driver reached into the glove compartment.

Crocker saw the glint of metal out of the corner of his eye.

"Weapon!" he shouted, reaching for the driver's arm. Two quick shots went off before Crocker grabbed hold of the man's wrist and slammed it hard against the dashboard three times until the pistol dislodged and slid to the floor.

Aware that Jared had been hit and was struggling to open the driver's door, he slammed the driver's head against the passenger-side window until he stopped moving. Blood covered Crocker's hands.

"Jared, wait!"

The kid was already out. Part of the fight-or-flight response. People were screaming and seeking cover. Almost simultaneously, Crocker heard a screech of tires and the sound of a vehicle slamming into another. Glass rattled across asphalt.

"Hey, Jared!"

A gasp from the onlookers, followed by a moment of silence that gave him a chill as he slid across the front seat and out the driver's-side door.

What the hell had happened?

He quickly took it all in. On the opposite sidewalk he saw a crowd of people, one of whom was shouting into a cell phone. He followed their eyes to the front of a blue-and-yellow bus stopped in front of him. Some were pointing.

Why isn't it moving?

Hurrying around the side of the bus, he spotted a figure lying on the ground. Legs first, then a torso in a pool of dark blood, then a face. Jared's light-brown eyes were open, a wry smile tugging at the corners of his mouth, but he wasn't moving, because the back of his head had been crushed. Brain matter spread onto the pavement.

Fuck! Oh, fuck….

Crocker knelt and checked his pulse. None. Around him onlookers muttered and prayed. He pulled off his black jacket and was using it to cover Jared's head when he heard a motorcycle start up across the street. The sound reverberated up his spine like an alarm.

Time to move!

Someone was pushing through the crowd behind him.

He didn't stop to look at who it was or consider where he was going to go. There was nothing he could do for Jared now. He stepped over his body, ran along the far side of the stalled bus with his head down, crossed at its rear through the traffic, and reentered the crowded bazaar.

Blood pounding in his temples, adrenaline surging, he had no time to stop and text an alert to Istanbul Station. Nor did he know the city well. Nor was he armed.

He had to exit the area, lose the assassination team, or kidnappers, or whoever the fuck they were.

Running for his life, he hurried through the bazaar. Grabbing a white cap with a red Turkish crescent and star embroidered on the crown from one of the stalls, he handed a fifty-lira bill to the boy manning it and continued on instinct honed through years of training.

Keep moving. Change your profile. Lose them. Contact Istanbul Station.

From the bazaar, he reentered the Meşale Café and strode directly to the men's bathroom. Blood covered his right hand and wrist. He washed it off and removed his black polo, exposing the white crewneck T-shirt underneath. Stuffed the polo in the trash, fixed the cap on his head backward, took a deep breath, and exited through the kitchen.

The space was tight and crowded with boxes and employees. A man in a white apron was smoking.

"Hey. Ne yapıyorsunuz?" the man shouted.

"Tourist. No problem."

"Yes, problem!"

He pushed through a greasy screen door to an alley. His heart beating fast, he ducked his head, turned right, and hurried back onto Kabasakal and into the open-air parking lot at the back of the mosque. There was more space here. He paused to take a look around and think.

Nothing but tourists and locals going about their business. Hearing a motorcycle engine behind him, he hopped a cement planter and entered a little shop that sold scarves, tourist mementos, and pottery. Didn't catch the name.

He had to try to get his bearings and use his burner cell to alert the Station. Jared was dead; he was on the run, possibly being pursued by unidentified assassins.

He peered out the front window looking for pursuers. An attractive middle-aged woman approached from his right, bringing with her the scent of oranges. Thick, dark-brown hair parted in the middle, a full-lipped smile.

"Can I help you, sir?" she asked softly.

"Uh, yes. I'm looking for a scarf for my wife." His heart jumped in his chest. He was sweating through the brim of his hat.

"Okay. Silk, cotton, or pashmina?"

"Pashmina, I think."

He struggled to appear normal, but the woman could see his chest heaving and sweat dripping down his neck.

"Are you okay, sir? Are you feeling all right?"

"I'm fine."

"Some water, maybe. Would you like a cup of water?"

She called to someone in back. Past the display in the front window, he spied a young man wearing a black motorcycle helmet parking his bike across the street near the mosque. He looked closer. Another young man—the one with the curly black pompadour—ran up to the motorcycle man and pointed vehemently toward the shop.

Fuck.

As they jogged across the street, Crocker turned to the woman, who was carrying a plastic cup of water. He grabbed her by the shoulders, causing the liquid to spill, and said, "You need to leave, immediately. You hear me? It's an emergency!"

The shopkeeper's expression quickly changed from concern to alarm. "What?" her eyes practically popping out of their sockets. "I don't understand. I—"

Crocker pointed to a sleepy young woman behind the cash register counter. In a stern voice he said, "Take her with you and leave by the back. It's *important.*"

"Who are you? What are you talking about?"

Crocker squeezed the woman's shoulders and said, "Something bad is about to happen. I need you to go out the back, now!"

"But—"

He turned her toward the exit, pushed her, and barked, *"Go!"*

The woman jumped back, spilling the rest of the water over her blouse, and glared at him, hands on hips. She was about to say something when a skinny man in jeans and a black motorcycle jacket and carrying a helmet burst through the door. Crocker spun to face him, saw the dark-haired man reach for something in his pocket with his free hand, and in one continuous motion raised his right leg and kicked him in the chest. The man grunted, flew into a display shelf of ceramic jars and plates, and as his back hit it, let go of the helmet, which smashed into the counter.

The shopkeeper screamed. She and her assistant scrambled away. Crocker grabbed the kid by the front of his jacket, reached down with his free hand and grabbed the helmet, and used it to smash him in the mouth. One, two, three times. Blood, teeth, and saliva flew everywhere. The man grunted.

That's for Jared!

He smashed him one last time to be sure he was out and was about to relieve him of whatever he was carrying in his pocket when the second man approached the front door, pistol drawn. Looked like a

Russian-made APB—the silenced version of an APS. Nickel-plated and nasty. He had his finger on the trigger.

Crocker reacted instinctively, pushing a display of pink pashminas onto him and diving at the young man's ankles. A bullet tore through the cascading scarves and grazed Crocker's back.

Fuck!

A split second later, Crocker's shoulder hit the man's legs two inches above his ankles—just like his high school football coach had taught him—and the man fell backward and crashed back-first through the glass door. His head hit the pavement hard.

Cr-ack.

Split like a fucking coconut; his hair still perfectly in place. Crocker saw the young man's pained expression and a trickle of blood. Neither attacker was moving.

He was already pulling himself up, looking to see if anyone else was coming, ignoring the shards of glass embedded in his forearm, the pain from his back, and the alarmed shouts of passersby and the proprietress in back.

Slipping on the wet floor, he quickly rifled through the first man's pockets. A folding knife, a chambered Glock 9mm, a thin leather wallet with 200 liras inside, the ignition key for a Kawasaki Ninja Sport. No license, no ID, no picture of his family or girlfriend.

A trained professional on a mission.

He pocketed the key, then removed the man's motorcycle jacket and pulled it over his bloody white T-shirt as best he could, ignoring the pain in the middle of his back. He slipped on the mess of blood, glass, and water, caught himself, and exited out the front door, stepping over the body. He strode as purposefully as he could past several stunned onlookers, mounted the bike, started the engine, put it in gear, cranked back the throttle, and rode to the end of Kabasakal with the motor screaming. Almost hitting a van head-on, he turned right, ignoring a policeman blowing a whistle somewhere behind him and a siren in the distance. People were pointing.

There was no good reason to stick around. The shopkeeper would call the police. The two punks would be hauled away to either a hospital or a morgue. A morgue, he hoped.

Bystanders would report that their target had been a middle-aged man wearing a white hat. Looked European. All this information would be passed on to the National Intelligence Organization, which would try to fit the pieces together. The newspapers would write their stories, which might or might not be accurate. Life would march on. It always did. The trick was to strike quickly and disappear.

Poor Jared. Nice kid. His poor family.

Jared had barely mentioned them, except that his father was in the lumber industry and he'd grown up in Oregon. Beautiful wild country, Crocker remembered as he wove through the midmorning traffic, adrenaline pushing him, a voice in his head demanding, *Who the fuck were those guys? In broad daylight, no less.*

Why? What did Jared know? Or who did he know? Fuck!

The front glass on his burner cell phone had shattered, but the device still seemed to work. At least he hoped it did as he punched the emergency number at Istanbul Station and waited for the phone to ring.

Pick up! Hurry!

A woman's steely voice answered, "Yes?"

"This is five-seven-seven," he shouted over the Kawasaki's roar. "I was just attacked and need directions to the Sultanhan Hotel."

"Where are you?" she asked.

"Downtown Istanbul. I'm headed northeast on Torun."

"Surveillance?"

"Previously, yes. But not anymore as far as I can tell."

"You in a vehicle or on foot?"

"I'm riding a motorcycle."

"Okay. Continue on Torun to Akbiyik, which turns into Kapi-ağasi, then Kadirga Limani. Take a right onto Piyer Loti. When you pass Peykhane Caddesi, look for the Sultanhan Hotel on the left. You got that?"

"I think so. How far away is it?"

"Seven minutes, eight, depending on traffic."

"Someone was with me. Someone who called himself Jared."

"Jared?" the woman replied.

"Jared. He's dead."

"Oh…"

All the doubts, second-guessing, grief, and guilt of the past two months had flown out of his head. Every fiber of his being was operating at total alert and was fully in the present. Although the wound on his back burned like hell and he felt bad about Jared, he felt sharper and more alive than he had been in months.

CHAPTER TWO

Everything you want is on the other side of fear.
—Jack Canfield

HOLLY HAD warned him. She had argued with him not to go. Dangerous missions not only risked his life, they also challenged the longevity of their marriage.

"I love you, Tom," she had said. "I really do. But I don't think I can take this anymore."

Holly meant his serving as a top-tier clandestine commando and the leader of Black Cell. Her words were drenched in sadness and regret. The corners of her mouth seemed to pull her entire face down into a tragic mask. Christ, he loved her. He didn't want this. He'd always seen them as two stalwart warriors, adoring each other and protecting their country. But life had changed her. Nasty shit had happened that neither of them had anticipated.

"Take what?" the family therapist had asked about Holly's comment. The therapist was a tall woman with straight, dark, shoulder-length hair, straight bangs, and dark-rimmed glasses. Dr. Stephanie Mathews. Dead serious and academic.

She'll never understand.

"The insanity of it all," Holly answered. "The constant danger and the not knowing."

He understood what she meant. CIA regulations prevented him from telling her where he deployed. He couldn't help that. And he never knew how long he'd be gone.

She knew the rules of the game. She'd lived by them and accepted them. Until now. She'd yearned for the same excitement he had. Until now.

Oh, Holly....

He hated seeing her this way—the doubt etched in fine lines across her forehead, the brightness in her beautiful blue eyes diminished, slumped in a chair, hands clutched in her lap.

Dr. Mathews had been recommended by the ST-6 psychologist, Dr. Petrovian, when, as a result of Crocker's last mission, cartel assassins had burned down the couple's house, injured him and Holly, and killed his daughter's friend Leslie Ames.

"Do you understand why Holly feels this way?" Dr. Mathews asked as she sat across from him with a pad on her lap and her legs crossed.

"Is that a serious question? Yes. Of course I do."

"But you aren't willing to change jobs."

"I've considered it. I have, but…"

"What?"

He wanted to explain to her that the attack on their house had only added to the determination burning in his stomach. It confirmed his belief that there were evil motherfuckers in the world—wolves like the cartel leader and his killers—who wanted to do serious harm to other people. And unsuspecting, trusting decent individuals like Dr. Mathews, Leslie Ames, and others, whom Crocker likened to sheep. It was his job as a sheepdog to protect them. He had failed, and that pissed him off.

He would do better next time; he'd be better prepared, he hoped. The world was much more dangerous than people like Dr. Mathews could imagine.

"How do you feel about what happened to your home, and Leslie's death?" Dr. Mathews asked.

Crocker lowered his head for a moment and looked across the hardwood floor to her ankle. Tattooed there were three little black lizards that looked as if they were crawling up her leg. On the credenza behind her a picture showed her standing next to a look-alike daughter.

"Terrible," Crocker answered, thinking, *What a stupid fucking question.* "Very, very angry." He told himself to calm down.

"Angry?"

"Yes, angry."

"What about guilt?"

"Yes, of course." He had offered to do anything he could for Leslie's parents—a thoughtful physician and soft-spoken librarian—but they refused to meet with him, or even answer the phone when he called. He understood. Losing a daughter had to be hell to deal with. He felt awful that he hadn't prevented it.

"Do you blame yourself?" Dr. Mathews asked, staring at him with big, dark eyes.

"Somewhat. Yes. The cartel assassins wouldn't have attacked my house if I hadn't gone on the mission. It was my job. I understand my job and the risks I take. I never expected blowback like that. Never in a million years. I should have. That's on me. My failure. But there's a high level of tunnel vision that kicks in on missions like that."

"You mean, you didn't anticipate that the cartel leader would attack your family?" she asked.

"That's correct, yes. I didn't see it coming. They killed my colleague's brother, too."

"Paul Mancini." Paul was Joe Mancini's brother. Mancini was Crocker's right-hand man.

"Do you feel responsible in any way?"

"Yes. Absolutely. Like I said…I should have considered it. I should have known it was a possibility that the cartel leader would go after our families. I was so focused on what I was doing, it didn't cross my mind."

It hadn't crossed the minds of his superiors at HQ, either. But he didn't mention that.

He parked the bike outside the hotel, waited a minute to see if anyone was following, then passed through the carpeted lobby, trying not to drip blood on the white marble patches. Sundry quick impressions registered in his head—stately, old world, regal, sophisticated, a faint smell of jasmine. White filigreed ceilings, blown-glass chandeliers.

He stood at the rear of the elevator, trying not to draw attention. A man in his condition didn't belong here.

He waited another thirty seconds for anyone to enter the lobby, then pushed the button for the sixth floor. A young European couple hurried from inside the hotel and entered just as the doors were closing. He looked them over carefully and relaxed when he realized they were too soft and distracted to be agents or operatives.

As the elevator ascended they spoke to each another in French, complaining about the size of their bed.

Enjoy your life while you have it. Forget the size of the bed, and make love on the floor.

He smiled at them briefly, exited at the sixth floor, found the stairway, and climbed to seven. Waited at the stairway door to see whether the elevator stopped there. It didn't.

Stood for several seconds listening outside room 732, wondering if it was unwise to even be here. Maybe he was still in shock. He punched the buzzer.

Jim Anders answered, wearing a blue oxford shirt with sleeves rolled up to his elbows, looking fit and rested. Early forties, medium height, clean-cut with a bodybuilder's physique. A shorter, younger, brown-haired woman in a blue business suit stood behind him.

"Welcome, Crocker. This is Janice Bloom. Janice is a targeter and analyst working on the Syrian account….Jesus—you okay?" he asked, seeing the blood on Crocker's white shirt. "What happened?"

"Hi, Janice," Crocker said. He turned to Anders. "We need to talk in private."

Anders shut the door and flipped the lock behind him. "Talk? Are you aware that you're bleeding?"

"Yes."

They were in a suite with a big living room containing a table and four chairs set in front of the window. Dark hardwood floors, maroon brocade curtains. A big bed was visible through a door to the right. Classy in an old-world way.

"Point me toward the bathroom and I'll clean up," Crocker said.

"Here?"

"Yeah." He grabbed Anders by the elbow. "Come with me."

"Okay. Janice, wait here. Call a doctor."

"No," Crocker said. "No need."

Anders pulled his cell out of his pocket. "You're bleeding, Crocker. For Christ's sake."

"It's a flesh wound," countered Crocker. "Janice, please call downstairs for some towels, hydrogen peroxide, bandages, and tape, and I'll do this myself."

Anders pointed to the bathroom by the front door. "Jesus, Crocker, what happened?"

Crocker closed the door behind him.

"Two punks on a Kawasaki," he said in a low voice. "I was with Jared." Then he remembered. "Fuck...."

They stood in the white marble bathroom. Anders's face reflected in the mirror looked alarmed. "What? Is he injured, too? Where is he? He's supposed to be here."

"Jared's dead."

Crocker pulled two shards of glass out of his right forearm as the news sunk in. When he looked up into the mirror he saw Anders hold his chest as though he'd been shot.

"*What?*"

"Jared's dead. I left him lying on the street with his brains spilled out."

"What the hell are you—Jared, the young case officer?"

Crocker held his forearm under warm water, wrapped it tightly in a towel, and waited for the bleeding to stop.

"They were attempting to kidnap him. There was a struggle. Someone pushed him in front of a bus. He fell. Crushed his head on the street."

Anders shook his head as if he couldn't quite comprehend. "What the hell are you saying? This is awful. Who attacked him?"

"Don't know. At least four, maybe five young punks. Middle Eastern–looking. I checked the pockets of one of them. Found no ID. It was a planned op. Orchestrated."

"Where?"

"On Torun, just around the corner from the Arasta Bazaar. A

crowded street, broad daylight. They attacked Jared, then came after me." Crocker pointed to his back. "Help me pull off this shirt."

The bloody fabric on the back stuck to his skin. Anders helped him peel it up slowly.

"Broad daylight…"

"Yeah, with people everywhere. Bold motherfuckers."

"Jared was one of our best operatives," Anders said sadly. "You sure he's dead?"

When the hem reached his neck, Crocker pulled it over his head. "He's dead, Anders. He's dead. Yes."

Anders looked as if he was tearing up. "It's hard to believe. Poor Jared. I…I…That's a real nasty gash."

"I was lucky."

Anders shook his head. "Don't say anything to Janice. Please don't. She and Jared were close. They trained together at the Farm; maybe they dated, hooked up, whatever. I'd better notify the Station."

Anders retreated to the bedroom, spoke in a low voice on the phone, and returned ten minutes later and closed the bathroom door.

"They follow you here? Were you able to ID them? They say anything to you? They identify themselves in any way?"

"No. No. No. No," Crocker answered. "I told you that already."

"So you saw nothing that could help us identify them?"

"I saw four of them. Two on a motorcycle; two in a van. All young guys, trained, tough."

The front door buzzer sounded.

"Who's that?" Crocker asked, getting ready to defend himself.

Janice answered it. A minute later she knocked on the bathroom door cradling towels, a bottle of peroxide, bandages, medical tape.

"You absolutely sure you don't need a doctor?" she asked.

"No, I can handle this myself. Thanks." She was pretty, with straight hair to her shoulders.

"Are we still doing this?" he asked Anders.

"What?"

"The meeting. The meeting you called us to. My colleague Akil is supposed to be here, too."

An alarm sounded in a far corner of his brain.

"That…uh, I don't know." Anders quickly looked at his watch. The news had clearly thrown him off his game.

Crocker said, "Maybe we should do it later."

Anders frowned and shook his head. "No, no, can't. Our source is bringing us critical information. Important evidence. My understanding is that he returns to Damascus right after this."

"Okay, then. I'll get ready."

"This is so goddamn disturbing," Anders continued. "I just spoke to Jared this morning. He was scheduled to go on R&R after the mission." His face was beet red, and he looked like he wanted to scream.

"What mission?"

"You'll soon find out."

"Seemed like a great guy."

"Dynamic, yeah. Smart, fun. A huge, huge loss."

As Anders was heating up, Crocker started to calm down.

"All right," he said. "If we're going through with the meeting, I'm going to have to borrow a shirt."

"The timing sucks, I know. But I've been led to believe that our source is bringing intelligence that needs to be acted on immediately."

"The darker the better. The shirt, I mean." Crocker's wardrobe leaned toward black, but this time he had a reason that went beyond convenience. A dark color would hide the blood from his back if it leaked through.

"Right."

Anders finished helping Crocker clean his back and secure the bandages. He looked at his watch again when they were done. "They're scheduled to arrive in fifteen minutes. I'd better tell Janice to order the drinks and snacks."

"They?"

"A Syrian businessman and his assistant."

"Go ahead. I'll wait." He thought of something and grabbed Anders's wrist. "What are you going to tell them about Jared?"

"Jared? Good question. I don't know if they're expecting him. I'll wait for him to ask."

"What's his name?"

"Manshir Talab. He's a friend of ours."

"You mean he's a source."

Anders nodded.

"Do we have any friends in this part of the world?" Crocker asked.

"Good question."

"I mean people we can trust with our lives?"

"I can't answer that definitively. I'd better go."

He left. Crocker had no appetite, but he was thirsty. So he twisted open the bottle of Evian he found near the sink and sat on the edge of the tub drinking and remembering his Black Cell/SEAL colleague Akil, who had arrived with him yesterday.

He should be here by now, Crocker thought as he checked his damaged cell.

He punched out a text to Akil. "Do a SDR. Where r u?"

Anders returned with a white T-shirt and a light-blue oxford that was almost identical to the one he was wearing. He didn't look rested and relaxed anymore. "This is the best I could find," he said, as if the weight of the world had fallen on his broad shoulders.

Not dark or black, but it would do. "Did you inform Akil about the meeting?" asked Crocker.

"Akil?"

"My colleague Akil. The big Egyptian-American guy. You asked me to bring him because of his language skills. Remember?"

"Yes, of course," Anders answered. "I texted him about forty minutes ago."

"He respond?"

"Yes. He's on his way."

As Crocker buttoned the shirt, he worried. *What if whatever organization that attacked me and Jared is lying in wait for Akil, too?*

He turned to Anders and asked, "How do I look?"

"The same, except maybe a little more buttoned-up than usual."

"That's too bad."

"Why?"

Crocker pushed past him. "No reason. I think I'll wait for Akil downstairs."

"Why?" Dr. Mathews had asked him during their second counseling session.

"Why what?"

He wanted to dislike her but couldn't. She had a gentle manner and didn't come across as judgmental. In the photos of her with her daughter, she appeared to be a kind, loving mother. No man in any of them.

"You've chosen a very unique and extreme way to make a living," she said. "I'm sure you know that."

"I do."

"Have you ever asked yourself why you chose to become a SEAL?" she asked. That's all they had told her. She didn't know that he was a member of ST-6 or about the existence of Black Cell. Only a handful of people in the CIA and the White House did.

Crocker looked at Holly, to his left, who lowered her head and wouldn't meet his eyes. He wanted to say that he resented being here and the doctor's last question. He wasn't the type of person who liked to dwell on psychological motivations. He did what he did, and understood why.

Instead of snarling back, he answered evenly, "I was a very energetic kid. I've always been drawn to adventure and danger. The town where I grew up in Massachusetts was full of motorcycle gangs and drugs. My young friends and I were drifting into that life. I started working out and running, and joined the navy at eighteen. From the navy, I passed the test to get onto SEAL teams. It turned out to suit me perfectly. I'm very grateful for the life it's provided me. And I love what I do."

Dr. Mathews nodded. "It's enormously satisfying to find a profession that suits you and gives you a sense of purpose, isn't it?"

"Yes, it is," he said, liking her even better.

Now he sat in one of the big, silk-covered armchairs in the lobby, wondering about Jared's family and how they would take the news about their son. Death, especially when it happened to someone he knew and liked, always affected him profoundly, drawing him deep inside himself.

That's where he was now, considering the unfathomable mystery of life and death, and how someone so vital and intelligent could vanish in a second, leaving behind an emotional vacuum and a lifeless shell.

Crocker was thinking about the sacrifice Jared had made for his country, while most young people his age were playing video games and couldn't find Syria on a map, when a tall, dapper-looking man strode through the lobby with a very attractive young woman by his side. She was dark-eyed and put together. His eyes followed her to the elevator. She walked as if she expected to be watched, the fabric of her dark skirt pulled tight against her full behind.

Realizing that he still hadn't heard from Akil, he reached for his burner cell phone and called him again. The call went directly to voice mail; he left a message: "Call me, knucklehead!"

Two minutes later his cell pinged with a text from Anders: "They're here! Soon as u return, we'll start."

"Waiting for A," he punched back.

"Do we need him?" came Anders's reply.

The question annoyed him. "Want 2 make sure he's ok. B there in 5."

Crocker called Akil's burner cell again. No answer.

He was getting anxious. The loss of another teammate would be too much. Looking again at his watch, he started to think that he'd been around so much death and destruction in the past year that maybe he was cursed. His teammate Ritchie had died in a helo crash near the Golan Heights. He'd been working with four FBI and DEA agents who were beheaded in Mexico. His teammate Mancini's brother was shot through the front door by cartel assassins—the same ones who had killed his daughter's friend Leslie. Now Jared. A lousy track record, for sure.

Another ten minutes passed before his cell pinged again.

It was Anders asking, "WTF are you?"

"I'm still waiting for A. Hold on."

"This is getting awkward," texted back Anders. "Maybe we should start without him."

Crocker got up and started pacing in front of the window that overlooked the entrance. His loyalty to the guys on his team was immense. Losing Ritchie had been like losing a brother. How many times since then had he dreamt of Ritchie running through the woods beside him, or imagining him with that mischievous grin on his face?

A white Mini Cooper with a red stripe down the roof and hood pulled to the curb. Through the window he saw a long-haired blonde at the wheel. She looked like a Scandinavian model. Gorgeous, but too boney and bloodless to be his type. Still, she caught his attention. He started to wonder why she was stopping in front of the hotel, and what she was doing in Istanbul. Suddenly a smiling, seemingly carefree Akil came into the picture, emerging from the passenger's side, bounding over to the driver's open window, and kissing her, long and hard.

WTF!

She pulled him close. Akil whispered something in the young blonde's ear that made her blush. She waved, put the little car in gear, and sped off in what might have been a scene from a James Bond movie.

Fucking Akil, Crocker said to himself, half relieved, half pissed. His teammate amused him, even when he was totally friggin' exasperating. Like now.

He stood waiting as the burly, good-natured SEAL hurried through the glass doors, winking at the doorman and pulling on the blue blazer he'd been carrying on his shoulder.

"You're late," Crocker barked.

"Sorry, boss. Something wrong? You look stressed."

They knew each other so well that they could read the other's mood.

"Yeah, I'm stressed, because you don't answer your fucking cell phone. You got it on you? It work?"

"Yeah. Oh, yeah. I was stuck in traffic. No signal," Akil explained with a pat on Crocker's back and a smile. "What's up? The powwow canceled?"

"I texted you five fucking times."

"Ease up, boss. I'm present and accounted for. Sorry I'm a few minutes behind schedule, but I had to take care of something."

"I saw. Let's go."

Crocker's irritation didn't dim in the elevator, even though he wanted it to. It didn't help that Akil quipped, "Nice shirt. When did you start shopping at Brooks Brothers?"

"Fuck off."

"Looks like somebody got out of bed on the wrong side this morning."

"No. Actually, I slept fine. It's what happened since that's got me annoyed."

"What's that?"

"I'll tell you later. No more bimbos, understand? No more fucking around. I need you to be present and alert. We got eyes on us. Killers."

"She's not a bimbo," offered Akil. "She's a visiting fellow at the archeological museum. Looks, brains, personality, and a fabulous tush all rolled into one."

"Stop screwing around."

"Okay. But honestly, how often in life do you find all three in one package?"

Crocker stopped in front of 732 and lowered his voice. "I'm serious, Akil. Cut the bullshit. I'm glad you met someone you like. Now forget her and focus."

"I got it, boss," Akil whispered back. "I figure we're about to get into the shit, right? So I wanted to have some fun first."

"We're in it already, deeper than you think."

"Have you experienced issues with PTSD yourself?" Dr. Mathews had asked two weeks ago.

Crocker twisted in the metal chair. He assumed that she already knew the answer, because he saw his carefully redacted psychological file on the table by her side, provided by Dr. Petrovian.

He nodded.

It contained the results of a recent personality test, which revealed him to be a combination of an aggressive and introverted intuitive personality type. That meant he liked to command and exercise power, but also tried to stay in the background until he felt the need to take over. He was active, adventurous, and someone who relied primarily on his instincts. Others with his unique slate of characteristics included Al Capone, Fidel Castro, and Jeffrey Dahmer.

The Al Capone part was a hoot. But the Castro and Dahmer associations were harder to swallow.

"Do you think your PTSD issues have anything to do with why you want to continue doing what you're doing?" Dr. Mathews asked.

He lied. "No, ma'am. Not at all."

The "ma'am" was a tell. He caught that. Warned himself not to use it again.

"Because research shows that PTSD is often triggered by guilt."

She'd hit the bull's-eye again. He flashed to the image of Ritchie's bisected body lying on the ground inside the Syrian border, and a cold flash blew through his body.

"I've heard that," he answered, shivering and quickly straightening his back. "But in my case, it's a nonissue. The reason I continue has more to do with service to my country and loyalty to my team-mates. They're critical to me, Doc."

Holly sighed loudly. She'd been uncommunicative so far during this session. Lost in her head.

"More important than saving your marriage?" Dr. Mathews asked.

"No, ma'am. I didn't say that."

He had a hard time keeping his eyes off her. Mr. Talab's secretary had been introduced to him as Fatima. She sat by Talab's side, almost directly across from Crocker, in a tight black skirt and matching jacket with a white blouse underneath. Red lipstick on full lips, contrasted with her caramel-colored skin and sparkling dark eyes.

He could feel the heat coming off her body, and had to resist the impulse to take her in his arms and rip her clothes off right there. He imagined himself pushing over the chair and taking her from behind, while reaching under her shirt and grabbing her breasts.

Hard and fast.

He stopped and asked himself, *What the hell's wrong with me? This is an operational meeting. I need to pay attention.* Maybe it was this morning's brush with death that made him preoccupied with sex.

She dabbed her lips with a napkin, caught him looking, and shot him a quick and intense glance dense with history and emotion. It traveled like an electric spark to his groin.

His burner cell phone vibrated, and he glanced at it in his lap.

"Stop eyeballing F like a t-bone steak!"

Akil, forty-five degrees to his right, grinned out of the side of his mouth. Crocker resisted the impulse to text something back.

He made an effort to ignore her, but her magnetic pull was strong. They were in the tub together; they were furiously making love on the carpet; she was screaming in ecstasy and covered with sweat.

Stop!

Anders, to his immediate left, continued to talk with Mr. Talab informally about his background. Crocker learned that he came from a prominent Lebanese-Syrian family that owned hotels throughout the Middle East. Educated in France, he maintained residences in Beirut, London, and Dubai, where his wife and two daughters lived. A sophisticated, well-traveled man, who spoke several languages.

Crocker immediately had questions and suspicions. *Why is a guy like him working for us? He doesn't seem to need the money. So what does he want?*

Out of the corner of his eye he saw Fatima recross her legs, a hint of silk and black garters.

He focused on Anders and Talab so hard that it almost hurt.

Anders asked if he still owned a small interest in the professional soccer team Al Ahli Club that played in the UAE League.

"Oh yes," Mr. Talab boasted. "We won the President's Cup last year. The Brazilian striker Grafite scored the winning goal."

He wished Jared was present to give him the skinny on these two. Anders, though highly intelligent, clearly didn't know them that well and operated more on a need-to-know basis.

Janice passed a silver tray with cookies. She had a thin gold bracelet on her wrist with a name engraved on it that he couldn't make out.

Crocker handed the cookies across to Fatima, who selected a round shortbread with raspberry jam in the middle. She craned her long neck left toward Talab, bit into it, and smiled.

He caught a whiff of her rosewater-scented perfume and wondered what her real relationship to Talab was. He knew that the role of women in this part of the world was fraught with compromise and religious restriction. The ones he had encountered in his many travels throughout the region almost never made eye contact with men they weren't related to.

This lady knew her way around and understood her effect on men.

Anders mentioned the mysterious disappearance of the Malaysia Airlines 777 over the Indian Ocean and the continuing search for wreckage.

Mr. Talab, who claimed to have a great deal of knowledge about flying Boeing aircraft, said he believed that the autopilot on the plane had been interrupted via satellite signal from a foreign government. He noted that this system had been installed in all advanced Boeing passenger aircraft after 9/11 to foil terrorists should they gain control of the flight deck.

He came across as a consummate businessman—confident, prosperous, and pleased with himself. Crocker thought his theory about Flight 370 was wack.

Anders cleared his throat and, pointing to Crocker and Akil, said, "Mr. Talab, these are two of the men from our special ops team. Perhaps you'd like to tell them a little about the situation inside Syria."

As Crocker sat up he felt Fatima's warm eyes looking him over.

"Yes." Talab shifted his long frame in the chair and recrossed his legs. "I can tell you that my family is part Lebanese, part Syrian, and we have done business in Syria for years. Damascus was my father's favorite city. We have investments there and many friends, which is why I travel there often."

Anders turned to Crocker and said, "Mr. Talab and President Bashar al-Assad went to school together."

They had Crocker's full attention.

"Yes. Yes, we did," Mr. Talab responded. "For two years we were classmates at the al-Hurriya School in Damascus. Bashar went on to study medicine. In those days he wanted to be an ophthalmologist. I traveled to London to get a business degree."

Crocker noted the familiar tone in which he talked about Assad.

"Interesting," Janice said. "How well do you know him?"

"Well, we don't travel in the same circles, but anybody who does business in Syria has to deal with the Assad family."

"I would imagine. Yes," Janice responded.

"They can be extremely charming one minute and cutthroat and brutal the next, especially when you cross them. It's also a family with a history of mental problems."

"I've heard."

The muscles around Talab's jaw tightened as he continued. "My younger brother Hamid found this out when he entered into a dispute with the president's cousin Fawwaz al-Assad over the ownership of a horse ranch outside Damascus. Fawwaz is an avowed thug, who later founded the death squads known as the Shabiha, who hunt down and kill opponents of the regime. He wanted the farm, but my brother didn't want to sell it."

Crocker had heard of the notorious Shabiha and wondered if they ever operated outside the borders of Syria. Maybe they were the assassins he had encountered earlier.

"What happened?" Janice asked.

"A week after my brother turned down Fawwaz's offer, he was pulled out of his bed one night, tortured, and brutally murdered. This happened in September 2009."

"I'm very sorry to hear that."

"I say all this, my friends, so you and your people understand my motivation, which is pure and simple—revenge. I hate the Assad dictatorship and deplore its arrogance and brutality, which now all the world can see."

Makes sense, Crocker thought, though he wasn't completely buying it.

"So do we," Anders said.

"That gives us the same goal."

Like other urbane, educated Middle Eastern men Crocker had met, Talab was hard to read, and Crocker wondered whether his motivation really was that simple.

Again he was momentarily distracted by Fatima, who sipped her tea quietly and listened. She seemed to have a personal agenda, too, which she was keeping to herself.

"I waited," Mr. Talab continued. "When anti-Assad demonstrations started in early 2011 as part of the Arab Spring, I saw little chance that they would succeed. But we have a large Sunni Muslim majority in our country that has been oppressed by the small Alawite Shiite elite for many years. Some small groups of these men took up arms. The Assad regime responded with customary brutality. Rebels were soon joined by thousands of defectors from the Syrian military."

"That happened at the end of 2011," Anders said.

"Yes. The rebels formed what is called the Free Syrian Army. By early 2012, they boasted twenty thousand members. That's when the civil war really began."

Anders nodded. "Yes."

Crocker remembered. The Arab Spring had come as a sudden outburst of anger, frustration, and hope sweeping across North Africa into the Middle East. It caught everyone by surprise, including the United States, which had seemed unsure how to respond.

"The FSA captured territory and the Assad military responded with cluster bombings, artillery, and rocket attacks," continued Talab. "Civilians fled to the borders of Turkey, Jordan, and Lebanon. And other Sunni governments in the area started to take notice. They hated the Assad regime, too, so they wanted to help the FSA. Because of my connections inside Syria, I was approached by some of their intel services. I started to pass money and arms to rebel leaders. I also started to raise money myself."

If Talab had done half of what he claimed, he was playing a very dangerous game. The Assad regime had a terrifying reputation for dealing with dissidents and enemies. Its military intelligence service, the Mukhabarat, was aggressive and deadly, trained and supported by Russia's SVR.

"Throughout 2012, the expectation was that the U.S. and its European allies would establish a no-fly zone in Syria and aid the FSA, which would bring about the fall of the Assad regime," Talab continued. "But we waited, and it never happened. For whatever reason, your president was more concerned with Afghanistan."

"True," Anders added with a bitter note in his voice.

"Absent U.S. leadership, different Arab governments started to act on their own," Talab continued. "They supported various leaders from various rebel groups. Also, other foreign terrorist organizations saw an opportunity to extend their influence. These included al-Qaeda–linked groups like Ahrar ash-Sham, the Suquor al-Sham Brigade, the al-Nusra Front, and the Islamic State of Iraq and Syria (ISIS). Their stated goal is to impose a government in Syria based on Sharia law."

Crocker knew that ISIS had become a major concern of the Turkish government because of its control of territory near that country's southern border. Just last week ISIS insurgents had surrounded the Suleyman Shah tomb, just fifteen miles from Turkey.

Maybe it was ISIS that had ordered the hit on Jared. Given the complicated rivalries within Syria, it was hard to tell.

"As you know, by the beginning of 2013, the Assad regime seemed about to fall, despite the support it was getting from Russia, China, and Hezbollah," Talab continued. "That's when its main ally, Iran, jumped into the ring."

They had done so full-scale, according to the intel reports Crocker had read. The Iranian security and intelligence services were not only advising and assisting the Syrian military, they had also deployed Islamic Revolutionary Guards Corps (IRGC) ground forces, the Qods Force, intelligence services, and law enforcement forces to fight the anti-Assad rebels. Major General Qassem Suleimani—the leader of Qods Force and a man Crocker and his team had tried to kill in early 2013—was personally leading and directing the Iranian military effort in Syria. Crocker thought that he'd love to run into him and silence the bastard once and for all.

"Now the situation is a mess, with all sides and groups controlling different parts of the country," Mr. Talab continued. "If I were to predict an outcome, I would say that Syria will eventually split into fiefdoms—Iran controlling the south, radical Sunni groups like ISIS sharing territory and towns to the north and west with more moderate FSA militias, and Assad and his Alawite allies keeping Damascus and the territory to the east."

The horror of all this, of course, was the impact on the Syrian people. Rockets, cluster bombs, even chemical weapons had killed almost one hundred thousand of them so far. Another million or so had become refugees.

"This is a regime armed with chemical and possibly nuclear weapons," Janice pointed out. "They're heavily armed, desperate and dangerous. What's even more alarming is the danger of some of the more advanced weapons falling into other undesirables' hands."

"Yes." Talab nodded.

"I know the Russians have promised to monitor the WMDs. But they can't be trusted. Besides, the Assads listen to no one."

"No, they don't."

Anders, who seemed to have grown uneasy with the direction of the conversation, cleared his throat. "Thank you, Mr. Talab. I know you've got something to leave with us and must go shortly. So we won't waste any more of your time."

Talab nodded to Fatima, who snapped open the black briefcase by her high-heeled shoe. "I leave you this, gentlemen," Mr. Talab said. "I'm sure you'll appreciate its dire importance. I thank you for your time and wish you good fortune."

Fatima handed him a DVD disk in a plastic case. Talab stood, flattened the hem of his jacket, and passed it to Anders.

"Thank you, Mr. Talab. We greatly appreciate all you've done."

At the door, Crocker saw Anders hand Talab a white envelope stuffed with what he assumed were U.S. dollars. Under circumstances like these, where the American side had very limited access, intel could be worth a lot of money.

Money, he reminded himself, invited treachery. And treachery, he understood, often resulted in death.

CHAPTER THREE

*I go on working for the same reason that a hen
goes on laying eggs.*

—H. L. Mencken

HOURS AFTER he got the order to deploy to Istanbul, Crocker took Holly out to her favorite restaurant, Il Giardino. They sat in the atrium under a giant ficus tree wrapped in tiny white lights. A fire danced in the wood-burning pizza oven in the corner. As they sipped fresh Frascati wine and Andrea Bocelli sang "Con te partirò" over the stereo, Crocker gently broached the subject.

"How's work?" he asked.

"Busy," she answered quietly. "We're completing a cybersecurity assessment of the embassy in Kiev."

Holly's job title was security threat analyst at the Bureau of Diplomatic Security (DS). DS played a vital role in protecting 275 U.S. diplomatic missions and their personnel overseas, securing critical information systems, investigating passport and visa fraud, and protecting the high-ranking foreign dignitaries and officials visiting the United States.

"The Russians can't help snooping, right?" Crocker asked.

"With Putin in charge, you know it." She glanced around to make sure no one was listening and lowered her voice to a whisper. "Everything in and out of there is heavily encrypted. But we're constantly updating security. It's a very high-tech game of cat and mouse."

Because of the analytic nature of her job, Holly was able to work remotely and spend only a few days a month in D.C. When in the capital she stayed with her colleague and occasional rowing partner, Lena. Lena's husband, a young navy ensign, had died when al-Qaeda hijackers crashed American Airlines Flight 77 into the Pentagon on 9/11.

Crocker was proud of Holly and the work she did. He was about to say something to that effect when the waiter arrived to announce the specials. Holly ordered the pollo alla Sorentina; Crocker chose the veal piccata.

She looked radiant in the gentle overhead light, and emotionally fragile.

He winced slightly and said, "Jenny's back in school and seems to be doing well. You're back at work handling important assignments. And I'm sitting on my butt feeling useless."

Holly's mouth tightened. "You've been training nonstop and working out."

"Yeah, but it's not the same. You know that."

"Tom…" She bit her bottom lip as if she knew what was coming, and reached for her glass.

He plunged in. "I've talked to the guys on my team, and they feel the same. It's been three long months."

"Manny, too?" She was referring to his right-hand man, Joseph Mancini, whose brother had died from a cartel assassin's bullet.

"Yes."

"And Davis?"

John Davis, the team's comms expert, had been badly wounded in

Mexico. He'd spent the better part of the past three months convalescing at home.

"He says he's tired of playing daddy and real antsy to get back."

"Playing daddy, Tom? Really? So, what are you trying to say?"

"It's time for us to go out again."

She ran a finger along the rim of her wineglass and sighed deeply. "When?"

"We leave in the morning."

"How early?"

"0400."

She nodded solemnly, but he could see that she was steaming inside. "Okay."

Throughout dinner she'd remained uncharacteristically quiet as he talked about possible vacation spots for the summer and plans to build a new house. Even when they returned to the bedroom of their temporary apartment and made love, her mind seemed elsewhere.

Part of him wanted her to get mad at him and tell him what she was really feeling. But they both knew, and understood, that there was no middle ground. He did what he did, and that wasn't going to change until he got too old to do it, or dropped dead.

He awoke at three, quickly showered and dressed. He thought Holly was still sleeping when he kissed her goodbye.

When she turned and looked up, he saw that she had been crying.

He leaned over and said, "I'll call you when I can. The security team will keep a constant eye on you and Jenny. So there's no reason to worry."

"I know, Tom."

"I love you." He kissed her again.

She nodded sadly and said, "I love you, too. Be safe."

*   *   *

The four Americans pulled their chairs into a semicircle around the TV to watch the video Mr. Talab and his assistant had left behind. Before slipping it into the VCR, Anders explained that it had been shot outside the city of Idlib by a twenty-two-year-old Syrian engineering student named Hassan.

"When?" Crocker asked.

"When what?"

"When was it shot?"

"About a week ago," Janice answered.

"Where's Idlib?"

"Northern Syria, about 120 kilometers from the Turkish border."

"Any more questions before we start?" Anders asked.

"Yeah," Akil said as he bit into an apple. "Why are you showing us this?"

"You're about to find out."

Filmed at night using an infrared filter, the video showed a half-dozen uniformed men carefully offloading five-foot-long stainless-steel canisters from a truck and carrying them down concrete steps into a tunnel. The video was grainy and jerky, and lasted about two and a half minutes.

When it ended Crocker asked, "What did we just watch?"

"Those were members of the Syrian National Defense Force, the Quwat al-Difa al-Watani," answered Anders. "It was formed in 2012, following massive defections from the army and air force, and is made up of Assad loyalists. It's a special militia filled with members of the country's minorities—Alawites, Druzes, Armenians, and Christians—and modeled after the Basij militia in Iran."

"What were they carrying?"

SEAL TEAM SIX: HUNT THE FOX

"We believe the canisters contain sarin gas."

As the former WMD officer on ST-6, Crocker knew more about sarin than he cared to. He'd searched for it in Libya after the fall of Gaddafi and in Iraq after the ouster of Saddam Hussein. He knew that it remained in an odorless, tasteless liquid state below temperatures of 150°C. In order to maximize its potential as a weapon, it was usually dispersed from a canister attached to a rocket or missile into droplets fine enough to be inhaled into the lungs. The sarin that reached the ground would eventually evaporate into vapor. Once it entered the body through the eyes or skin, it shut off the nervous system, causing involuntary muscles like the diaphragm to stop functioning. It had been discovered by Nazi scientists, who dubbed it Substance 146 and found it to be hundreds of times more deadly than cyanide. A variation of insecticides using organophosphate compounds, sarin could be made relatively easily using more than a dozen recipes. One recipe used isopropanol, known as rubbing alcohol. Another involved mixing methylphosphonyl dichloride with hydrogen or sodium fluoride.

In 2012 the United States and other countries had tried to block sales to Syria of the chemicals used in the manufacture of sarin. By that time, however, the Assad regime had already stockpiled large amounts of them.

A lethal dose could cause death in a minute. Iraqi strongman Saddam Hussein discovered this in 1988, when he directed a sarin attack against the Kurdish village of Halabja that killed five thousand people. More recently, UN inspectors discovered that the Assad regime had used sarin against rebels occupying the Ghouta suburb of Damascus.

Janice said, "Assad's military has been stockpiling the stuff for years. As military bases are overrun, there's a very good chance of it falling into the hands of rebels, particularly ISIS and those groups allied with al-Qaeda."

"For a number of real obvious reasons, we don't want that to happen," added Anders.

"No, we don't," echoed Janice.

"What are the odds?" Akil asked, finishing the apple and tossing the core in the trash.

"Odds of what?"

"Odds of AQ or ISIS getting their hands on the sarin."

"Better than even," Anders answered. "We know they've tried as recently as a month ago, when Turkish antiterror forces raided an ISIS safe house in the province of Adana. They arrested twelve terrorists and captured a cache of weapons and documents. Among the weapons they found a canister of sarin that had been seized from a base outside Damascus."

Akil asked, "Any idea what they are planning to do with it?"

Janice looked at Anders, who nodded. She said, "NSA has picked up coded chatter on some ISIS al-Qaeda websites from someone who calls himself the Fox. His goal he says is to give ISIS an international profile by attacking the West."

"That's messed up," Akil said.

"Especially when the WMDs they need are within reach," Anders added.

Crocker leaned forward. "What do you need us to do?" he asked, already anticipating the answer.

"First, I need you to assess whether or not you can insert into Syria and recover the sarin canisters in the tunnel outside of Idlib before the city falls to ISIS, which could happen any day," answered Anders.

"There's nothing to assess," Crocker said.

"Meaning what?"

"Meaning, it needs to be done, so let's get to it."

"That's not what I asked," Anders countered. "I want you to explore the possibility. Evaluate contingencies and capabilities, and assess options."

"You already said that there's no time."

Anders frowned. "The problem is, Crocker, that without reliable partners or assets inside, we're not sure how to get you inside Syria, or where it's safe to operate."

"We'll figure that out."

"How?"

"We need to talk to people who know what's going on, on the ground."

"I'll call our liaison in Turkish MiT," replied Anders.

"Good."

"When are the rest of your men arriving?"

"They're scheduled to land at 1700."

"Then let's arrange a meet tonight."

The room at the Hotel Nena Istanbul, only a block and a half away from the Sultanhan, was lavish by SEAL standards. From the rooftop restaurant where Crocker and Akil snacked on hummus, black olives, and Efes Pilsen, they took in a panoramic view of the city, from the port located on the Asian side, to Bosphorus Bridge, Topkapi Palace, Hagia Sophia, the Blue Mosque with the Golden Horn in the background, and the Prince Islands in the Sea of Marmara.

"Pretty damn impressive, right?" Crocker asked.

After six years of working together in places like Pakistan, Yemen, Paraguay, and Afghanistan, he thought of Akil as a younger brother, even though their backgrounds were wildly different. Crocker came from a hardscrabble town in Massachusetts; Akil was born Muslim in a town outside of Cairo, emigrated to the States with his family, and joined the U.S. Marines. SEAL teams had bound the two men together in ways most people couldn't understand.

"Yeah," Akil offered, holding up his hand to shield the late afternoon sun. "There's a whole shitload of history out there."

"More than we can comprehend."

"You notice how the Ottomans stuck the minarets on the Hagia Sophia?" Akil asked, pointing to the glistening multidomed monument.

"I did."

"Randi told me about it. Started as the seat of the Greek Orthodox church in the fifth century, was converted into a Roman Catholic cathedral at the end of the Roman Empire, became a Muslim mosque when the Ottomans ran the city, and after World War I it was turned into a museum."

"Randi, the blonde I saw you with earlier?" Crocker asked, thinking about how the mission to recover the sarin was going to work.

"Yeah. Puts everything in perspective, right?"

They'd need a reliable escort, weapons, a good cover, comms, vehicles. He saw Akil looking at him, waiting for an answer. "Who, Randi?" he asked.

"No, the Hagia Sophia," Akil answered. "I mean all the blood that was shed over the place by the different religious groups. And now it's a museum."

"Yeah."

After World War I, Turkish nationalist and president Mustafa Kemal Atatürk started to transform Turkey into a modern, secular state. Now, it seemed to Crocker that the current prime minister, Recep Tayyip Erdoğan, who was an Islamist, was trying to take it backward, arresting journalists, banning YouTube and Twitter, and dissolving the long-standing separation between religion and the state.

Akil, seeing the faraway look in Crocker's eyes, asked, "You okay with the shit that went down this morning?"

"Not really," Crocker answered, "but what am I gonna do, cry?"

"You want to talk about it?"

"Not really."

"I hear he was a good guy."

"Jared? Yeah. Good sense of humor and a big fire in his belly. You would have liked him."

"He tell you much?"

"About what?"

"The sarin. The hottie in the suit. The op."

"Nah. Never got around to that."

Akil raised his bottle of Turkish beer. "Here's to the kid."

"Jared."

"Here's hoping he's in a better place."

"Yeah."

Back in their room, Crocker had a message from the desk clerk informing him that his friends had arrived and were staying in 321. He called and invited them up, then dialed Holly, who didn't answer.

He left a message on her cell phone. "I'm safe. Will call again soon. Love to you and Jenny."

As he looked out the window at the minarets in the distance and listened to the muezzin call evening prayer, he wondered if Dr. Mathews would consider him selfish for taking the mission.

A voice in his head said, *How can I be selfish when I'm doing this to protect people?*

That didn't change the problems they were having in their marriage, or the faraway look in Holly's eyes when he'd kissed her goodbye.

The awkward doubts disappeared the moment Mancini walked in, sporting a foot-long beard and hair that curled over his ears. The energy he brought with him was palpable.

"What the fuck happened to you?" Crocker asked.

"Life," the linebacker-sized SEAL responded through a gap-toothed smile. "I grew some hair. How's your leg?"

The cartel assassins who had bombed Crocker's house had shot him in the thigh before he took them out.

"Still barks some, but it works."

The two men embraced for the first time in three months. Crocker noticed that Mancini had a new tattoo on his forearm. It was a heart with his brother's face in it and the words *"In Memoriam Amantem"* (in loving memory).

He felt something tighten in his chest.

Behind Mancini (who was the weapons, logistics, and tech expert on the team) followed Suarez (explosives) and Davis (comms). The last time Crocker saw Davis he'd been lying in a hospital in Guadalajara recovering from a bullet wound that had shattered his collarbone. He looked fit, tan, and healthy now.

"Glad to see you're back," Crocker said, squeezing his hand. "Been working out?"

"Yeah, boss, I've become a CrossFit fanatic. I missed you guys...."

It meant a lot coming from a man of few words.

"How's the family?"

Light-haired Davis had a matching blond wife and two young sons. Looked like a family out of a J. Crew catalog, except that the dad was an adrenaline junkie, conspiracy theorist, and secret New Age follower who believed in aliens and communicating with the dead. He was convinced, for example, that Hitler and the Nazis had made contact with aliens.

"Good. All good."

"Anybody hear from Cal?" Cal was the sniper and sixth member of Black Cell.

Mancini, who had clicked on the TV and was surfing through the channels with the sound muted, nodded.

"He wanted to come, but Doc wouldn't clear him. Even though he bitched to Sutter, he wouldn't sign off." Captain Sutter was the commander of SEAL Team Six and their boss.

Suarez, who was the newest member of the team, handed Crocker a white envelope. "Your wife asked Sutter to give you this."

"Thanks and welcome. Your family good?"

"Healthy and relatively happy, boss. Praise be to our savior Jesus Christ."

"You still believe in the virgin birth?" Akil asked.

"You still a Muslim who chases anything with a pair of tits?" Suarez asked back.

"Hoo-ah."

They banged knuckles and bumped chests.

Inside the envelope was a wallet-sized photo of his daughter, Jenny, and an invitation to her graduation. A reminder that, one, his daughter (from his first marriage) was graduating from high school, and, two, that the ceremony was being held in a week. Crocker didn't want to miss it. He noticed that there was no accompanying message from Holly.

"You guys staying in one room or two?" Akil asked, referring to Mancini, Suarez, and Davis.

Suarez glanced at Mancini and answered, "Two. He snores and farts so much we gave him his own gas chamber."

Akil laughed. "Talks to himself, too. Weird shit about making love to computers and robots."

"You fucking sissies are lucky to associate with me," Mancini shot back. "Maybe if you listen, some of my knowledge and erudition will wear off on you."

"What the hell is erudition?"

"Maybe not." Then, to Crocker, "What's up, boss?"

"Looks like we might be going into Syria to recover some WMDs."

"I figured Syria might be on the agenda. You got details?"

"Hopefully we'll get them later tonight."

Mancini slapped his hands together. "I'm ready to get it on!" Then, nodding toward the others, "Not sure about these jerk-offs."

"Bring everything you've got, I'll bring it ten times stronger," said Akil.

"Really, Akil? Really? What are you bench-pressing these days? You up to a buck-fifty?"

"You know what they call muscle-bound guys in tight shorts who like to hang in the gym together?"

Mancini got in his face. "What? You really think you're ready?"

Suarez: "Get a room, guys. Work it out."

Akil tossed a pillow at Suarez that missed his head and knocked over a lamp on the desk where Crocker was sitting, studying some of the reports Janice had given him.

Crocker barked, "Come on, Akil. What are you, five years old?"

"It's Manny's fault." To Mancini: "Don't you know that all the self-improvement shit isn't good for you? You need some primal rage."

"Believe me, brother, I got plenty of that." Then, to Davis: "You might want to buy some Clairol and die your hair black. They eat blonds like you for dinner in this part of the world. Which reminds me…. This is a great restaurant city, and I'm famished. Anybody up for dinner?"

"First intelligent thing you've said," Akil responded.

The first time he'd seen Holly, almost fifteen years ago, he was struck by her poise and physical beauty. He remembered thinking she seemed like a perfect partner—smart, friendly, attractive, and fit. It had happened at an ST-6 picnic at a teammate's house. She stood next to a teammate's wife, holding a glass of wine. The sun glanced off her cheekbones and highlighted the waves in her long, auburn hair. Though he later heard that her marriage to her first husband (also a member of ST-6) was on the rocks, she looked completely in control of herself and happy.

He had lost sight of her for a few minutes in the smoke from the barbecue, then she was miraculously by his side, smiling at two-year-old Jenny. Almost too close for comfort. In proximity, her effect on him was even more powerful. Big blue eyes that were both intelligent and kind, a fit, womanly body stylishly adorned in a tight light-blue T-shirt and matching checkered shorts.

"Sweet girl," she said, referring to Jenny. "How old?"

"I'll let her tell you."

Jenny held up two fingers. "Two and a half."

"Really? What's your name?"

"Jen-ny."

"Pretty name."

Later he'd seen Holly around the neighborhood and at other ST-6 functions. Heard she was a good mother and a decent athlete, including serving as captain on a women's championship rowing team.

Six years after that, after Crocker's first wife moved out, he dated for two years—an Australian skin diver, a Hispanic FBI agent, an anesthesiologist who was into rock climbing. He was starting to think about settling down again when one of the ST-6 wives informed him that Holly and her husband had split up. She suggested that the two of them might like to keep each other company.

They met at the Starbucks in the Red Mill Commons. He felt awkward at first, discussing his training for an upcoming Ironman competition and thinking that he was boring her, but she quickly put him at ease. She knew the SEAL life and the kind of people who were attracted to it. She explained that she had left her husband because of his drinking problem, which had led to abusive behavior and infidelity.

She said, "He refuses to deal with his personal problems, and I couldn't put up with them anymore. It's as simple as that. I wish him well. It's time to move on."

Crocker, who still felt bad about his first marriage, appreciated her no-nonsense practicality. His ex-wife was someone who could never decide what she wanted and was therefore impossible to please. She'd hated it when they were assigned to a base overseas, then didn't want to leave. She wanted a child, but didn't enjoy being a mother. It had driven him crazy. Holly seemed more solid emotionally and mature. They got together for coffee a few more times, then started dating.

It was so natural, because they liked the same things—being outdoors, working out, movies, and quiet restaurant dinners. After three months of dating, he moved in with her and her teenage son, Brian. When they discovered that Brian was taking and selling drugs, Crocker sat the kid down and tried talking sense into him. Brian started to take school seriously and seemed to be getting his life together when, one night, he was shot by a drug dealer friend, and slipped into a coma.

As horrible as the situation was, Holly dealt with it with incredible strength and dignity. When Brian's brain and body started to swell because of damage to his spine and internal organs, the doctors told her that they had to unplug the respirator that was keeping him alive. She sat with Brian and held his hand when the doctors pulled the plug. He couldn't imagine the pain she was in, but she handled it amazingly well. Her values were solid: God, country, family.

Crocker's love and admiration grew. She became his rock—the partner who made his life fuller and more fun, and made everything work.

The first crack in her confidence came two years ago when she and a DS colleague were kidnapped while doing an embassy security survey in Libya. She was held for three days and forced to watch her male colleague being tortured and killed. She was still recovering from that trauma, a year and three months later, when cartel gunmen planted a bomb at their house. Holly had just driven Leslie Ames and Jenny back from a soccer tournament in Richmond. Leslie died in the explosion, which also lodged shards of glass and wood in Holly's liver.

She recovered quickly. But the emotional impact seemed to linger. She spent more time in her room alone and didn't want to talk. Sometimes he caught her crying. Crocker cheered her on, telling her that they'd build a new house and live even better than before. He kept waiting for her to snap out of her funk.

Dr. Mathews had told him to be patient. She also warned him that it might take years. She said, "Each one of us has an emotional limit."

Maybe Holly had reached hers. Maybe she'd never be the same optimistic, confident woman she had been before.

"I can live with that," he told Dr. Mathews. "As long as she doesn't expect me to change."

But she did.

He faced a choice: continuing as the leader of Black Cell, or staying married to Holly. He feared that he couldn't have both.

CHAPTER FOUR

In order to attain the impossible, one must attempt the absurd.
—Miguel de Cervantes

FORTY MINUTES later, the five members of Black Cell were on their way to the Amedros Café on the other side of Divan Yolu, a touristy street that ran down the center of Sultanahmet, the old section of the city. Crocker, Mancini, and Suarez, dressed in casual attire, walked on one side of the street, Davis and Akil following on the opposite side, with both groups keeping an eye out for surveillance. They had progressed a block and a half, checking out the shops and the people strolling, and Crocker was thinking that it would be fun to explore the city sometime with Holly when his burner cell phone pinged.

He reached into his black 5.11 Tactical cargo pants and discovered that it was Akil, who had texted "*87!"

Suddenly the environment turned hostile. "Again? Fuck."

"What's the matter?" Mancini asked.

"We're being followed."

"Who? Where?"

"Don't know."

Again the opportunities for countersurveillance weren't ideal because of the large number of tourists walking the narrow streets. And the SEALs weren't armed, which was a big disadvantage. Nor did they know the city.

"Follow me," Mancini said, nodding left and entering a hotel lobby. He was quick on his feet for a man built like a linebacker, which he had been at Boston College. As they stood near the front desk eyeballing the people who entered, Crocker's cell pinged again.

"Akil again?" Mancini asked.

"No, it's Anders."

The text from Anders read "Meet at the gym in 30?" According to their prearranged code, the thirty minutes had to be halved, and "the gym" meant Anders's room at the Sultanhan Hotel.

He pecked back "OK," and decided not to tell him about the surveillance. He and his men were totally capable of dealing with that.

"What's up?" Mancini asked, continuing to watch the people coming and going.

"Anders wants to see me. I'm taking Akil. You're gonna have to eat without us."

"I think I lost my appetite. Two guys in jumpsuits, eleven o'clock."

Crocker quickly checked them out. The jumpsuits were too stylish and colorful. Seemed like two dudes going out for an evening run.

"Doubt that," he countered as the men exited through the revolving door.

Mancini grinned. "You're right. My appetite for food is hard to kill. You want me to order you some kabobs and bring 'em back to the room?"

"Unnecessary. But first you've got to shake whoever is following."

"Of course. You, too."

Crocker nodded and consulted his Suunto watch. "Be alert. If they're the same guys I tangled with this morning, they're deadly fuckers."

"Got it. Suarez and I will go first. We're gonna exit out the back."

"Cool."

Crocker consulted the tourist map he carried in his back pocket, then called Akil and told him to meet him on the corner of Divan Yolu and Bab-I Ali. He took an elevator up to the roof, lingered there for five minutes listening to two British women discuss who they considered sexier, Jon Hamm or Daniel Craig, then descended the stairs and exited out the back.

It was a beautiful, warm night with a sweet breeze. He found Akil standing in a tourist shop called Hookah John that sold rugs and knickknacks.

"What'd you see?" Crocker asked.

"Two guys riding in a dark-green Renault 19."

"What's that?"

"A boxy looking hatchback similar to a VW Passat."

"What did they look like?"

"Young, clean-cut. One wore a black leather jacket. They both had short black hair. No facial hair."

"You see them now?"

Akil shook his head.

"Follow me."

They entered the heavy foot traffic on Divan Yolu, then hurried to catch the tram at Çemberlitaş, near the Grand Bazaar. They rode it in the direction they'd come from and got off at the Sultanahmet, checking around them. No dark-green Renault in the vicinity. No one who looked suspicious.

"I'll go first," Crocker said. "You follow on the other side of the street."

"Roger."

Ten minutes later they entered the Sultanhan Hotel lobby. Janice stood near the elevator wearing a black jacket and black pants, with her hair pinned back.

"We were followed," Crocker said.

"I know. Those are Colonel Oz's men. They were sent to provide security."

"Two clean-cut guys in a Renault 19 wearing civilian clothes, black jackets?"

"Sounds right."

"Who is Colonel Oz?"

"He's a section leader with MiT. You're about to meet him. I've got a vehicle waiting."

She led the way through a narrow hallway that exited into an alley. Akil elbowed Crocker, thrust his chin toward the rear of her tight pants, and smiled.

Crocker leaned into him and whispered, "Grow up."

Two beefy guys in black suits waited by the black Suburban. They had buds in their ears and looked like Scorpions—CIA private security personnel. Probably ex-military. Both of them appeared to have been bench-pressing serious weight and doing 'roids. Veins stood out on their necks.

Janice climbed into the front with the driver—bull-necked, shaved head, with a tattoo of an inverted cross behind his ear. Crocker and Akil slid into the back with the second Scorpion. Crocker sat wondering whether the inverted cross stood for atheism, humanism, the occult, or devotion to Satan as expressed by one of his favorite bands, Black Sabbath. Depended on the context, he supposed.

As they left the alley, Janice turned to face them. "Anders set up a meet with a couple of guys from MiT. They'll brief you."

"When are we gonna see the guy who shot the video we watched earlier?" Crocker asked.

"The engineering student? We're arranging that now."

"I want to talk to him."

They left the historical/tourist area and turned onto a well-lit freeway that cut through the northern hills and suburbs. Akil's eyes closed, and he seemed to be taking a power nap.

Crocker glanced out the darkened windows and followed the full moon in the cloudy sky. "Nobody told us about the security," he said. "We thought we were being followed."

"Our oversight," Janice answered. "After what happened this morning, we're not taking any chances."

He phoned Mancini to update him. He and the rest of the team were already at the Amedros Café. Crocker heard singing and rhythmic slapping in the background. His teammates hadn't forgotten how to have a good time.

As he put the cell away, Janice asked, "You been doing this long?"

"Three years in the navy; sixteen on the teams."

"I admire you guys a lot."

"Thanks."

He knew her type—dedicated, serious, probably a screwed-up personal life. Sometimes young women like her overdid the tough act as they tried to fit into a field dominated by men.

"What about you?" he asked.

"Eight years in."

"Overseas?"

"No, mostly at HQ."

"Nice."

He imagined a town house in Reston where she lived alone. Probably dated within the Agency. Looked like she ran and worked out.

"We have a friend in common," she announced. "John J. Smith."

Crocker smiled. John Smith was the alias of a CIA officer who ran Shkin Firebase on the Afghan-Pakistani border. Crocker remembered him as a tireless worker with a positive, can-do attitude. He had heard that Smith had gotten into trouble with management for running unauthorized ops into the Pakistani tribal areas.

"What happened to John?" he asked.

"Last I heard he's living near Tampa, running a private executive protection and recovery outfit."

From the wistful expression on her face, he concluded that they had either dated or had had a thing.

"Married?"

"Yeah, to some Colombian girl. They have a baby."

"Good for him," Crocker said, thinking he should call him when he got back to the States.

So many of the guys he had served with as SEALs or with the Agency overseas resurfaced in private security and military companies (PMCs) like Academi (formerly Xe, and before that, Blackwater), L-3 (formerly Titan Corp), Aegis Defense Services, and others. Ten years ago his former SEAL teammate and workout buddy Scott Helvenston was in Iraq as an employee of Blackwater. He and three colleagues were escorting trucks from a food catering company over a bridge near Fallujah when insurgents attacked their vehicle with rocket-propelled grenades. The four men were killed, their bodies burned and mutilated, and two were strung up on a bridge over the Euphrates.

All these years later, Crocker was unable to get the image of the crowd celebrating over the charred bodies out of his head.

There was a lot of ugly shit in there that he'd like to expunge.

*   *   *

They had turned off the freeway and were entering an industrial area. The Scorpion at the wheel guided the vehicle into a gated compound with two tall smokestacks, turned to Janice, sitting beside him, and said, "This is the place."

Judging by the railroad cars loaded with rock, it looked like a metal smelting operation of some kind. Behind one of the large buildings stood a streamlined office structure with cars outside. Three local men wearing street clothes and wielding automatic weapons indicated that they should stop. After Janice addressed them in Turkish through the open window and showed them an ID, they pointed to a place to park.

The long, low-ceilinged room was crowded with people and smoke. Groups of Turkish officials stood conferring and puffing on cigarettes. Through the haze and to his right, Crocker saw Anders standing next to a tall, bald man with a walrus mustache.

What are all these people doing here? Typical second-world shit. Invite everybody and their cousin.

Anders appeared to be the only other American. He waved at Crocker and said something to the bald man, who slapped the table and blurted out something in Turkish.

Three of the Turks put out their cigarettes and took places at the table. The other dozen or so nodded in the direction of their leader and left. The lone female among them paused near the door and looked back at Crocker. He thought for a second that it was Fatima wearing an olive pantsuit and a black headscarf. But this woman had a nose that stuck out like Gibraltar.

Mr. Talab wasn't present.

"All these people work for MiT?" Crocker whispered to Janice, feeling somewhat awkward. He was in the country clandestinely as John Wallace, a security consultant, and didn't like being seen in the company of a known CIA employee, especially by so many people.

She shrugged. "I don't know."

The bald man at the head of the table barked something in Turkish, then shifted quickly to English. As he did, his tone softened.

"Welcome, to you all. Particularly you, Mr. Wallace, and your associates. My name is Colonel Ozgun Ozmert. Call me Colonel Oz. Everybody does." He spoke with a slight British accent and smiled a lot. Reminded him of the actor Yul Brynner.

"Thank you, Colonel. It's good to be here."

"You're very welcome. My good friend Mr. Anders has asked me to answer your questions and to assist you in any way I can."

"I appreciate that."

Colonel Oz held out his hand to a thin man in a dark suit and white shirt to his right.

"First, one of my assistants, Inspector Evren, would like to ask you one or two questions about the unfortunate incident this morning, if that's permittable."

"Go ahead." Again he felt exposed and uncomfortable. *What's the purpose of this meeting?*

Oz continued, "Let me say, first, that political violence of that kind has been rare in Istanbul. We've made sure of that. But with the war in Syria and all the problems that has caused us, these unfortunate incidents have become more frequent."

"Understood." Crocker reminded himself that the Turks were U.S. allies. He had worked with them before and found them cooperative and helpful. He attributed his acute sensitivity to the incident that morning near the Blue Mosque.

Inspector Evren rubbed his hands together and in a pinched voice asked, "You sure you don't mind if I ask you these questions?"

Crocker, who hadn't expected this, looked at Anders, who nodded.

"No. Not at all," he said, feeling strange talking about something he hadn't had time to process fully in front of a group of strangers.

"First, all of us express our deep condolences about Mr. Munoz," Evren said. "Many of us here worked with him and considered him a friend."

Crocker assumed he was talking about Jared. "Thank you."

"The initial attack took place on Torun Sokak?"

"Just around the corner from the bazaar. That's correct."

"How many individuals were involved?"

"I saw four men altogether. Two in a van and two on a motorcycle. I noticed the two motorcycle men on the sidewalk first. I observed that they were following Jared. I was behind him. When I turned onto Torun Sokak, I saw that Jared had been pushed into a van. I rushed to his aid. He was killed while trying to get away. I encountered the two motorcycle men again when they attacked me in a shop on Kabasakal."

By the time he had finished, Crocker noticed that his heart rate was elevated and he had started to perspire.

"Thank you, Mr. Wallace. We're very sorry for your trouble. You might want to know that we were able to capture one of the wounded men from the van."

"Oh. I'm glad to hear that."

"I can also tell you that one of the men you fought off in the shop on Kabasakal is dead from a wound to his head."

"Good."

"We interrogated the wounded man and believe he is a member of Shabiha. These men are paid assassins working for President Assad in Syria."

Crocker wasn't surprised. "I've heard about them, yes."

It made sense. Jared had been in Syria helping the FSA rebels who were trying to destroy the Assad government.

"We are very sorry for your trouble, and apologize deeply."

"If you need me to identify anyone, or to provide you with further details, I'm happy to comply."

"Thank you, Mr. Wallace," said Colonel Oz. "Now, please, so we don't waste your time, let's talk about the situation inside Syria and answer your questions."

"Yes."

He pointed to another man at the table. "Mr. Asani here is our director of intelligence for Idlib province. His English isn't very good, so he submitted this report."

Colonel Oz proceeded to read it, and Crocker took notes.

Three hours later, when Crocker returned to the hotel, his brain was so fried he couldn't think. He passed out as soon as his head hit the pillow and woke up two hours later. Although his body begged for more rest, his mind had rebooted and was eager to process the information it had received.

With shadows dancing across the ceiling and rain splattering against the windows, he reviewed what he had learned from MiT officials. The battle of Idlib had started in March 2010, when elements of the FSA—mostly Sunni defectors from the Syrian Army—seized control of the city. Several weeks later, the Syrian Army fought back, launching a ferocious artillery and air assault that dislodged the rebels from some neighborhoods and sent civilians fleeing toward the Turkish border.

The city had been a military battlefield since, with the Syrian Army controlling the center and east of the city, and periodic attacks, counterattacks, and street-to-street fighting by the rebels who occupied the north and west. While rebel groups also held most of the territory and towns around the city, their ability to retake all of Idlib was severely compromised by the infighting among them.

Mr. Asani likened the current situation to gang warfare. "Alliances shift almost daily. The different militias squabble like teenage girls but mainly disagree about two things: the presence of foreign fighters or jihadists, and the future of Syria."

The Islamic State of Iraq and Syria (ISIS) were the most militant Islamists, dedicated to imposing a medieval-style Islamic caliphate, run under a strict interpretation of Sharia law, in any territory under their control. They were known to assassinate rival rebel commanders they suspected of conspiring against them, including a popular doctor and rebel brigade commander who had been tortured and killed in December.

Other al-Qaeda–affiliated groups such as the al-Nusra Front were more moderate and willing to compromise. On the other side of the political spectrum sat the FSA, whose objective was the overthrow of the Assad regime and the establishment of some form of representative government.

In late 2013, ISIS and FSA had fought pitched battles north and west of Idlib that had resulted in as many as a thousand casualties. In December ISIS seized an FSA weapons warehouse along the Turkish border.

Alarmed by the infighting, nations supporting the rebels gathered in Ankara in late December. Attending this meeting were representatives of Turkey, the United States, Saudi Arabia, Oman, and Qatar, and more than a dozen other rebel groups. These countries promised additional support if the groups they supported pledged to work together. The FSA (backed by Turkey), SRF (Syrian Revolutionary Front, backed by Saudi Arabia), the Army of Islam (backed by Qatar), the Syrian Martyrs' Brigade, and ten other groups signed an agreement to cooperate under the banner of the Syrian Revolutionary Front to push back ISIS and liberate Syria.

Bolstered by new equipment, money, and a renewed sense of purpose, Syrian Revolutionary Front units had made major inroads in the past several weeks, pushing ISIS back to an area northwest of Aleppo.

Crocker realized that the ever-shifting rebel alliances only complicated Black Cell's mission. Because Assad's army still controlled parts of the city and various rebel militias continued to fight for control for the area around Idlib, infil and exfil would be problematic. Entering via helicopter or parachute was probably out of the question. Even more difficult was the challenge of removing the canisters. Since Idlib was far from the coast, they would have to enter and leave by truck.

Mr. Asani explained that the road from the Turkish border town of Reyhanli was considered safer, but it was at least twice as long as the route from Yayladaği, farther west. Both roads presented multiple challenges, including mines, IEDs, and roadblocks. Also, there was a danger that the Syrian air force could mistake vehicles as belonging to the rebels or rebel sympathizers, perhaps ferrying arms or other supplies, which meant that they could travel only at night.

As the minutes passed and Crocker's body begged for more rest, he considered two other problems. The first had to do with the number of individuals (particularly the ones in MiT) who were now aware of his and his team's presence. Given the religious nature of the conflict in Syria and the political/religious struggle currently raging in Turkey, it was impossible to know these individuals' loyalties.

Second, because of the sketchy nature of the information about the situation on the ground, there was no way to know what they might encounter once they entered Syria. And there would be no one to call for help.

CHAPTER FIVE

My mama always said you've got to put the past behind
you before you can move on.

—Forrest Gump

EARLY THE next morning he was driven to the American consulate, which involved crossing the Galata Bridge and following a highway that snaked alongside the Bosphorus north toward the Black Sea. Last night's storm had cleared the air, leaving deep-blue skies and puffy cumulus clouds on the horizon.

He was thinking of home and walks along Chincoteague Beach, holding Holly's hand. During the last session in Dr. Mathews's office, she had accused him of loving his job and his teammates more than his family.

"Not true," he had told her then. But now he admitted she might be right. The truth was that while he loved his wife and daughter and enjoyed spending time with them, the satisfaction and excitement he got from being in SEAL teams was hard to beat.

Inside the consulate auditorium, the U.S. ambassador (who had flown in from Ankara) was quoting from Aristotle as he talked about the differences among intellectual, physical, and moral courage. He said that Jared Olafsen had possessed all three, which had made him an exceptional officer. Then he read from Senator John McCain's book *Why Courage Matters*: "Physical courage is often needed to overcome our fear of the consequences of failure. Moral courage, more often than not, confronts the fear of the consequences of our success."

When Janice stood at the lectern, she got more personal. She and Jared had entered the Agency in the same class, and she described him as the most vital person she had ever met. "Wherever he went, he made friends," she said. "And whatever he did affected people. He certainly had a major impact on my life."

Finally, an American minister closed with a reading from John 15 that ended, "Greater love has no one than this, that a man lay down his life for his friends."

Crocker filed out with the twenty or so others, feeling unmoored and unsettled, wondering what was going to happen next. He found Anders waiting in the hallway. Standing beside him was the station chief, who had also flown in from Ankara—Taylor Grissom, a tall, long-faced man with a mane of silver hair.

Anders introduced them.

"I've been to too many of those things lately," Crocker said, referring to the service.

"They're tough," Grissom responded as he studied something on his cell phone. Without looking up, he asked, "Why are you and your men here and not in Ankara?"

"Because this is where we were told to report," Crocker answered, trying not to let Grissom piss him off.

"Why's that?"

Anders saw that Crocker was getting annoyed, and cut in. "Because Jared, the person who was coordinating this, asked us to meet here."

"For what purpose?" Grissom's eyes were still directed at the little screen on his phone.

"There were people he wanted us to meet."

"Did he tell you who?"

"We sat with some of them, including Mr. Talab, yesterday," Anders responded.

Grissom glanced up and grunted, "Talab, yeah." As he texted something with his thumbs, he added, "I'm headed back to Ankara, and I suggest that you two accompany me."

"Why?" Anders asked. As Deputy Director of Operations, he was really Grissom's boss.

"Because that's where all our targeters and planners are located. I have no problem coordinating this with the Turks, but I don't think we should depend on them—if we do this at all."

Crocker was confused. "Given the stakes, my men and I have been treating this as a 'go' mission."

"Nothing is a 'go,' " Grissom answered, "until we've worked out the logistics and it's approved by the White House."

Annoyed that this trip might become nothing more than a long, nightmarish fishing expedition, he followed the two Agency officers but paused before entering the elevator. "What should I tell the rest of my team?" he asked, glimpsing the Yale University graduation ring on Grissom's index finger.

"Tell them to wait here for the time being. We'll have them deploy directly to the border if and when necessary."

Crocker had been to Ankara only once before, and that had been in the dead of night. What he saw of it now was more modern and a lot less charming than Istanbul. Take away the domes and minarets, and they could be somewhere in Germany.

Anders leaned into Crocker to show him iPhone footage of his fourteen-year-old son striking out the side in a Little League game as the bombproof SUV they rode in entered a heavily fortified compound off one of the major thoroughfares, Atatürk Boulevard.

"His coach has clocked his fastball in the high seventies."

"Impressive," Crocker said. What he was thinking was that Anders should really be more concerned about what all that strain was doing to the kid's developing elbow and shoulder. He tried to be positive. There were two sides to everything. It was good that Anders was proud of his son, and impressive that the kid had developed strong pitching skills at an early age.

He kept his thoughts to himself in the elevator that took them up to the fourth floor of the reinforced concrete vault that housed the CIA station. It smelled of lime disinfectant. The office Grissom led him to was windowless, with a large computer Smart Board filling one wall. Standing beside it stood an Asian woman wearing thick glasses, a plaid skirt, white blouse, and a lopsided grin. A vase of yellow tulips and a picture of her crouched beside a golden retriever rested on her desk. She seemed shy and eager to please her boss.

Grissom, who was reading a message on his phone, asked, "What have you got for us, Katie?" without looking up.

She punched a key on her laptop, which caused a large map of Idlib and the surrounding area to appear on the Smart Board. "I've been talking to various people, including assets on the border and inside the country," she said with a smile. "What they're seeing the last couple of nights is a great deal of rebel activity to the north, east, and west of the city and in the suburbs. That activity corresponds to the state of the weather. Clear skies mean light rebel activity. Cloudy, and they most likely attack with fervor."

"Fervor, is that a technical term?"

She grinned. "Sort of, sir. I use it a lot."

Without looking up from his cell, Grissom asked, "What kind of activity are you talking about?"

"Anti-Assad militia units have engaged the Syrian military defenders with rockets and artillery. The fighting is intense and the militias are making steady progress forward."

She seemed like a typical analyst—smart, articulate, but removed from the fray. She also remained perky in spite of her boss's gruff demeanor, which Crocker admired.

"What about the air force?" Grissom asked as a rail-thin young African American man entered and stood against the wall.

"That's the interesting part. In the past, in a situation like this, we'd see Syrian fighter jets, attack helicopters, and tanks counterattacking. But they're staying away this time. Why? Because the rebels are armed with Croatian-made antitank weapons and Chinese-made MANPADS."

Anders turned to Crocker as if to say, *This is a friggin' mess.*

Katie pressed a key on her laptop and a video played on the Smart Board of a bearded rebel firing a shoulder-held antiaircraft missile and downing an Mi 8/17 helicopter.

"You recognize that weapon, Crocker?" Grissom asked.

"Yes, sir. That's a Chinese-made FN-6."

"You ever fire one?"

"Yes, I have."

"How would you describe it?"

"Powerful, deadly, reliable, and user-friendly."

Grissom turned to Katie and growled, "Who'd you say is providing them?"

"The Saudis, sir."

"Let's just hope to God those damn things don't fall into the wrong hands, and we don't see them taking down commercial air-liners," offered Grissom.

"The FN-6 is only accurate to about five thousand feet," Crocker added. "So jetliners would only be vulnerable if they were taking off or landing."

"So?"

Crocker wanted to reach past Anders and slap him.

Katie cleared her throat and adjusted her glasses. Before she had a chance to speak, Grissom cut in. "With regard to the sarin canisters, which is our concern now, based on what you've told us, what's likely to happen is that the Syrian Army forces will withdraw east or south, taking the sarin with them and making the mission unnecessary. Isn't that a correct assessment?"

"Well...not really, sir," Katie answered.

"Think about it," Grissom barked back.

"I have."

"Think hard."

The thin African American man leaning against the wall behind them spoke for the first time. "What Katie hasn't told you yet is that ISIS units under command of Mohammad al-Kazaz have taken advantage of the FSA–Syrian Army engagement to make a sudden push for the air base."

Crocker later learned he was dealing with the Station's liaison with NSA. That organization was using high-tech cell-phone scanners to track the movements of the various rebel commanders and try to fix the position of their forces—a tricky practice that Katie and others didn't think they should depend on. The problem remained, as always, no reliable sources on the ground.

"So? Doesn't that make my argument even stronger, that the army will withdraw and take the sarin with them?" asked Grissom.

"I believe that's unlikely, sir," Katie responded.

"Why is it unlikely?"

"Because Assad's forces are surrounded."

Crocker looked at Anders, who shook his head as if to say *The situation is even more dangerous than I thought.*

"What air base are you talking about?" Grissom asked, as he scratched his scalp.

The male NSA officer stepped forward, pointed to the map on the Smart Board, and said, "That red marker is just outside Abu al-Duhur military air base, and shows the approximate location of the sarin storage tunnel. There are FSA and ISIS units positioned here, here, here, and here."

The places he pointed to formed a virtual circle around the airport.

"Shit," Grissom blurted. "How close are they?"

"According to the latest intel, approximately a half mile east. The fighting is heavy along these roads." Katie pointed to several arteries on the map. "We're hearing reports of rockets, mortars, house-to-house fighting. And as always, more civilian casualties."

"Are there still civilians in Idlib?"

"It's hard to imagine," Katie answered. "But civilians continue to live in Idlib and the little town of Abu al-Duhur, which is closer to the airport. We believe that both towns are controlled partly by the FSA."

Grissom stood with his hands on his hips and thrust his chin out to study the Smart Board.

"You think Assad would rather see their troops get captured or slaughtered than risk a few helicopters to pull them out?"

"That's my opinion, yes," said Katie.

Grissom's face was turning red. "I don't want to rely on your opinion. I need facts."

"According to intel we got through FSA sources, the majority of the aircraft at the base, including all helicopters, have already been moved. So it appears that unless Assad orders the helicopters back, the troops there are trapped in a situation where they're either going to have to defend the base or surrender."

Grissom pivoted back to Anders and Crocker, who were now standing to his right.

"What do you make of this?" he asked gruffly.

"Katie and Logan are the experts," Anders answered. "If the intel they have is accurate, we face a very serious dilemma."

"What about you?" Grissom asked, thrusting his chin toward Crocker. "What do you think?"

"I think we'd better move quickly, before those chemicals fall into the hands of the terrorists, whether they're al-Qaeda–affiliated or ISIS."

Minutes before midnight the same day, Crocker sat in the passenger seat of a Toyota Land Cruiser rolling through the hills and valleys of Turkey's easternmost Hatay province. What he saw passing in the dark were fields of olive trees, tobacco, and new wheat dotted with hamlets and towns.

Closing his eyes, he dreamt he was in Syria, not far from the Golan Heights. He and Akil were walking toward the Israeli helicopter that had crashed during their mission to recover a downed Predator drone. He saw Ritchie's severed body lying alongside the Black Hawk. This time when he turned it over, Ritchie coughed, blinked, and said, "Boss, come closer."

"What, Ritchie?"

With his last breath he whispered, "Life is tenuous."

Then he turned his head away and sighed.

Crocker had told Ritchie and Cal to remain on the helo while he and the other three SEALs jumped. His order had resulted in Ritchie's death and Cal's very serious injury. Cal was healing now. But as for Ritchie, there was no way to make what had happened right, or to turn back the clock.

The sharp braking of the vehicle jolted Crocker awake. He looked over at the strange thin face behind the wheel and wondered for a moment if he'd been captured.

"I'm stopping here to check the tires," Logan said casually. "Yayladaği's about fifteen minutes away."

"Yayladaği?" Crocker asked, temporarily confused about their destination.

"Yayladaği. The Turkish town on the Syrian border."

He looked out the window and saw a red-white-and-blue NigGaz petrol station lit by flicking fluorescent light. Then he turned back to the light-skinned African American man named Logan he'd met at the Ankara CIA Station. "What's wrong with the tires?" he asked, as he got his bearings.

"Low pressure, according to the indicator," Logan answered, climbing out.

Crocker stood on the concrete, stretched, and watched the boy with the tattered Valencia CF T-shirt fill the tires. Air scented with rosemary refreshed his lungs.

If Akil were here, he thought, *he'd say something clever about the T-shirt.* Akil was an international football fanatic. His favorite squad: FC Barcelona. Favorite players: Andrés Iniesta and Leo Messi.

Crocker had little interest in team sports, and what with Black Cell, working out, and family had practically no time to follow them.

Logan emerged from the white station clutching two bottles of honey and handed them to Crocker as they reentered the vehicle.

"What's this for?" Crocker asked.

"It's a present from you to Colonel Oz. He's our host and a connoisseur of fine honey, not the processed junk they sell in most markets that has none of the good bacteria and enzymes."

Crocker had never heard of processed honey. "How do you tell the difference between the good stuff and the processed?"

"Well, labels are deceptive. So usually smell or taste, unless you know where it comes from."

Logan explained that starting about ten years before, the Chinese had flooded the market with cheap processed honey. In order to avoid importation taxes in various countries they deliberately cooked out the pollen, which was the element that could prove the country of origin in lab tests.

"That's messed up."

"It's commerce. Chinese merchants dilute it with water and high-fructose corn syrup. They couldn't give a shit about human health."

"A lot of people don't," said Crocker, looking out the window at a sign warning that the Syrian border was twenty-five kilometers ahead. He was a physical fitness fanatic who stayed away from excessive carbs, sugar, and processed foods. The older he got, the more he appreciated the need for feeding his body with high-value nutrients.

They topped a promontory covered with groves of olive trees. As they descended into a long valley Logan pulled to the shoulder and stopped. He pointed past Crocker to their right. Filling the oblong field were rows of hundreds of white tents with the Turkish red crescent and star insignia on their roofs.

"That's Yayladaği Refugee Camp Number One," Logan announced. "It holds about twelve thousand refugees and is currently being expanded."

"It's as large as a village."

"It *is* one, in a sense, because the Syrians come here and don't leave. They want to return home but can't, because there's nothing to go back to. Back in Syria, they'd die from attacks or hunger."

Crocker had seen dozens of other refugee camps in places like Ethiopia, Jordan, and Somalia. They always struck him as sad, filled with people who had been torn from their lives and were facing an uncertain future.

"Looks well tended-to from here," commented Crocker, noting that the camp resembled the rows of tobacco they'd passed before—except that these neat lines were formed by tents with families in them.

"This one's state of the art," Logan said. "Every tent is equipped with its own satellite dish and electric hookup to power, lights, heaters, refrigerators, stoves. The camp is run by its own internal government, with an elected governor and citizens' council. Pretty orderly, by all reports, and well administered."

"Nice."

"The Syrians living there are tremendously grateful."

Logan pointed to a group of low stucco buildings at the bottom of the opposite hill. "That's the old tobacco warehouse. It's now used for classrooms, a medical clinic, and laundry."

"So it's completely tricked out."

"These refugees are the lucky ones," Logan continued. "They arrived here more than a year ago. Now it's a hell of a lot harder to get in."

"I can imagine." Crocker had heard that the huge exodus of people from Syria had severely taxed governments and NGOs in Jordan, Lebanon, and Turkey. And it continued.

Logan pressed down on the accelerator and steered the SUV back onto the highway. "Last fall, the Turks were receiving as many as fifty thousand refugees a month," he said. "They've been generous but have reached what the government has called the 'psychological limit.' Now border guards stop anyone who doesn't have a valid passport, which eliminates most poor Syrians."

"So what do they do?"

"Some of them sneak across the border at night. Others camp out in villages where there's no fighting."

The poor always seem to get the short end of the stick whenever things turn ugly, Crocker said to himself.

With that grim reality in mind, they rolled into Yayladaği, a town of six thousand nestled in a sweet green valley surrounded by pine-tree-covered hills. Many of the houses and buildings featured red-tiled roofs that reminded Crocker of Tuscany. In the center of town rested a domed mosque.

They passed it and stopped at the gate of a compound with two large Turkish crescent-and-star insignias painted on the walls. An armed guard checked their passports and waved them in.

He slept for five hours, awoke in the dark, put on a pair of shorts and ASICS he kept in his bug-out bag, and went for a run through the deserted streets. Pre-dawn and dusk were his favorite times of the day, because they grounded him in nature. Back home in Virginia, he liked to run a fourteen-mile loop through First Landing State Park near the Chesapeake Bay Beach, with gulls and egrets flying overhead. Here his footsteps echoed through still streets and under rooms filled with sleeping children and parents. A slight tremble stirred the air in anticipation of the new day, less than an hour away.

This was his form of meditation, a way to release toxins from his body and guilt and second-guessing from his head. His mind focused on the present—the gentle swish of a breeze sweeping through the streets, the thump of his heart, a motor coughing and igniting.

Feeling refreshed and exhilarated, he started to loop the town a third time. Passing a school on the southern perimeter, he spotted ahead a mustached man dragging a suitcase held together with rope and leather belts. The man looked over his shoulder, saw Crocker approaching, and waved at someone to his right to go back. He ducked behind a whitewashed wall, desperation writ large all over him.

When Crocker got to within fifteen feet of the spot, he heard a girl cry out. Past the corner of the school gymnasium, he saw the same man lifting a girl onto his back. She had a pained expression on her face. A teenage boy climbed out of a drainpipe that ran under the track to help the middle-aged man, who Crocker assumed was his father.

Crocker called gently, "Stop." Then using the equivalent Arabic term, he said, *"Waqf."* It was the best he could manage, since he didn't speak Turkish.

The boy, who looked to be about thirteen, reached into his pocket, produced a folding knife, and grunted a warning at Crocker.

Crocker stopped. It wasn't as though he felt threatened. He knew he could disarm the kid in an instant, but he raised his hands instead and said, "It's okay. There's no problem. I want to help you."

The older man grunted and, unable to bear the weight of the girl any longer, started to lower her. She let go of his shoulders and slid down to the ground, landing with a yelp of pain.

Crocker thought he understood the situation. "Syrian?" he asked. "You're Syrian?"

"Syria," the boy nodded back. He had deep circles under his eyes and the gaunt look of someone who hadn't slept or eaten in days.

Crocker pointed to the girl, now moaning on the ground and holding her leg. "Your sister?"

"She…my sister. Yes."

"Is she hurt?"

"Her foot. Bad foot."

"Maybe I can help."

The boy held up three fingers. "Three days…we walk. Khan al-Asal."

Crocker didn't know if this was the boy's name or the village they came from. "This your family?"

"Family. Yes. Mother, father, sister, brother."

Crocker hadn't seen a mother. He pointed to the sister, then at his own eyes, and said, "Your sister. Can I look?"

The father grunted a warning, and the boy pointed the knife at Crocker's chest. Simultaneously, a stout woman with a black scarf over her head stepped out from behind the side of the school.

She must be the mom.

"Doctor?" the boy asked Crocker.

"Medic."

"What…medic?"

"Like a doctor. Yes."

The kid looked confused. Crocker reached into the pouch around his waist and removed two Bonk Breaker energy bars, which he offered to the kid.

The boy lowered the knife, took the bars, and handed them to his mother and father. They ripped the packaging open and passed them to their children. The girl ate hers, but the boy handed his back. The father split it and handed half to his wife, who wolfed it down.

As Crocker knelt beside the girl, he detected the foul odor of infection. Slowly and carefully he undid a black scarf that had been wrapped around her foot. She winced, while the others leaned in and watched.

"You come far?" he asked.

"Far. Yes."

Crocker found considerable swelling, a puncture wound on the sole of the foot, and two spots of gangrene—a quarter-sized one near the heel and a small, lighter colored one in the arch. The puncture was deep and required surgery.

The mother, seeing the discolored skin, covered her face with her hands and started to cry.

"Waqf," Crocker whispered to her.

The woman nodded. Mother and daughter possessed the same dark, almond-shaped eyes.

"Has she had spasms or clenching of the jaw?" Crocker asked, wondering whether the girl had displayed any symptoms of tetanus poisoning.

The boy shook his head. "I no understand."

"Fever? Hot?"

"Hot, yes."

"And shaking?"

Behind him blue lights washed over the street and nearby buildings, and a vehicle braked to a stop. This produced looks of alarm from father and mother. The former lunged forward, grabbed his son by the collar, and pushed him toward the drainage pipe.

Crocker turned and saw a black jeep. Three men in black uniforms and hats stepped out. He didn't know if they were Turkish police or military, or how exactly to handle the situation.

Both mother and father rushed toward the officers, holding out their arms and pleading in Arabic.

Standing in his running shorts, Crocker told them, "I'm an American official. A medic. This girl needs immediate medical attention."

They didn't seem to understand him, nor did they appear impressed. One of the Turkish officers pushed him back gently; another grabbed the boy by the arm and pulled him out of the drainage pipe. They stood surrounding the family and speaking to one another in Turkish as the girl remained on the ground.

One of the Turks asked the father a question in Arabic, and the father responded with a look of defeat.

Crocker had no ID on him, but he tried again. "American," he said pointing at his chest. "I work with Colonel Oz. This girl needs to go to a hospital. Hospital, you understand?"

One of the officers stared Crocker in the eye and barked, *"Pasaport!"*

"Not on me. Back at the military base."

Realizing the futility of staying, arguing, and maybe being detained, he backed away and said to the son, "I'll get help. What's your name?"

"Hakim."

"Wallace. I'm going now to get help."

He sprinted back to the MiT compound and found Colonel Oz standing on the front steps smoking a cigarette and speaking on his cell. The sun had started to rise over his shoulder, casting a golden light on the structures around them.

"You might want to conserve your energy," Colonel Oz said, a smile tugging at the corners of his mouth as Crocker caught his breath. "Your colleagues will arrive within the hour."

He turned to the clock on the tower to his left. If the time displayed there was correct, they would be there by 0745 local time.

"Colonel, as I was running just now I found a Syrian family—

father, mother, and two kids. The girl is young. She's gotten a very serious infection on her foot that requires surgery. While I was examining it, three Turkish officials arrived in a black jeep. They were about to detain them."

"Where?" the colonel asked.

"Near a school in that direction." He pointed past the building they stood beside.

"Fatih Terim Lisesi," Colonel Oz concluded.

"That sounds right."

Oz punched a number into his cell with thick fingers.

"I memorized the license plate number."

"Good," the colonel said. "I'll call now and take care of it." Crocker repeated the number, which Oz translated into Turkish as he spoke into the phone.

"Thank you," Crocker said. "Later, I want to go to the hospital or clinic where they take the girl and make sure she's treated correctly."

The colonel nodded and said, "We have to locate them first."

CHAPTER SIX

Blessed are the meek, for they shall inherit the Earth.
—Matthew 5:5

HE STOOD in the shower, staring at the spaces between the green tiles and thinking how fortunate he and his family were to be citizens of the United States. Most Americans didn't appreciate how lucky they were, nor did they understand the thin line between peace and chaos. When he got home, he'd tell the story of the refugee family to Jenny. He tried to imagine himself and his family in the same situation, fleeing their home with as many possessions as they could carry.

As he pulled on cotton pants and a T-shirt—all in his customary black—a Turkish military aide arrived to inform him that Colonel Oz requested his presence in a room on the second floor.

"Me alone, or my whole team?" Crocker asked.

The aide looked confused. "Your team, I think."

He found Mancini, Akil, Davis, and Suarez sitting on sofas on the second floor, drinking hot tea from glasses and cracking jokes about Davis's dyed black beard and hair.

"Don't you think he looks like an Arab pinup boy?" Akil asked.

The dark hair made Davis's blue eyes stand out more than usual.

"Have you seen Colonel Oz?" Crocker asked.

Mancini shook his head. "Not since we arrived. Why?"

"What about Logan?"

"Logan? Don't think I've met him."

"What do you call a Turkish baby?" Akil asked in a low voice as Crocker craned his neck looking down the hall.

"What?"

"A kebaby."

Crocker groaned. "That sucks."

"What do you say to a crying Turkish baby?"

"What?"

"Shish kebaby."

Crocker shook his head and groaned again. "Even worse. You guys drive here?"

"Unfortunately. We've been listening to his bad jokes for the last hour," Davis complained.

"I would have tossed him out of the vehicle."

"We considered it."

Mancini asked, "Boss, what's going on? You look like you got a lot on your mind."

"We need to get ready to deploy into Syria tonight."

"How?" the always practical Mancini asked. "What's the plan?"

"There is no plan, as of yet. We just have an objective and a timeline, but no approval."

"Let's not do what we did in southern Mexico," Mancini commented. In that case, with the minutes ticking down to a deadline, Crocker and his men had launched a raid before they'd gotten White House approval. Fortunately, they had saved a U.S. senator's wife in the process, otherwise Crocker might have been drummed out of the service.

"Hopefully Oz will have more intel when I find him."

"He's getting his head polished," Akil joked.

"Not funny."

"Seriously, boss, some cultural advice," Akil offered. "Don't get impatient. Turks don't like that. Pride and honor are important to them."

"Thanks."

He hurried down to the end of the long hall. All the offices and rooms were empty, except for one in which a man with his feet on his desk was reading a report.

"Excuse me, do you know where I can find Colonel Oz?"

The Turkish soldier picked up a phone and called someone. After he hung up, he led Crocker over to the window and pointed to a low adjoining building on the left.

"Kahvalti," he said in Turkish.

"I don't understand."

The Turk mimed sipping a cup of coffee. "Colonel Oz…"

The Turkish orderly led them across an empty cafeteria and entered a private dining room where Colonel Oz sat at a round table with Mr. Asani and Logan watching a TV propped in the corner. Logan looked bored and uncomfortable.

Seeing Crocker and his men, Oz stood and pointed to a buffet set up on a table along the wall and said, *"Buyrun, takilin"* (Help yourselves). Before the SEALs had heard the translation, they were filling plastic plates with boiled eggs, cheese, green olives, *sucuk* (dried sausage), and *börek* (thin dough filled with meat, cheese, and chopped vegetables).

"These people know how to eat," commented Akil as he bit into a piece of *börek*.

"Good," Mancini said. "Check out the baklava."

"Isn't *baklava* a Greek word?" asked Davis.

"No, Turkish. Dates back to ancient Mesopotamia."

They found places at the table and filled cups from white pitchers of Turkish coffee and green tea. Colonel Oz's eyes never wandered from the TV, where a buxom blonde with elaborate makeup and a tight lavender outfit was interviewing a bearded man in a white suit.

"Who's the babe?" Crocker asked as he sat next to Logan.

"Don't know."

Crocker couldn't understand what the man on TV was saying, but he noted his extreme self-importance and theatricality.

"What about the guy in the white suit?"

"His name is Harun Yahya."

Crocker had never heard of him. "Who is he?"

"Harun Yahya? The messianic leader of an apocalyptic Islamic sex cult, and a close friend of Prime Minister Erdoğan."

"Really?" Crocker asked in disbelief. "I never thought I'd hear the words *Islamic* and *sex cult* in the same sentence."

"Harun Yahya is an important man in Turkey and considered one of the most influential figures in Islam. Kind of a cross between L. Ron Hubbard and Hugh Hefner."

"Who's she?" Davis asked from the other side of Logan, pointing to the woman in lavender.

"Don't know her name, but she must be one of Harun Yahya's so-called kittens. He's into kinky sex and cocaine, and has written something called the *Atlas of Creation,* which espouses some weird form of creationism, that he's sent to academics and biologists all over the world. Those who have bothered to read it dismiss it as pure BS."

"Sounds like your kind of thing," Crocker said to Davis. "You ever hear of it?"

Davis shook his head.

As they watched, one of several lavender-spacesuit-clad kittens did a slow pirouette and broke into song, an off-key Turkish version of "The Impossible Dream" from *Man of La Mancha*.

Colonel Oz applauded and started to laugh. He rose halfway to his feet as though he was about to say something when a massive explosion blew the glass out of the cafeteria window, threw him back against the wall, and lifted the others out of their seats. Glass flew everywhere. Chunks of plaster from the ceiling crashed onto the table. Eggs, tea, and coffee spilled onto the floor.

Crocker found himself on the floor gasping for breath. He brushed the dust away from his eyes and mouth, and did a lightning-fast appraisal of the damage. When he saw that the ceiling wasn't going to cave in, he hurried over to Oz, who lay near the wall holding his chest and coughing.

"What the fuck was *that?*" Akil shouted through the dust and debris.

"Car bomb, probably," Mancini responded, picking a sliver of glass out of his thigh. "The explosion originated to our left."

Men were scrambling, moaning, and coughing. Some crawled under the table.

Crocker, his eardrums ringing, shouted, "Clear everyone to the courtyard in back!"

He heard no gunfire or sounds of a follow-up attack.

With Oz leaning on him and wheezing, he turned to him and said, "We're going outside to get fresh air and find out what's going on."

Oz nodded.

Mr. Asani, who was bleeding from a cut to his forehead, took Oz by the arm and led him out while Crocker accounted for his men. Except for a few minor cuts, they were all intact.

The courtyard, which occupied the space between the military headquarters building and barracks, quickly filled with half-dressed soldiers carrying AKMs (modernized Kalashnikovs) and Spanish-made G3 7.62x51mm NATO assault rifles. MiT officials in black were barking orders into handheld radios and cell phones, and medics were ministering to the wounded. Nobody appeared to be seriously hurt.

"The bomb went off in front of Turkish police headquarters down the street," Asani reported. "From what I hear, the whole front of the building collapsed."

Crocker knew that meant casualties and wounded. "You wait here," he said, turning to Mancini. "I'm going to see if I can help."

Akil chimed in, "I'm coming with you."

With a borrowed medical kit and two Sarsilmaz Kilinç 2000 semi-automatic 9mm pistols, he and Akil hurried left along the main street.

As he ran, the thick, stomach-turning smell of Ritchie lying on the ground hit Crocker again. His throat turned dry and he started to feel sick. Leaning on the hood of a parked truck, he felt the muscles in his abdomen convulsing and he threw up.

"Go back, boss," Akil said. "I can handle this."

"No, I'm okay."

"No, you're not. Wait here. I'll get you some water."

"Screw that."

Three short blocks later they reached the Turkish police building. Pushing through the throng of onlookers and stepping around the six-foot-deep crater and smoking ruin of what was left of the truck that had carried the bomb, they confronted the pancaked façade of a modern six-story building.

"Holy shit!" Akil exclaimed.

Crocker had seen too many scenes like this.

The sickening smell of ammonium and burning plastic lingered in the air—a telltale sign of an ammonium nitrate car bomb. Half-dressed Turkish firefighters were trying to extinguish a furious blaze on the third floor. Scattered around them lay bodies, parts of bodies, the twisted remains of furniture, glass, and rubble. People trapped in the building called for help.

"What do we do now?" Akil asked.

"Follow me," Crocker said, crossing to a passageway along the far side of the building where rescue workers in blue-and-red helmets were carrying out people on stretchers. The heat and dust were oppressively thick. Pushing forward, they climbed through the rubble to the back. All the windows there had been blown out, and although the six stories were still intact, the whole structure looked about to collapse.

Men from inside a basement floor were shouting in Turkish and waving pieces of clothing. Crocker and Akil knelt in the broken glass and lifted out a stretcher bearing a wounded man through the broken frame of a window. They handed it up to rescue workers, grabbed an empty stretcher, passed it inside, and got ready to take the next wounded individual.

After the fourth one, Crocker's arms were aching and sweat was dripping from his brow. "There are prisoners trapped downstairs," he heard a woman behind him say in English.

"Where?"

"Over there." She pointed to a pancaked section of the building to their right.

He stood and acknowledged the woman in the blue Turkish EMS uniform. "Thanks."

Stepping over a chunk of smoldering, undistinguishable flesh, he pulled at Akil's sleeve and pointed to the little space in the collapsed concrete where a man was attempting to pull himself through. His shoulders were stuck and he grimaced in pain.

"Calm down," Crocker told him. "We'll get you out."

"American?" the trapped man asked, his face covered with white dust and vivid red blood dripping from the top of his head.

"Canadian."

"Toronto Maple Leafs or Montreal Canadiens?"

"The Leafs, of course."

Together, the SEALs used their legs to pivot a chunk of concrete to the right so it continued to hold back the debris above it but opened enough space for the man to worm through.

He smiled and embraced them, even though his right foot was a mess. A relief worker with a Canadian patch on his shoulder led the man off. *Weird coincidence*, Crocker thought, his throat and nostrils clogged with dust and smoke.

The space they had opened allowed more prisoners to squeeze out. Crocker was helping one with an injured arm when he recognized the face of the Syrian boy he had seen earlier with his family.

"Hakim."

"My friend! My friend! Mr. Wallace."

He knelt in the rubble, cleaned and dressed a cut near the kid's elbow, and asked, "Where's the rest of your family?"

"Hospital. They go to hospital."

"Good. What's your last name?"

"Gannani."

"Hakim, stay with me. You can be my assistant. Okay?"

"Yes." The boy smiled, revealing a large space between his upper front teeth.

Crocker found Akil on his knees, still passing empty stretchers to the workers inside. Wiping the perspiration from his forehead, Crocker said, "I'm taking this kid to the hospital and will meet you back at headquarters."

"Who's he?"

"I'll explain later."

"When?"

"I'm going now."

"I mean, when will you be back at HQ?" Akil asked.

"Soon as I'm finished."

"Remember, we've got a mission."

"I know. I'll be no more than an hour."

He and the boy worked their way to the front of the building, stopping to disinfect and bandage wounds and clean faces. Crocker directed Hakim into the back of a blue-and-white medical van. A young female nurse with pale blond hair leaned on his shoulder and sobbed throughout the five-minute ride uphill.

"You're doing good work," he said to her in English. "These people need you."

She nodded and wiped her eyes. "Nona."

"Wallace."

"Polish."

"Canadian."

Cute girl. No more than twenty-five.

He lost her in the chaos of the hospital—a parking lot and entrance lined with stretchers; inside, stressed-out EMS workers, doctors, and nurses shouting orders in Turkish and Arabic and running to and fro.

He saw a little girl lying on her back fully conscious, with her stomach, liver, and intestines exposed. He held her hand, grabbed a doctor, and locked his eyes on her dark-brown ones as they wheeled her into surgery—heroism and tragedy all around him. Everyone pitching in to save lives.

Crocker worked his way down a green corridor, administering help where it was needed—setting one man's broken femur, removing broken teeth and debris from a soldier's throat, handing out bottles of water to people in shock. Hakim ran upstairs to try to locate his family.

Time flew past, with more wounded arriving by the minute. Then, as though someone had turned off a tap, the flow of incoming stopped and the entire hospital and all the people in it seemed to relax.

Crocker was leaning over a gurney applying a cold compress to a minor burn on an old man's arm when Hakim tugged the back of his shirt. From the expression on his face, Crocker could tell that he had found his family.

"Where?" Crocker asked.

"Floor three. Room 312."

"Good. I'll be there in a minute."

Ten minutes later, he climbed the steps and found a large rectangular room packed with beds and cots. Some patients rested on mats on the floor. The Syrian family stood beside a bed in the far corner by a window covered with old mustard-colored curtains. The sun through the curtains cast a golden hue over their heads and shoulders.

Mother and father greeted him with hugs and kisses. Both pointed proudly to their daughter, lying on her back with her eyes closed. An IV drip fed her right arm, and her left foot was wrapped in bandages, indicating that the doctors had treated it in time.

Crocker nodded with relief and turned to the faces of Mr. and Mrs. Gannani beside him, each clutching one of his hands and smiling and weeping at the same time.

"I'm very glad," he said.

"Allahu akbar," the father muttered. God is great.

"Yes, *Allahu akbar,*" Crocker repeated. It didn't matter that he was Christian and the Gannanis Muslim. They were all giving thanks— whether they were referring to a divine creator, karma, or random good luck. The Gannanis had no home to go back to, no country, and little more than the clothes on their backs, but they were grateful to be together with their children and alive.

Through Hakim, the parents asked Crocker about his own family and nodded with affection and muttered blessing to Allah as he described Holly and Jenny back in Virginia.

After he had confirmed with a Turkish doctor that the girl's foot had been saved and she was out of danger, it was time to say goodbye. Mrs. Gannani insisted on pressing a little white embroidered handkerchief into his hand as a token of thanks. They hugged and kissed him again. He wished them well and walked back to the military compound feeling fulfilled in an important way.

Maybe what Jared had said back in the Meşale Café was right. Maybe larger commercial interests really were pulling the strings. But he lived by his own code, and that included protecting humble people like the Gannanis wherever they lived in the world, even if that made him naive, or romantic, or a renegade in some people's eyes.

CHAPTER SEVEN

Success is going from failure to failure
without losing your enthusiasm.
—Anonymous

WITH A renewed sense of purpose, he huddled with Logan, Colonel Oz, and Mancini back at the military headquarters to plan the mission. They quickly decided that the men of Black Cell would need some kind of cover to give them the best chance of reaching Idlib without resistance. Mr. Asani suggested that they play the role of foreign humanitarian workers delivering medical supplies to the besieged city, which the clinics badly needed.

"That will work," Crocker said. "But we're going to need uniforms, medical supplies, and the proper kind of trucks to pull that off."

Logan used the phone and fax in one of the offices to communicate with Ankara Station. Returning to the conference room, he reported four things: One, Anders was on his way to Yayladaği. Two, Ankara Station would coordinate with the Canadian consulate to produce identities, passports, other documents, and even appropriate clothing for the five men. Three, the president still hadn't approved the mission. And four, FSA Elite Battalion soldiers under the command of Captain Zeid were on their way from nearby Rey-hanli to help escort Black Cell into Syria.

"What do you know about Captain Zeid?" Crocker asked.

"He's a former Syrian Army 17th Regiment soldier who defected in early 2012," Colonel Oz answered. "One of about five hundred. They formed the core of the armed resistance against Assad."

"Can he be trusted?"

"As much as you can trust anyone fighting in Syria," Oz answered.

"How much is that?"

"About sixty percent."

By 1500 local time, the men's physical dimensions were recorded and photos were taken and sent back to Ankara. By 1720 hours a helicopter had landed at the back of the compound, with the re-quired uniforms, passports, documents, and other gear. Also aboard were Anders, Mr. Talab's assistant Fatima, Janice, and the young engineering student named Hassan who had shot the video of the soldiers carrying the sarin canisters into the tunnel.

Fatima, on whom Crocker focused first, wore a tight olive uniform with no insignia. As she and Hassan retreated to a nearby office to confer via telephone with Mr. Talab, the rest of them discussed ve-hicles. It was assumed that Captain Zeid and other members of the FSA escort would be traveling in their own truck or jeep. The ques-tion then was, how many vehicles did Crocker and his men need, what was available, and of those available, which ones best suited the mission?

Mancini spelled out their needs. "Since we're going in as human-itarian workers delivering medical supplies, we need delivery-type trucks. They also have to be big and strong enough to accommodate the sarin."

"How many canisters are we talking about?" Crocker asked.

Logan, who had carefully studied Hassan's video, answered, "Anywhere from six to ten."

"Then we need two trucks," Crocker responded.

"Cobras?" Colonel Oz asked. The Cobra was a Turkish-made armored vehicle.

"No," Crocker said. "Armored vehicles will attract attention."

"But they offer more in terms of safety," Anders added.

"I'm thinking more along the lines of covered extended-cab pickup or transport trucks," said Crocker. "Something that will pass for medical transport."

"Yeah. One that doesn't have visible ordnance mounted on it," Mancini offered.

Oz: "We've got the Turkish-made 25 Kirpi 4x4."

Mancini said, "I'm gonna have to see it."

"Follow me."

Behind the barracks, Colonel Oz pointed out various vehicles in a fenced-in, guarded lot. Crocker and Mancini picked out a mine-resistant, ambush-protected 25 Kirpi 4x4 and a 2.5-ton BMC covered transport truck. Then Crocker changed his mind and decided in favor of an extended-cab Ford F-250 pickup and Mercedes Sprinter van.

"Why, boss?"

"They're more low-profile. If we're going in in-alias, we gotta play that all the way."

"But they give us no place to take refuge if we're attacked."

"We'll manage."

The Sprinter was beige, but the pickup sported military camouflage, which Crocker didn't like.

"You have one in a neutral color?"

"You want leather seats and air conditioning?" Colonel Oz asked back with a grin.

"Yeah, tilt-back steering and moon roofs, too."

Oz chuckled. "I'll have my men check with the highway department. Their trucks are gray."

"Solid. And find a cover for the pickup."

"Canvas okay?"

"Aluminum is better. Slap some crosses on them if you can, so they look official."

"You want petrol in them, too?" asked Oz.

"That would be nice. We're also going to need to load them with medical supplies," Mancini added.

"Medical supplies....I'll talk to Dr. Ebril."

Crocker: "Who's he?"

"Head of our medical department."

"How many klicks to Idlib?" Crocker asked.

"Klicks?" Oz asked.

"Kilometers."

"About one hundred twenty-four kilometers. Without delays, it should take no more than two hours."

"That's seventy-seven miles, boss," Mancini said, doing the conversion in his head.

"He's our combination computer, dictionary, encyclopedia, technical manual, and atlas," Crocker said, nodding toward Mancini.

"Where's Cape Arnauti?" Oz asked, testing him.

"It sits at the northwestern tip of Cyprus," Mancini answered. "Nice beach and offers excellent snorkeling, but the roads suck."

"Impressive," responded Oz. "I could use someone like him."

*   *   *

That task completed, Mancini went to the arsenal to look at weapons. He chose his favorite HK416 assault rifles, but these were the A5s, with the 5.56x45mm NATO-caliber ammo. He made sure they had M320 grenade launchers attached to the rails and AAC M4-2000 suppressors. Backing them up, he selected two MP5 machine guns, a Browning M2HB .50-caliber heavy machine gun, and a couple of Soviet-made RPG-7Ds with a variety of warheads—PG-7VRs for taking out tanks and armored vehicles, OG-7Vs for fragmentation, and Gsh-7VTs for penetrating bunkers. As sidearms, they'd pack the SIG Sauer P226s that they were familiar with.

Back in the conference room of the main building, Crocker started to feel the tension building in his stomach. Anders had brought Phoenix IR strobe beacons, grenades, SOG knives, Tri-Fold handcuffs, M3X weapon lights, tactical wristbands with a pouch that contained maps of Idlib and Arab-language translations, and INVISIO M4 in-ear conduction headsets. The latter used bone-sensing conduction to allow operators to whisper to one another, while eliminating ambient noise.

The last two items were black T-shirts with red Doctors Without Borders (DWB) insignia and Dragon Skin SOV-4000 Level V body armor, which was lightweight, tough enough to withstand up to twenty direct hits from an AK-47, expensive as hell, and not available to the general public. Each vest was made of overlapping ceramic disks enclosed in a sonic skin textile cover and weighed about five pounds.

Pointing to the DWB insignia, which featured a figure in motion, Akil said, "This dude looks like he's running."

"So?" asked Crocker.

"I don't run from anything."

"We'll see what happens when the Syrian Army or ISIS is on your ass."

*　　　*　　　*

Everyone assembled to listen to Hassan talk about conditions in Idlib and the location of the tunnel. He was in his early to mid-twenties, with round glasses, short bushy hair, eyebrows, and beard, and spoke perfect English, which he had learned attending one year of engineering school at the University of Delaware. Dressed in jeans and a striped Izod shirt, he looked like a nervous, determined grad student, Crocker thought.

"University of Delaware. That makes you a Fightin' Blue Hen," Akil said.

"How the hell do you know that?" Mancini asked.

"I dated a coed from UD once."

"You mean you got her too drunk to notice your ugly mug and slept with her."

"All right, guys," Crocker warned, nodding toward Janice, who was still in the room. "That's not funny."

"No, it's not," said Janice.

"Sorry," Mancini responded.

"He gets all macho when he's not being browbeaten by his wife," added Akil.

"Enough," Crocker said.

"Fighting blue hens have a reputation for being ferocious cockfighters," said Hassan.

"I'm not touching that," said Akil.

"Me either," added Mancini.

"When's the last time you were in Idlib?" Anders asked, turning to Hassan.

"Uh...two weeks ago," he answered. "Two weeks exactly."

Anders pointed to Janice, who hit a key on her laptop that projected a satellite map of Idlib on a screen at the front of the room. "Can you show us the exact location of the tunnel with the canisters?"

Hassan turned to Fatima, who was sitting to his left, shrugged, and muttered something in Arabic. She said something back.

"Is there a problem?" Anders asked.

"He never said the tunnel was inside the city of Idlib itself."

"Then where is it?"

Anders knew this information already, but wanted to make sure Hassan's story remained consistent.

"It's located in the province of Idlib, farther southeast," Hassan answered. "Near the town of Abu al-Duhur, inside the perimeter of the Abu al-Duhur military air base."

Fatima nodded. "Can you show us on the map?" asked Anders.

Hassan moved the cursor on the laptop and zoomed in closer. Two long runways appeared against a flat green-brown landscape. A rectangular building rose in the distance, the only major building in sight.

"That's the air base headquarters," Hassan said, pointing.

"Where are the aircraft and barracks?" Crocker asked. "Where's the control tower?"

"The control tower, I believe, is housed in the headquarters building," replied Hassan. "The aircraft and barracks are contained in four large underground bunkers. Here, here, here, and here."

"Is the base still operational?" Mancini asked.

Hassan looked confused. "If you mean, is the Syrian air force still flying planes and helicopters from there, the answer is yes."

Katie at Ankara Station had told them the aircraft were no longer stationed at the air base. If they made it there, they'd find out who was right.

"What kind?" Crocker asked.

"MiGs and helicopters."

MiG-25s and 29s; Mi-24 and SA 342 Gazelle attack helicopters," Oz answered. The latter were small, versatile, French-made, and originally designed for reconnaissance, sometimes armed with HOT-3 antitank missiles. Crocker had seen them deployed by Saddam Hussein during the First Gulf War and by the Serbians in Kosovo.

A military aide with an elaborate handlebar mustache pushed in a cart with tea, olives, cheese, and crackers.

"And where exactly is the tunnel?" Crocker asked.

"The entrance is here, near Bunker 3," Hassan answered, pointing at the map. He seemed precise and intelligent.

The entrance wasn't visible on the satellite map. Crocker did make out a sandbag guard station and a tank stationed nearby.

"If we go in, we're going to have to create a diversion," Mancini offered. "Maybe an attack on one of the other bunkers."

"C4 here and here," Akil remarked, standing and pointing to the two ends of Bunker 3.

"We'll leave that to Suarez," offered Crocker. Suarez, who wasn't present, was the explosives expert on the team. He and Davis were currently checking the gear Anders had brought via helicopter.

"How stable is the area?" Crocker asked.

"You mean safe? It's not safe at all." Hassan pointed to the map. "Most of the area west of the air base is controlled by ISIS. You know who they are, right?"

"Since they overran Mosul in Iraq, they've been a constant subject of discussion by counterterrorism experts on CNN. So, yes."

"If we can, we should avoid them," said Hassan.

"We'll try."

"Most of the territory between the border and Idlib is controlled by different FSA commanders," Hassan continued. "Some of them are Jabhat al-Nusra, but I know most of those guys, and they shouldn't give us problems."

"Isn't Jabhat al-Nusra allied with al-Qaeda?" asked Crocker.

"Most of these guys behave like gang leaders. They have two things in common. They all hate and are trying to overthrow the Assad regime, and they're all Sunni Islamists. The jihadists of ISIS are the most extreme. But most leaders cooperate. What differentiates them in terms of power has to do with who has the most weapons and money at a particular time. If you're a militia leader and you have cool weapons and lots of cash, you attract men to fight with you."

"So what you're saying is that a particular antigovernment fighter might be allied with FSA one week, al-Nusra another, and ISIS the next," Mancini offered.

"Yes. The makeup of ISIS is slightly different. They have more foreign fighters and religious fanatics. If they see infidels like your-selves, they'll probably kidnap you and sell you for ransom, or cut your heads off."

"That's not happening," Akil commented.

"How do we get from Idlib to the air base?" Crocker asked, trying to shift the focus to practical tasks.

"We follow Highway 60 through the city of Idlib until we reach a local road. I'll show you," Hassan answered, nodding toward the map.

"What about the town of Abu al-Duhur, north of the air base?" asked Crocker. "Who controls that?"

"Some FSA groups have been attacking it, but it's still firmly un-der the command of the Syrian Army and the pro-Assad Shabiha militias."

At the mention of the Shabihas, Crocker felt a shiver go up his spine.

He sat cleaning and reassembling his NATO-issue HK416 and listening to the Stones' *Exile on Main Street* on his headphones when Colonel Oz walked in to inform him that Captain Zeid had arrived. Glancing at his Suunto watch, which had adjusted automatically, he saw that the local time was 1944.

"Do you think these guys are necessary?" Crocker asked as he set the weapon on a nearby cot.

"Yes, we do."

Crocker liked to maintain as much operational silence as possible. The more people who knew about a mission, the greater the possibility word would leak out. Barging into the middle of a civil war to steal WMDs from an unfriendly army was risky enough. He didn't want combatants waiting for him and his men when they got there.

"You know this Zeid guy personally?" Crocker asked.

"No, but I know his reputation, which is good."

They found him in the conference room with his military boots propped on a chair, leaning back and smoking a Camel. Seeing Oz and Crocker, he clenched the cigarette in his teeth and slowly rose to his feet. He wore a clean camouflage uniform with a Syrian flag FSA patch on the shoulder and stood about five ten. A good-looking guy with an ugly scar over his right eye and well built. His casual manner threw Crocker off at first. Given the ferocity of the war across the border, he had expected someone more battle weary and intense.

His companion, a large, pot-bellied man introduced as Babas, didn't have the bearing of a military man, either. He looked like a guy you'd find in the back of a restaurant kitchen scraping plates.

"I thought there were going to be three of you," Crocker said.

"My other man, Marai, he is excused to go to a wedding. His sister."

"I see you speak English."

"A little, yes."

"That's good, because my Arabic sucks."

"Maybe no good. I don't know."

He turned to Babas, who laughed and said, "He like America woman. He want to marry…Scarlo Johasten." He formed an hourglass shape with his hands for emphasis.

"You mean Scarlett Johansson. I think she's taken."

"Taken? Who take her?"

Crocker looked at Oz and said, "We should get moving. Are these guys ready to roll?"

Oz muttered something to Zeid, and the two men started to argue in Arabic.

Crocker nudged Oz's arm and asked, "What's going on?"

"He says they can get you as far as Idlib, but after that you're on your own."

"What about getting out?"

"He says they'll wait for you in Idlib."

"Idlib, yes," Zeid interjected. "But after that…is very bad."

"Why?"

"Not bad…dangerous. Why you go?" Zeid asked. "You bring medicine? Medicine better for Idlib. Much better."

Before Crocker had a chance to answer, Oz pulled him into the hallway.

"What's the problem?" Crocker asked.

Oz rubbed his head. "He wants money."

"Of course he does. But he doesn't know the real purpose of our mission, does he?"

"No, but I'm sure he's suspicious."

They found Janice and Logan eating lamb stew in the cafeteria.

"Where's Anders?" Crocker asked.

"He had to leave. Why, is there a problem?"

"Zeid is here, and he wants to get paid."

Janice answered coolly, "We were prepared for that. How much?"

"Twenty thousand," replied Oz.

"Dollars?" Crocker asked.

"Yes."

"Tell him we're offering ten."

Oz nodded and did an about-face. Crocker followed, asking, "Do we really need Zeid and his friend?"

"If you want to get past the roadblocks, yes."

"What about Hassan?"

"I don't know anything about him, but Zeid knows his way around."

Soon after they returned to the conference room, Zeid casually agreed to the adjusted sum of ten thousand. He stubbed out his cigarette and offered his hand. "We do this together, my Canada friend."

"Yes. Be ready to leave in two hours." Crocker pointed to the ten o'clock mark on his watch. He was hoping they'd receive the necessary approvals by then.

"I think eleven is better."

"Why?"

Zeid smiled. "So my friend Babas can enjoy his dinner."

Babas made a silly face and nodded.

"Eleven, then, but this isn't a joke."

Zeid changed his expression from smiling to serious. "No joke."

* * *

The revised PLO (platoon leader's order) called for them to assemble in the yard at 2215 hours, depart at 2300, reach the air base by 0100, recover the canisters, and return to Yayladaği before sunrise. It was 2015 now, so Crocker gave his men an hour or so to rest, check their gear, and attend to any personal business before they met to go over the PLO again.

He stood in the officer's room he had been given stripped to the waist, checking the list of first-, second-, and third-line gear each man would be carrying, when he heard a knock on the door. He set the yellow legal pad down on the desk and said, "Come in."

He was hoping it was Janice telling him that the go order had come from the White House. Instead, Fatima pushed open the door partially, stood in the opening, and asked, "Do you mind if I interrupt you for a minute, Mr. Wallace?"

Her hair was pulled back and the top button of her uniform was open, revealing the tops of her breasts. Seeing the various scars across his stomach and chest, she gasped. He grabbed a black tee from the chair and pulled it over his head.

"Mr. Wallace…"

"Just Wallace. What's up?"

Somewhat awkwardly, she thrust forward a sealed bottle of Johnnie Walker Red Label scotch she had tucked under her arm and offered it to him. "Mr. Talab sends his apologies for not being here to see you off, and asked me to give you this," she said rapidly in thickly accented English.

Partially concealed under her top, just behind the curve of her left hip, he made out the outline of a pistol.

"Thanks," he said, noticing that the bottle had been warmed by the heat from her body. "It's nice and warm."

"What did you say?"

"I said, you have warm hands. Sit down. Tell me about yourself."

She sat on a metal chair and crossed her legs, but didn't seem to know where to put her hands. She folded them in her lap, looked at them, then lifted her head and said, "Mr. Talab asked me to thank you ahead of time for the brave service you're about to do for the people of Syria."

"Tell him he's welcome."

Her eyes were beguiling and dark, set above high cheekbones and framed by manicured arched eyebrows. He wondered why she was really there and what she was thinking.

"What brings you to Yayladaği?" he asked.

"Oh, Mr. Talab sent me."

In the corner by the sink he found two plastic cups, rinsed both, and dried one with the hem of his shirt. Then he cracked open the bottle, filled one of the cups with two inches of scotch, and offered it to Fatima. "Let's drink a toast."

"Oh....Yes."

"To a free Syria."

"Yes."

She took a long sip, noticed that his cup was filled with water, and stopped. "But..."

"I can't," he explained. "I'm leaving on a mission."

"Yes, but...."

He pointed to her cup. "And you're not a strict Muslim."

She shook her head and looked embarrassed. "No. Yes. I was born Muslim, but I'm more...liberal."

"You were raised here in Turkey?"

"No. No, I grew up in Damascus. You know the city?"

He had been there once on a reconnaissance mission but didn't want to talk about that. "So you probably haven't had much contact with Americans."

She bristled slightly. "We were taught in school to hate Americans. But I never felt that way myself."

"I'm glad. We're nice."

His smile seemed to calm her. She grinned back. On a strictly physical level, they were attracted to each other, but he had a feeling that wasn't what this was about.

"Before the fighting, I had a very good life, you see. Friends, parties, school. I went to the beach in the bathing suit I wanted. I could drink. I could go to school, drive a car, walk the streets by myself. If the Islamists take over, all that is finished, and it will be impossible for me to live in my own country."

"I understand," he said, gazing into her sad but defiant eyes.

"Freedom is like ice cream, Mr. Talab says. You taste a little, and you want more."

"What do you think will happen?"

"In Syria? I don't know. Assad is not going to live forever."

Crocker wasn't sure what she meant by that. Was she opposed to the armed effort to depose him? Was she saying that Assad was better than the possible Islamic alternative? It seemed so.

Seeing his confusion, she added quickly, "I hate the regime, of course, because of what they have done. But now we Syrians have to protect ourselves, because everyone wants a piece of that cake that is our country."

"You mean the Iranians?" he asked, leaning forward. He was referring to the aggressive role of the Iranians and their Hezbollah proxies who were defending Assad.

"The Iranians, the Lebanese, the Israelis, the Kurds, the Turks. Maybe even the United States."

Crocker shook his head. "The U.S.? I don't think so."

"No?"

He finished the water and set the cup on the floor. When he looked up, he saw her rising to her feet and reaching for her left hip. Instinctively, he lunged at her and went for the pistol. As he grabbed her right wrist and pulled it down, he realized that she wasn't reaching for the pistol but merely adjusting it. But it was too late.

Holding her right hand with his left, he reached under her uniform tunic and removed the weapon—a hot-pink Beretta Nano 9mm—from its nylon holster.

"What's this for?" It looked silly in his hand.

She pulled her wrist free and contorted her mouth. She also tried to twist away, which only added to the friction between their bodies. "What are you doing? You hurt my wrist."

He could feel her heart beating in her chest. "Why are you carrying a loaded pistol?"

"Do you like to hurt women?"

"No. I don't like it when someone I don't know walks into my room carrying a concealed weapon."

Their eyes met, a mere six inches apart. In close proximity he could smell the tahini on her breath and feel her full breasts against his chest.

"Maybe I carry it because I'm in a war zone where we have many enemies."

Good answer.

"What do you really want?" A moment after he said it, he realized that his question was loaded with all kinds of innuendo, which she seemed to be considering now in a private corner of her mind.

"I want lots of things. Things you can't give me, Mr. Wallace."

Said like a woman.

"But there is something…"

Of course there is. "What?"

She bit her bottom lip and said softly, "Look after Hassan."

"Hassan? The student?"

"Yes. He's my half brother," she said gently. "Very intelligent, but naive about people and politics. Someone who studies diagrams and numbers. I don't think he understands the risks out there. The darkness in the human soul."

It was a mouthful, said with a seductive sincerity. He let it sink in and settle.

"You want me to protect him?"

"Please."

Someone tapped on the door. Seconds later he heard Davis's voice.

"Boss?"

"Just a minute."

His eyes never left hers. Hers were filled with yearning, and fire.

"You think we can trust him?" Crocker asked.

"Yes. He's a good person."

He nodded. "Then I'll make sure he gets back safely."

She leaned forward and kissed him on the lips. "Thank you."

It wasn't a quick thank-you, more a long, full kiss that offered promise. Promise perhaps of more, if he brought Hassan back safely.

Wow.

She pulled back a little and waited to see if he understood, which he did, and to measure the effect she had on him, which was considerable.

"You'd better go now," he said in a deep voice.

"Yes." She stepped back, adjusted her tunic, and smiled warmly. "I hope we meet again."

"Me, too. And don't forget this."

He handed back the pink Beretta.

"You can take it if you want," she said.

"A pink Beretta? No thanks."

They assembled near the Ford F-250 and the Mercedes Sprinter van—both beige with blue crosses painted on the hoods, front doors, and sides. The pickup bed wore an aluminum cover, and the Sprinter featured a twenty-three-foot-long cargo bay.

Hassan, Crocker, and Akil stood alongside the F-250; Mancini, Davis, and Suarez waited beside the Mercedes. Captain Zeid and Babas leaned on a green Mitsubishi jeep fifteen feet in front of them, smoking cigarettes and trading jokes with Colonel Oz.

Crocker pulled himself away from the story Akil was telling about his childhood in Cairo to check with the colonel.

"Any word from the truck with the medical supplies?"

Oz waved toward him. "It's coming. Five minutes. No worries. You worry too much."

He held his tongue and looked at his watch: 2319. They'd be lucky to leave before midnight. Janice sat inside, in an office near the satphone, waiting for the approvals from Washington.

Zeid muttered something in Turkish, and Oz threw back his head and laughed. Crocker thought it might have been a sarcastic comment about him and his men but didn't really care. He was more concerned about the okay from D.C., and wondered if it would ever come. There was nothing he hated more than getting geared up for an op and waiting while the suits at Langley and the White House made up their minds.

"You spoke to the driver?" he asked Oz, unleashing some of his annoyance on him.

"What driver?"

"The driver of the truck with the medical supplies."

Oz pointed the radio clutched in his hand toward the gate and the town in the distance. "See, here. It's coming, my friend. Relax."

Easy for you to say.

All Crocker saw were low clouds and the murky lights of houses. He was about to say something about trust and accuracy when an old Mercedes 2.5-ton roared through the gate, made a half circle in front of them, and stopped.

Two men hopped out, waving their arms and shouting in Turkish. Oz met them halfway and yelled back.

"What's the problem?" asked Crocker.

"There is no problem, except that this fucking goat herder is late because he ran out of fuel."

"It doesn't matter," Crocker said, checking his watch again. "Did he bring the supplies?"

Oz shrugged and shouted at the driver, who was climbing into the cab. The driver shouted back and pointed his stubby arm toward the back of the truck.

Crocker unlatched the doors and pulled them open. The tall cargo area was half-full of boxes of medical equipment—gauze, tape, Israeli bandages, IV bags, and syringes mostly, and some medicine. It would do.

He heard Janice shouting from the top of the back stairway. "Wallace! Hey, Wallace!"

"What?"

She flashed a thumbs-up.

"Green light?"

"Yes."

He turned back to his men and said, "Looks like we're going into Syria."

Akil shouted back, "Sweet!"

CHAPTER EIGHT

Change calls the tune we dance.
                    —Al Swearengen, *Deadwood*

A **LIGHT RAIN** started to fall as they rolled through the elaborate white-and-red structure that housed Turkish customs, Zeid and Babas in the open jeep in front of them flashing their headlights and shouting at the guards. On the Syrian side stood two grim-looking old men shouldering M1 rifles.

Babas shouted, *"Subhan Allah!"* (Glory be to God!)

The guard waved back. *"Mawt al-Assad!"* (Death to Assad!)

They entered gentle verdant hills that reminded Crocker of western Virginia, one of his favorite locales. Except here the shoulders of the rough two-lane highway were littered with broken suitcases, empty boxes, strollers missing wheels, an ice chest, a smashed TV, pieces of clothing, plastic bottles and containers, and other junk that had been discarded by refugees and subsequently picked through by scavengers. Evidence of the thousands of civilian lives that had been upended. Families pulled apart; kids ripped out of communities and schools.

The barbarity of the Assad government against its own people hit home. Crocker had read somewhere that the Syrian president and his wife had met in London, where they were both studying. She was a stylish woman who advocated for women's rights and education, and they were parents of three children.

How could educated, civilized people justify horrors like this?

Low-lying clouds and precipitation limited visibility. The houses that dotted the hillsides appeared dark and uninhabited. Some were destroyed; others showed the ravages of war—collapsed roofs, walls decimated by artillery shells or rockets. Anti-Assad and jihadist slogans had been spray-painted in black on the remaining standing walls, forewarnings of an uncertain post-Assad future.

Crocker wasn't here to dwell on moral turpitude or political uncertainty. His focus was the mission, which was clouded with its own challenges. If he and his men did their jobs well, no one would ever hear about Captain Zeid, Fatima, Mr. Talab, or the sarin canisters. People back home would sleep peacefully in their beds and not have to worry about the terrors lurking in this corner of Syria.

The landscape ahead appeared like a moonlit painting—still and eerie. An owl hooted in the distance.

"This entire area is controlled by the FSA," Hassan announced from the passenger seat.

"That's good, right?" Akil said from behind the wheel of the crew-cab pickup with its faded gold interior.

"Yes. It should be."

More uncertainty. It was good to be moving. A low growl rumbled through the clouds.

"What's that?" asked Hassan nervously.

"Sounded like thunder," Crocker answered from the backseat, a loaded 416 with an M320 grenade launcher on his lap, a SIG 226 tucked near the door panel, an RPG-7 rocket launcher on the floor.

"You sure?"

"Deadwood, this is Breaker," Crocker heard through his earbuds.

Breaker was Davis's radio alias. *Deadwood* was one of Crocker's top TV shows, Al Swearengen his favorite character. Davis in the Sprinter was in charge of comms.

"What's up, Breaker?"

"Nevada reports no Pred flights tonight on account of the weather. Just got that. I repeat, no Pred support."

Nevada was the name of the duty officer at Ankara Station, where Anders waited. Janice had stayed behind in Yayladaği and an S&R (search-and-rescue) team remained on alert at Incirlik NATO air base in southern Turkey. Logan was back in Ankara, monitoring rebel commander cell-phone and text message chatter for the NSA.

Crocker hadn't expected drones or air support, with the Assad air force controlling the airspace and D.C. not wanting to get drawn deeper into the conflict.

"Nothing much the Preds could do anyway," he answered. Six months ago he'd lost Ritchie on a mission to recover a downed Pred not far from here. He didn't like the fact that some people put so much stock in technology and downplayed the value of human courage, training, and intelligence.

"Guess not," Davis replied.

War isn't a fucking video game, Crocker said to himself. Even though he had heard that the next generation of weapons out of DARPA would include robots equipped with cameras that could run, fire, carry equipment, and defuse bombs, they would never have the flexibility and intelligence of highly trained operators.

Loud EDM music washed back from the jeep, which remained uncovered even though the rain and wind had picked up.

"Goofballs," said Akil.

"It's a strange war from a sociological perspective," Hassan said as he wiped his round glasses on the front of his blue Adidas sweatshirt. "If it wasn't for the destruction and death, sometimes you'd think these guys were on a playground playing."

"Some fucked-up game," commented Akil.

The red brake lights ahead flashed, and the jeep slowed to a crawl. Through the mist ahead Crocker saw several trucks blocking the road and a gathering of people with rifles.

"Deadwood, Breaker here. What's up?" he heard through his earbuds.

"Company. Looks like a roadblock. Hopefully they're friendly. Stay alert. Over."

From the seat in front of him, Hassan said, "We can expect more of them."

"Rebel roadblocks?"

"Yes."

"Want do they want?"

"Depends. Talk, trade gossip, maybe inspect the trucks, maybe they will ask for money."

"Whatever it is, let's try to get through quickly."

Akil eased to a stop directly behind the jeep. Zeid was already out embracing a man in a blue rain parka. A skinny man with a very prominent nose and Adam's apple wandered over to Akil's side of the truck holding an AK. He asked him casually for cigarettes.

"None of us smoke," Akil answered in Arabic.

"No cigarettes. You sure you guys aren't Islamists?" the man asked with a smirk.

"No, Canadians," Akil replied in Arabic.

The man looked at Crocker in the backseat and asked in English, "Mossad?"

"No, not Mossad. Canadian medical workers," Akil answered.

"Mossad," the man repeated confidently, nodding and turning away.

The smell of roasting lamb wafted back. Crocker got out, stretched, and waved to Zeid, who was standing with a group that included a woman with short dark hair.

"What's the delay?" Crocker asked.

"There is no problem," Zeid answered.

"If there's no problem, why aren't we moving?"

"They want to check us out."

"Who are these people?" Crocker asked, nodding to the hodge-podge ahead.

"Some...they are journalists and photographers...they wait for escort. Others...FSA. Assad airplanes no fly tonight. So people wait here...for news. For information."

"We don't have time to sit around."

Five minutes later an engine started and one of the parked trucks backed out of the way so they could pass. The man who had called him Mossad mock-saluted Crocker as they drove past.

"Wise guy."

"Typical," said Hassan. "They believe every Westerner is a spy for the Israelis."

Crocker tightened his grip on the SIG 226. There was a strange casualness to this conflict that bothered him.

Past the roadblock, they climbed a curved incline to a little agricultural hamlet that had been completely decimated by bombs. Buzzards picked dried flesh off the bones of an animal carcass that lay beyond the burned shell of a small Fiat sedan.

"This is the work of Assad's air force," Hassan said. "If there are different gradations of evil, like in Dante's *Inferno*, they belong in the lowest circle of hell."

After three more minor delays—two FSA roadblocks and an old Volvo truck loaded with metal scrap that had blown a tire, causing it to roll over—Hassan announced that they were two-thirds of the way to Idlib. Crocker's mood brightened. He felt the adrenaline building in his blood.

Akil was telling a story about the first time he had gone to an American movie, as an eight-year-old who had recently immigrated to Michigan. The film was *Superman*, starring Christopher Reeve, Marlon Brando, and Gene Hackman. He was a guest of his new friend Clyde Ketchup and his father.

"You know that scene where Lois Lane is in a helicopter that's taking off from the top of the *Daily Planet*, and it crashes, and the ledge it landed on is breaking, and Lois is trapped and trying to get out?"

"I think so, yeah," Crocker said, keeping an eye on the road ahead.

"Well, it was so real to me that I stood on my seat and started screaming: 'Superman, hurry! You have to save Lois! Save her now!' "

"Crazy kid."

"Mr. Ketchup had to take me into the lobby. I was so excited, it took me a couple days to realize what I had done wrong."

"You haven't changed," Crocker cracked.

"Reeve and the actress who played Lois Lane were great. I'll never forget them."

"Margot Kidder," Crocker remembered.

"Great bod; terrific smile. Whatever happened to her?"

"Next time you're in Hollywood, you should look her up."

"She's probably a grandmother now."

"Hasn't stopped you before."

A minute later he braked again as they approached more trucks blocking the road and more armed men. This time when Captain Zeid got out of the jeep, the men he embraced wore long black beards and looked decidedly fiercer.

"Islamists," Hassan muttered under his breath, pointing to the black-and-white banner flying from one of the trucks.

"Let's waste 'em," Akil responded.

"Stay calm," warned Crocker.

"I am calm. But I can feel their hatred from here."

Through the open window Crocker tried to see what was going on ahead. Three men with black beards and black headscarves approached, carrying automatic weapons. He lowered the 416 below the seat but kept one hand on the stock.

As the jihadists spoke to Hassan, Crocker wondered what they wanted. He had $500 in cash concealed in the soles of his Merrell boots and flash grenades hidden under the seat.

"Deadwood, this is Breaker."

"Hold on, Breaker. We've hit an Islamist roadblock this time. Should be moving soon. Over."

"Here's hoping you're right."

Most people in his situation would have freaked out, but Crocker and his men remained calm, their heartbeats steady. The men of Black Cell had been selected, in part, because their bodies produced an abnormal amount of an amino acid known as neuropeptide Y (NPY), which regulates blood pressure and also works as a natural tranquilizer, controlling anxiety and buffering the effects of stress hormones like norepinephrine, also known as adrenaline. It gave them a major physical advantage in pressure situations.

One of the bearded men leaned in the open passenger window and asked in Arabic, "Journalists?"

"Humanitarian workers," Akil answered.

"British?"

"No, Canadian."

"Jewish?"

"No."

"Christian?"

"I'm Muslim," Akil said.

The bearded man bowed. "Thanks be to Allah. Allah is great."

"Yes," Akil repeated, "Allah is great."

"How do you pray?" the man asked. "You show me."

"I'm not going to show you," Akil answered. "But if you want to know if I'm Shiite or Sunni, I'm Sunni, born in Egypt."

"Go with God, my brother. Allah is great."

As the three men shuffled away, Hassan said under his breath, "They're foreigners. Probably from Iraq."

"Is that a problem?" Akil asked.

"I hope not," Hassan responded. "We're all supposed to be fighting for the same cause."

Crocker remembered that Fatima had told him that her half brother was naive about politics. How could foreign jihadists not be a potential problem, given the nature of their mission?

Recorded Arabic chanting drifted back from where the bearded soldiers were gathered.

"That's Anasheed," Hassan explained.

"What's that?"

"It's kind of like jihadist rap. Words with percussion. The lyrics have to do with Islamic beliefs and some current events. There's no musical accompaniment, which they believe gets around the prohibition in the Ahadith that says music is sinful."

"What's the Ahadith?" asked Crocker.

"The sayings of Mohammad."

"Translate the lyrics."

"Oh, sons of Zionists, the wrath of God awaits like a powerful lion. Let them shed our blood and it will run over the soil, but they will never settle in the land of pilgrimage—"

Davis, through the earbuds, cut in. "Deadwood, this is Breaker. Nevada recommends that we abort."

"Abort?"

"Yes, that's what they said. Abort. Over."

"Who's they?"

"Grissom and Anders."

"Did they say why?"

"Because we haven't reached the target, and we're already meeting ISIS resistance."

"Tell Nevada that this isn't ISIS resistance. Not yet. Tell him that we came expecting resistance, and we'll probably meet it. But we're not going to let that stop us."

"Roger."

"Call them back and tell them. And ask them to stop calling us with bullshit."

"You sure you want me to convey the last part?"

"No. Erase that."

"Good call, boss. Roger and out."

Captain Zeid started toward them, paused to light a cigarette, and stopped. He grinned and shook his head as though he was starring in his own movie.

"Extremists...don't smoke," he said, slipping the Marlboro back into the pack.

"What's the holdup?" Akil asked.

"We might have some problem," Zeid said casually.

"We kind of deduced that, Sherlock."

"What's the problem?" asked Crocker.

"ISIS is about to launch an operation, so they won't let anyone through. They think we could get in the way. End up what you call collateral damage."

"Nice of them to be concerned," said Crocker. "Did you explain that we're delivering medical supplies to some clinics in Idlib?"

"I told them this, yeah."

"What did they say?"

"They have orders from their leader not to let anyone pass."

"Tell 'em we'll take full responsibility if anything happens."

"I did."

"Then tell them I want to talk to their leader."

Zeid nodded. "That's not a problem; he's on his way."

"Now?"

"Yeah."

"Who?"

"Not sure. But they are part of a group...loyal to Mohammad al-Kazaz. Maybe one of his lieutenants."

Crocker's attention perked up. Al-Kazaz was a feared leader of ISIS and a member of al-Qaeda with close ties to Ayman al-Zawahiri, the Egyptian cleric who had cofounded the movement with Bin Laden back in 1989. He was born and raised in the nearby city of Aleppo, jailed by Assad for ten years, and was rumored to have fought alongside Bin Laden in Afghanistan. He had recently brokered a peace between al-Nusra militia groups and those allied with ISIS. In the jihadist world a major player, and according to Ankara Station the guy who had been posting plans to attack the West on jihadist websites that called him the Fox.

"Al-Kazaz?" asked Hassan. "Oh, no."

"Okay if their leader wants to inspect the trucks?" Zeid asked.

"As long as he doesn't mess with us and is only interested in looking at the cargo in back," Crocker responded.

Zeid explained that militia commanders sometimes traded men, weapons, pieces of land, even hostages and captured boys like pieces of candy.

"So he might want a portion of the medical supplies?" asked Crocker.

"Either that or he will want to take one of you for his harem."

"That's not happening," Akil remarked.

"Don't worry. You're too ugly anyway."

Ten minutes later Akil and Mancini were leaning back on the hood of the Sprinter, talking about the new Israeli Tavor TAR S21 assault rifle, equipped with a MARS integrated laser pointer and 4X sight for precision firing, that they had all test-fired recently. It was as if they were back at the firing range at the ST-6 base in Dam Creek.

"I prefer the ergonomics of the Galil ACE," Mancini said, referring to another advanced Israeli-made assault weapon. "And it can fire seven hundred rounds a minute, so it packs a nice punch. Yo, boss. You ever see a Soviet Korobov TKB-022?"

"You mean that short gas-operated automatic with the reddish-brown plastic housing developed in the sixties?"

"That weird-looking gizmo, right."

"Got a chance to fire one once at Fort Bragg. Had this messed-up ejection chute that pushed out spent cartridges above the barrel."

"Awkward."

"Looked cool, but never went into production, as far as I know."

"Nah. Never did," Mancini said, shaking his head. "The Soviets had some real talented weapons designers. Korobov was one of them."

Hearing the growl of approaching motorcycles, they grew quiet. A current of excitement passed through the air and hit Crocker in the stomach. He quickly measured the distance between where he stood and the SIG 226 in the truck's backseat.

These guys were ISIS and AQ—in other words, Islamic terrorists. Part of him wanted to waste them right there.

The motorcycle engines stopped and were followed by shouts of *Allahu akbar* that sent shivers up Crocker's spine. Boots squished the fresh mud as four jihadists hurried toward them with Zeid leading the way.

"We're not letting them into the cab without a fight," Crocker whispered to his teammates beside him. "Pass that down the line."

Mancini nodded. "Got it."

They'd disarm the bastards before they knew what was happening. Then they'd really be fucked.

Crocker took a deep breath. He stood facing a broad man wearing a thick black robe, his head covered with a black bandana with a jihadist slogan printed on it that hung down his back, ghetto-style. An AK-47 slung over his shoulder and a six-inch knife in a sheath on a belt across his chest. Their eyes met for an instant and Crocker recognized a grizzled, determined veteran who wasn't afraid of anyone or anything.

"*Sadiq,*" the man grunted. Friend.

"*Sadiq,*" Crocker said back.

The man strode to the back gate of the Sprinter, which was now open. Crocker saw that the jihadists were unloading boxes and stacking them on the ground.

"We gonna let them take our cargo?" whispered Akil.

"Let's see what they want first."

Two of the jihadists handed their weapons to the others and lifted a dozen boxes, deep frowns on their faces as they walked by. Bandages and syringes mostly.

The last two stopped in front of Crocker, who was guarding the cab door. Captain Zeid stood behind them.

"Okay?" Zeid asked tentatively.

"Yeah. What's this dude want?"

Crocker looked into the face of the leader in front, measuring the distance between himself and the man's Adam's apple, where he intended to thrust his forearm should he try to push past. Break the thing and leave the bastard gasping. The man's face communicated both fierceness and exhaustion, from his gray eyes, to the droop of his broken nose, to the thick gray beard. But there was something in his frown-lined forehead and ironic half smile that made him appealing.

The militia leader muttered something in a hoarse voice, and Zeid jumped forward and pointed at Crocker. Crocker recognized the word *balad* (country), but couldn't make out the rest.

The grizzled militia leader stepped closer until Crocker could smell the intense garlic on his breath. His ruddy skin, gray eyes, and other features made him look more European than Arab. Like a rugged alpine climber.

He waved his hands as if trying to communicate an important thought. *"Fahima...kalla. Tabib?"* he asked in Arabic. Doctor?

Crocker tried to follow. "What the fuck's he want now?"

Zeid: "He wants to know if you're a doctor."

"Tell him no. I'm a medic."

Zeid translated. The militia leader nodded, then reached out and put an arm on Crocker's shoulder. If that wasn't unexpected enough, he also rattled off a plea using thanks to God and *min fadlak* (please), and, surprisingly, *khoya* (brother).

"Did he just call me 'brother?' " Crocker asked.

"He did, yes," answered Zeid.

"Is he…Mohammad al-Kazaz?"

"Yes."

The mission was getting stranger by the second. "This dude is serious ISIS and AQ. I don't get it. What's he want from me?" Crocker asked.

"He's asking you to help him," Zeid answered. "Someone he knows is wounded. As a humanitarian, a brother in arms, he asks you by the grace of God to accompany him to a house nearby to see this person."

"Does he understand that I'm not a doctor, but a medic with limited supplies? Tell him that."

"He knows already."

"Tell him again."

Captain Zeid did. Al-Kazaz puffed out his chest and nodded.

"If I agree to go with him, will he let us through?"

Zeid translated and came back with al-Kazaz's answer. "He says he'll even guarantee your safety."

"If I can't save this person, which could likely happen, will he hold me responsible?"

"No," the militia leader said.

Crocker had dealt with all kinds of questionable characters in every dark corner of the planet. This time his instincts told him that al-Kazaz would be true to his word. Besides, if he didn't accept the challenge, he and his men might be unable to recover the sarin, which might then fall into the jihadists' hands.

His only other major concern was time. Quickly checking his watch, he figured that they had maybe two hours to spare.

"Just a minute," he said, opening the cab door behind him and removing the backpack that contained his emergency medical kit. He slung it across his back and nodded.

"Okay. Tell him I'm ready."

Al-Kazaz grinned and nodded.

"No, boss," Akil warned. "Bad fucking idea."

Mancini: "He's a terrorist. What happens if he kidnaps you and holds you for ransom?"

"If he does, proceed without me."

"Boss, fuck that. He wants to cut your head off."

"It's the only way they'll let us through."

"No, boss. The risk isn't worth it."

"Wait here. Behave yourselves. I'll be right back."

CHAPTER NINE

For by grace are ye saved through faith; and that not of
yourselves: it is the gift of God.

—Ephesians 2:8

HE CLUNG to the back of the Yamaha 450 dirt bike as it ripped up a narrow path, rain pelting his face, like a teenage kid on a nighttime adventure wondering if the fat lady was about to sing. Maybe he was taking his last wild ride. Maybe he should have heeded Holly's pleas and never gone on this mission. Maybe she was right when she'd suggested in one of their sessions with Dr. Mathews that he had a death wish.

No, part of him argued back. *I love life. I celebrate it and defend the freedoms it offers.*

Whatever the truth, it was too late now. He was heading into something he had no control over, holding on to the back of a motorbike ridden by the enemy.

Someone had once told him that people were divided between those who took action and worriers. The worriers were often more intelligent because they considered all the possible dangers and outcomes before they did anything. But those who took action got a hell of a lot more done.

133

He was definitely heading into something now, recalling all he had learned in hand-to-hand combat and at SERE (Survival, Evasion, Resistance, and Escape) school. No way was he going to be kidnapped, interrogated by some fucking jihadists, and held for ransom or beheaded—even if he only had a SOG knife on him.

Refreshed by the wet night air and exhilarated by his circumstances, he focused on the vague outlines of a house ahead. He saw yellow light peeking through windows half hidden by the branches of cypress trees.

He wondered how Holly and Jenny would manage without him. Pretty well, probably. Holly seemed like she was halfway out the door, and Jenny was only a few days away from high school graduation. It's not as if they hadn't considered the possibility before. They'd have a new house and plenty of money from his bereavement allowance and navy pension.

The strange things that pass through your head at times like these.

"Man plans, God laughs." It was a Yiddish saying an ST-6 commander had repeated to him when they were pinned down on a beach during his first mission to Somalia.

He remembered it now as the bike braked and slowed to a stop. Two men ran out of the house to greet al-Kazaz. He pointed behind to Crocker. A tall man in a black robe and long black beard bowed to Crocker, then took his medical pack and led him inside.

So far, so good. They seem friendly.

At the door two armed jihadists frisked him and took his knife. One pointed to a cell phone and asked Crocker if he had one on him.

He shook his head. *"Kalla."* No.

The main room was lit by candles. He saw dirty mattresses on the floor, a radio transmitter in the corner, PRKs and AKs propped against one wall and a framed and filigreed Islamic quotation leaning against another. Al-Kazaz waved him forward and ducked into another room.

It stunk of feces, paraffin, and rotting flesh. A man with a gaunt face was on his knees beside the mattress, praying. Past his shoulder, newspaper was taped over a window. An Arabic slogan had been scrawled in black paint across the wall.

If this is where the ISIS leader is planning attacks against the West, the West has nothing to worry about, Crocker said to himself.

Al-Kazaz stood beside him and pointed to the swaddled figure on the bed.

Ibn, he whispered.

Crocker thought it meant "son." He nodded. Whoever it was, he was clearly important to al-Kazaz, who knelt beside the gaunt-faced man alongside the bed and started to pray with him. Their low voices merged into one.

The still figure lay on his back, his face and head covered with towels. A simple brown blanket had been draped over his torso and legs. Kneeling beside al-Kazaz near the head of the bed, Crocker started to remove the coverings.

As he did the smell grew thicker and more intense. Setting aside layer after layer, he reached dried blood and the boy's badly damaged and swollen face. His neck had been injured, too. He appeared young, maybe early teens, with thin wisps of mustache and beard.

First thing Crocker noticed was that the kid's breathing was very shallow, because whatever had hit him had entered his neck, damaging his larynx. As with other gunshot wounds to the face he'd seen, there had probably been a substantial loss of blood. This was confirmed by the kid's rapid, thready pulse and low body temperature. Fortunately, his cervical column and major arteries hadn't been compromised. Still, he was a mess.

Crocker took a step back to assess the damage. Compressible hemorrhage, tension pneumothorax, airway and ventilatory damage were the leading causes of preventable combat death. He would have to close the wound, clean out the infection, and remove the bullet or shrapnel that seemed to be resting near the boy's temporal bone along his right jaw if the kid were to have any chance of surviving.

It would be a delicate procedure, and judging by the kid's weakened condition, there was a high likelihood that his body wasn't strong enough, or he had lost too much blood, to withstand it. Also, since he was working with a DA-Med bag, the tools he had were limited. Nor was he in an operating room.

Al-Kazaz stopped praying and rested a hand on Crocker's shoulder. *"Labass?"* (What do you think?)

There was no point trying to explain the challenges. His Arabic wasn't good enough for that. Besides, he had accepted the assignment and had no choice but to see it through the best he could.

"Bad-a." (I start.)

"Inshallah." (By the grace of God.)

"I need clean towels and hot water," he said in English, pointing to the aluminum sink in the corner and the dirty towel hanging beside it.

"Tahir! Tahir!" (Clean! Clean!) Crocker growled, grabbing one of the towels. "And the water… *Harr.*" (Hot.)

Al-Kazaz nodded.

"You understand?"

He nodded again, then barked orders at the gaunt-faced man, who hurried off on bare feet and came back five minutes later holding a basin of near-boiling water.

Crocker washed his hands, donned nitrile gloves, and proceeded.

Using the cervical collar he had in his kit, he tilted the boy's head back and held it in place. Then he used a clamp to hold his mouth open and inserted his middle and index fingers to sweep the mouth and throat for bone fragments. He located several broken teeth, removed them, and in the process noted that the kid's tongue was swollen, indicating that it had probably been injured, too.

Crocker faced more immediate challenges.

The boy's pulse remained rapid and his body temperature low, indicating that he was on the verge of going into hypovolemic shock. That meant he had to get some fluids into him, fast.

Among the supplies al-Kazaz had purloined from the Sprinter were several hypertonic saline solution drips. Saline wasn't as effective as blood or plasma, but it would have to do. He hooked up one of the drips to a vein in the boy's left forearm and monitored his pulse, which slowly started to stabilize.

"Hasan" (good), Crocker said, handing the bag to the gaunt-faced man and showing him how to hold it.

"Alhamdulillah" (thanks to God), al-Kazaz said.

Given Crocker's limited supplies, the best he could hope to achieve was to remove the bullet, disinfect everything, and close up the wounds to the face and neck, providing adequate drainage. After that, systematic doses of penicillin and the body's natural defense and healing mechanisms would have to do the rest.

What he didn't want to do was tax the kid's system to the point that he succumbed right in front of him. In part because of the lack of ventilation, Crocker had already sweated through his black shirt and pants.

A tall man offered him a glass of tea and another glass with water. Crocker downed the water, nodded to the man, and replaced the glass on the tray. *"Shukran"* (thanks).

The man bowed and backed away.

Crocker replaced the nitrile gloves with a fresh pair and considered the next problem—closing up the wound to the kid's larynx. He decided to sew it up before he administered morphine, because of the respiratory-depressing effects of the drug. Inserting a rubber shuttle in the kid's mouth, he showed al-Kazaz how he wanted him to hold the patient down by the shoulders.

With the kid immobilized on the bed, Crocker carefully cut away the damaged tissue around the larynx. Luckily, the cartilaginous skeleton was stable and the only serious damage was a fracture to the thyroid cartilage. Given the poor light, it was impossible to determine whether the projectile had done any damage to the kid's vocal cords or the larynx nerve.

There was no wire in the basic Tac Med surgical kit contained in a pocket of the Med Pack, so Crocker used a needle and strong nonabsorbable CRS suture to repair the cartilaginous fracture. He wasn't a surgeon, but he closed the fractured cartilage as well as he could.

Then he stood back and watched with satisfaction as the kid's breathing returned to near normal. *So far, so good.*

He mopped the sweat from his own brow, then administered a shot of morphine, waited for it to take effect, and used a smaller-gauge suture to close the larynx skin. That completed, he took another drink of water and started working on the boy's face, a chore that was much more painstaking. The projectile had traveled along the hard palate and done damage to the soft tissue along the jaw.

Crocker had to perform a surgical debridement to remove as much dead, damaged, and infected tissue as he could. As he did, he was careful not to dislodge any blood clots that might result in significant new blood loss. It was difficult, tense work. The closest experience to this he'd had was working on an injured goat when he attended Special Forces medical lab at Fort Bragg, North Carolina.

The light wasn't ideal and the conditions sucked, but Crocker worked his way along the palate to the mandible bone, where he located the bullet, a .22-caliber probably fired from a pistol and more or less intact. He disinfected everything and started to sew up the wound, al-Kazaz beside him, praying in Arabic, whispering encouragement, and even using a towel to mop the sweat from Crocker's brow.

An hour after he started, he applied the last bandages to the boy's face and neck, and rechecked his pulse and breathing. Both had improved. When he tried to straighten up, his neck barked. He cracked it, left, then right, and flexed his shoulders.

Miraculously, the kid appeared to be okay. Some luster had returned to his eyes. But the chances of him surviving in his current location were minimal at best.

Crocker looked back at al-Kazaz, who was grinning broadly, and said, "That's it. I think I'm done. *Intaha.*" (Finished.)

"Sadiq" (friend), the burly al-Qaeda leader said, pulling Crocker into his arms and kissing him on both cheeks. This was the savage terrorist who had beheaded many of his enemies and spread fear throughout Syria and Iraq.

Crocker pointed to the box of penicillin and used his fingers and watch to explain the dosage. "Two, every four hours."

Al-Kazaz nodded.

"As soon as you can, move him to a hospital."

He looked confused.

"Mustasfa" (hospital), Crocker said.

"Mustasfa, na'am." (Yes.) Al-Kazaz nodded, embraced him again, and escorted Crocker into the living room, where he wrote a note on a piece of paper that Crocker hoped would guarantee safe passage

through any ISIS roadblock, then handed him something wrapped in a blue velvet cloth.

"What's this?"

Inside was a brand-new five-inch wooden koppo martial stick—a pocket self-defense tool.

"Ihsan" (gift), al-Kazaz answered. *"Shukran, shukran."*

Wait till I show this to my teammates, was the first thought that came to him. As exhausted as he was, the irony still pleased him immensely. *A terrorist has gifted me with a koppo martial stick. Imagine that!*

Back in the Ford F-250, Crocker dreamt it was a beautiful spring morning. He lay in his bed in Virginia Beach listening to the birds chirp outside. Golden puffs of pollen swirled through fresh new leaves. He saw the green flash of a hummingbird and lifted himself to get a better look.

The bird represented good luck, according to Holly. *Beautiful,* he thought. The creative magic of nature; amazing variety and wonder.

The Ford hit a pothole and jolted him awake.

"What the fuck!"

He looked sternly at Akil, behind the wheel.

"Sorry, boss, but you kept calling me sweetheart, and the road's real torn up."

Through the windshield he saw that they were winding down from the hills onto a flat dry plain. A few lights sparkled in the distance through the mist.

He didn't remember the return ride on the motorcycle or any events since then. He flashed back to the kid and his swollen face in the candlelit room, al-Kazaz looking pleased, tears welling in his eyes. No threats, no *Once we finish our work in Syria, we will attack the West.* Just genuine gratitude.

"Boss, you with us?" Akil asked.

"Sort of. Yeah."

Looking to his left, he saw his medical bag on the seat, which confirmed that the whole thing hadn't been a dream.

"What happened to al-Kazaz?" he asked.

"We had to rip him off your back at the roadblock."

"Get off."

"Seriously. The guy was embracing you so much, we were afraid he'd never let go."

"But he did."

"Yeah, waved us through. Wished us good luck."

Crocker remembered the koppo martial stick al-Kazaz had given him and found it stuffed inside the medical kit with the folded note. *Crazy surreal place*, he thought.

Hassan was telling Akil how the Assad regime used malware to penetrate opposition websites. Syrian intelligence would distribute a link to a video of Assad soldiers beheading someone. When you clicked on it, it would prompt you to update your Adobe Flash software. Instead of Flash you'd be downloading malware, which would take control of your computer.

"Sophisticated mofos," Akil said.

"That's Idlib," Hassan said, pointing toward the left to the lights ahead.

"Already?"

Crocker quickly checked his watch: 0148 hours.

"How much farther to the air base?" he asked.

"Another ten, fifteen minutes tops."

If they could secure the sarin within an hour, or even two, it would give them ample time to return to Turkey before dawn. The problem was that they had no detailed map of the air base, which consisted largely of a runway and underground bunkers, and no definitive intel on the deployment, number, and disposition of Syrian Army troops and pro-Assad forces. Without the above, it was hard to even conceive of a plan until they got there.

"Breaker, Deadwood here," he said into his head mike. "We're approaching the road to the air base."

"Copy."

A huge explosion lit up the sky in front of them and shook the ground.

"What was that?" Hassan asked.

"A big bomb or rocket," Crocker responded.

"Could be one of those Chinese FN-6s, right?" Akil asked.

"Maybe."

The jeep in front of them pulled over to the shoulder and braked to a stop. Captain Zeid walked back and leaned in the driver's-side window. As Crocker got out, he caught a whiff of rotting animal in the grass behind him.

"That's no-man's-land ahead," Zeid said. "Dangerous territory. Assad and ISIS fight there. It's as far as we go."

Crocker wanted to grab him by the neck and call him a coward, but restrained himself. They might need his and Babas's help getting back.

"Where's the cutoff?" he asked, hearing something stir in the brush behind them.

"The cutoff for the road to Abu al-Duhur?" Zeid responded. "You will see it; maybe three hundred meters ahead."

"What happens then?" Crocker asked, peering past Zeid to the high grass and brush behind him. Something was in there. He sensed it.

"We wait for you over there." Zeid pointed to the burned-out remains of a petrol station fifty feet ahead and on the left.

Seeing something move in the grass, Crocker held a finger to his mouth, removed the SIG Sauer P226 stuffed in a back band of his pants, and flashed a series of hand signals to Akil. Moving simultaneously, the two men slid down a gravel embankment and circled through the low scrub brush and grass in a crouch, Crocker from the rear of the pickup, Akil from the front. The smell of putrefying animals was so thick it stuck in Crocker's throat. On his right something moved, and he jumped and grabbed a kicking, struggling person. After pinning his ankles, he brought his right hand up to the boy's throat. Caught him in half scream, yanked him up to his knees, and quickly swept him for explosives or weapons. The kid wasn't armed, but he had a black stocking pulled over his face.

"What the fuck's he doing?" Crocker asked.

The kid grunted something.

Akil held an older man, who wasn't bothering to resist and wasn't armed either.

The two of them wore filthy clothes and sneakers. The older man had a pair of surgeon's shears and two different types of pliers hanging from a belt around his waist. Both carried black sacks that hung behind their backs.

Crocker and Akil dragged them over to the trucks, where Zeid leaned lighting a cigarette.

"Scavengers," he said with disgust. "If ISIS finds them, they cut off their balls."

Akil reached into the sack the trembling old man was carrying and retrieved a handful of teeth with gold fillings, earrings, pins, and rings.

Zeid booted the old man in the ass so he fell forward. Then he held a pistol to his head. The man whimpered as he pointed into the bushes and offered an explanation in Arabic.

Crocker pushed in front of Zeid and said, "Leave him alone. What did he say?"

"Assad's troops stopped a truck of refugees," Akil translated. "Raped the girls and women in front of the men, then shot them. Every last one."

Zeid aimed a kick to the older man's stomach, then said, "These pigs loot the bodies."

Crocker shoved him back this time. "Leave him alone! How old's the boy?"

"*Sitta,*" the boy grunted. He was only six years old.

"Claims he's the old man's grandson. They're all that's left of an extended family of twelve, originally from Aleppo. The men joined the resistance. When the pro-Assad gangs found out, they tortured and raped the women. Some of them drowned themselves in the river. Others were killed and beheaded. The boy had his eyes gouged out."

Crocker removed the black stocking from the kid's head and held his chin up. Indeed, his eyeballs were gone and the sockets covered with scar tissue. He reached into his pocket, found a twenty-dollar bill, and pressed it into the old man's hand.

"Here, take this.... May God be with you."

"*Alhamdulillah....Alhamdulillah.*"

"Leave 'em. We can't afford to waste any more time. Let's go."

CHAPTER TEN

*It's just a job. Grass grows, birds fly, waves pound the sand.
I beat people up.*

—Muhammad Ali

THEY LAY in tall grass within the base perimeter, all wearing
night-vision goggles and holding weapons. A rocket whined overhead as Crocker calmly counted the seconds in his head. "Five, six,
seven—" *KA-BLAM!*

The explosion sucked the oxygen out of the air, creating a wind
that pulled at the green stalks. It was followed by a second blast less
than a minute later.

They were waiting for Suarez and Akil, who had run ahead to recon the approach to the tunnel. ISIS rebels approximately 1,000 feet
behind them had kept up the barrage for fifteen minutes now. Their
target: the big rectangular building that housed Abu al-Duhur air
base headquarters and the control tower. That structure stood about
a quarter mile ahead and to their left. When Crocker raised his head
above the three-feet-tall grass he saw black smoke streaming from
the top left of the structure.

"They hit it," he announced.

"What happens now?" Davis whispered back.

"We wait for Suarez and Akil."

He had no idea how many of Assad's forces remained there or what their response was likely to be. Nor was he aware how long the ISIS rebels planned to keep firing missiles.

Would they follow up the barrage with a land assault? He hoped not, because that might interfere with Black Cell's objective—the tunnel that held the sarin canisters, which was about 900 feet to Crocker's three o'clock, at the opposite end of a long underground bunker, B3, that housed Assad's aircraft and crews.

The whole setup was odd. Aside from the large main building there was nothing to indicate that there was, or had been, an air base here. Everything else, except the airstrip itself, was disguised under bunkers covered with the same grass that carpeted the pancake-flat plain.

"Deadwood, it's Romeo," Crocker heard through his earbuds.

"You guys stop for pizza?"

"We're almost finished. Be there in three. Over."

"Time's a-wasting."

Mancini, Davis, Crocker, and Hassan had parked the trucks in a drainage culvert fifty feet away and now lay on their stomachs with their backs against an old mud wall that rose about four feet.

Four more rockets sailed overhead and exploded before Crocker saw Akil's Phoenix IR strobe beacon in the grass ahead. Soon both men were kneeling before them, breathing hard and drinking water from the bladders they carried strapped to the back of their waists.

Suarez removed his NVGs and used an iPad and stylus to sketch the setup in and around B3.

"The tunnel is right where Hassan told us it would be, boss," he said pointing to the screen.

The men gathered closer.

"Let's hope the canisters are still inside," said Davis.

"Better be," Akil responded.

Suarez pointed over his left shoulder. "One of the four main bunkers starts about two hundred yards over there. It's huge. Really massive. At the end of it is like a concrete parking area with sandbags and a gate. Part of that gate has been destroyed. We couldn't tell if it had been hit by rockets or had withstood a more coordinated attack."

"Where's the tunnel?" asked Crocker.

"The entrance is right there, past the bunkers. Six to eight concrete stairs that lead down to a locked door. Nothing much."

"Think you can breach it?"

"Yeah. Easy."

"What's in the hangar?" Crocker asked.

"B3 also appears partially damaged," Akil chimed in. "Maybe from a previous attack. Looks like it's being used for storage. Trucks, parts, barrels of fuel, random shit."

"No soldiers inside?" Crocker asked.

"A few guards. The main focus of the base seems to have shifted to bunkers 1, 2, and 4, farther north and closer to the main building."

"Got it."

"Access to the tunnel aside from the stairs?" asked Crocker.

"We located an air vent here," Suarez said, pointing to a location on his sketch just south of B3. "We think we can squeeze in through there."

"Good. What's going on behind us?" Crocker asked, pointing to the ISIS missiles behind them.

"The jihadists appear to have gotten their hands on a BM-21 Grad missile launcher system," Suarez reported.

"It's a truck-based Soviet system built back in the sixties," Mancini, the weapons expert, added. "Nothing especially high-tech, but with enough bang to do damage."

Crocker nodded. "I can see that."

"I think they're firing Egyptian-made Sakr-45A missiles," Suarez said. The Sakr-45A was an eleven-foot missile with a range of about twenty miles.

"Why are they so close? Don't those babies have range?" Crocker asked.

"Because they're idiots," Akil answered, "who like to film what they're doing and post it on YouTube."

"You mean they're filming this shit now?" Davis asked. "At night?"

"Fuck, yeah. You'd think they were having a party. Every time they fire a fucking missile twenty guys jump in the air, dance and shout 'Allahu akbar!' And every time they hit something, they go crazy."

"Zero operational training."

Akil: "They don't think they need it. Allah is on their side."

"Allah or not, they're about to get their asses kicked," Suarez added.

"Meaning?"

"Meaning the Assad forces are massing a counterattack. They're moving out armed columns here and here," he said, pointing to the map he'd drawn. "They're gonna outflank the rebels and cut off their escape."

"How many?"

"Maybe two squads with tanks and armored vehicles. They might not be flying because of the low cloud cover and the missiles, but they're still here and they look plenty strong."

"Good work," whispered Crocker. "We'd better move fast."

"Agreed," responded Suarez.

"Akil and Davis, you get in the tunnel through the vent. Suarez and I will attack B3. Manny, you back the pickup up to the entrance and get ready to load the sarin."

"Yes."

"What about me?" Hassan asked.

"You wait here with the other truck."

"What about the jihadists? What if they find me?"

Crocker removed the letter he had gotten from al-Kazaz and handed it to Hassan. "Take this. The jihadists are gonna start running away when they're attacked, and they're not gonna run toward the base."

"Okay."

Crocker also handed him his SIG Sauer 226. "Take this just in case. All you have to do is unlatch the safety, here, then point and shoot."

"I don't know."

"You'll be fine. We'll be back soon."

Twenty minutes later Crocker lay on his belly to the rear of B3 waiting for Suarez to set the C4. The body of a dead Syrian Army guard lay in the grass to Crocker's right. He had finished him with a swipe of his SOG knife against his throat. Quick, lethal work.

Several hundred yards behind him a vicious battle raged between Assad military forces and ISIS. Lots of automatic weapons fire and the occasional explosion, like the one now that lifted him six inches off the ground and lit up the low clouds so that for an instant the entire landscape turned white.

Crocker extended his forearms and eased himself down. Based on the sloppy military tactics of the jihadists, he had to believe they were losing and would soon be retreating. When that happened, Assad's forces would return.

He pushed the button that lit up the dial of his Suunto watch. Already 0243. Things were proceeding too slowly for comfort. If they wanted to get back to the border before sunup, they had to pick up the pace.

"Manny, Deadwood here. What's happening?"

"The StunRays are in place." The StunRays were special hand-held hardware Mancini had brought along.

"Good."

"Rojas?" Crocker asked into his head mic.

"I need two more minutes."

"Time's fucking precious."

"I know, boss," Suarez whispered from two hundred feet inside the hangar, where he had found a pile of propane tanks near some parked vehicles. He was trying to orchestrate the biggest possible diversion.

"Breaker, can you hear me?" Crocker asked.

"Breaker? Report."

"We're…" His voice broke up.

"Breaker. Breaker?"

Davis's voice came through. "I read you."

"What's your status?"

"We're in, boss."

"The tunnel?"

"Roger."

"Excellent. Romeo with you?"

"He's bitching like usual. Scratched his pinky."

"The canisters there?"

"We count six of 'em."

"Only six?"

"How many did you expect?"

"Wait. Here comes Rojas. Hold on."

He saw Suarez hugging the opposite wall, moving as fast as possible while trying not to be seen. Through his NVGs, Crocker eyeballed the clearance in all directions, rose into a crouch, and signaled Suarez to join him on the south side of the bunker.

When Suarez arrived, his chest heaving, he readied the radio-controlled detonator in his hand.

"C4's set. Time to blow?"

"Hold on. Let's move alongside the bunker first. Maintain a safe distance."

They proceeded another hundred feet and stopped. All the action behind them seemed to have shifted farther north and west, which was ideal for their escape.

Crocker, into the head mic: "Manny, report. Ready with the truck?"

"Near the gate, Deadwood. Ready. Over."

"Breaker and Romeo?"

"In the tunnel. Ready."

"All right. Signal to launch!"

Suarez lowered the black button and a split second later, the bunker emitted a tremendous roar that shook the ground and sent a huge column of light, flames, and debris shooting out the back. Crocker and Suarez didn't stick around to watch. They ran the rest of the two hundred yards in a crouch toward the opposite end—the front entrance to B3—hoping to meet Mancini soon after he entered the gate.

Mancini, meanwhile, drove the Ford pickup up to the gate and came out of the cab shouting gibberish at the two guards, who started running toward him. They readied their AK-47s and ordered him to the ground. He stepped behind the cab and pushed a button that activated the six XL-2000 StunRays he had bolted to the forward stabilizer bar of the truck.

To say the light they emitted was intense was a huge understatement. An aircraft landing light put out about one-tenth the light of only one of these little devices. The collimated beams of incoherent optical radiation temporarily blinded both Syrian guards. In fact, the light was so bright they became completely disoriented. One soldier covered his face with his arm and stumbled backward.

Mancini put them both down with suppressed blasts from his M7A1. Then he got back into the Ford, rammed through the fence, swung it around, backed in, and lowered the gate. It was like picking up furniture at Walmart.

"Vehicle in position," he barked into his head mic. "Let's do this! Over."

Cradling the M7A1, he knelt beside the back gate of the truck and got ready to start loading. A Syrian guard to his left opened fire, and he responded.

"Clear?" Davis shouted from the steps to the entrance to the tunnel where he waited with Akil. Both men were drenched with sweat.

"Clear!" Mancini shouted back, now that the guard had run away. "What did you guys find?"

"We've got six of these babies."

"Hand 'em over."

Mancini set down the M7A1 and took two of the forty-pound canisters at a time, one under each arm, and started to load them into the back of the pickup. Each canister was wrapped in black plastic.

"Where's Crocker?" Akil asked when Mancini came back for the second round of canisters.

"Dragging ass, per usual."

Akil smiled.

They worked fast as military sirens sounded in the distance. By the time Crocker and Suarez arrived, everything was loaded.

"That it?" Crocker asked.

"Done. Where the fuck were you?" Akil responded.

Mancini pointed to a Russian S-125 Pechora missile system on a truck parked at the entrance to B3. "Looks like two more there!" he exclaimed.

"Two more what?"

"Warheads. They contain sarin."

Crocker saw that they matched the size and shape of the canisters in the truck bed.

"I can dislodge them," Mancini said. "Spare some civilian lives."

"How long?"

"Give me five to seven."

Crocker glanced at his watch and nodded. "Five. Davis, you help him."

The rest of them guarded the pickup as the fierce battle raging in the distance moved north. As Mancini handed down the first warhead, an armored vehicle appeared from the other side of B3, speeding toward them.

"Incoming!" exclaimed Akil. "Three o'clock!"

"Keep your heads down and cover my ass!" Crocker shouted.

The .30 cal on the armored truck opened up, bullets tearing into the concrete around the pickup and ricocheting. Crocker knelt and fired one of the PG-7VR rounds from the RPG-7 he'd been carrying.

Whoosh!

The PG-7VR maintained a straight line four feet off the ground.

The first 64mm round detonated against the vehicle's reactive armor block, and the second 105mm warhead penetrated the gap created to take out the vehicle itself—just as it was designed to do.

Within seconds the truck was a ball of flaming white-hot metal.

"Bingo."

"What next?"

"How about we get the hell out of here?"

Seven minutes after the "launch" order had been given, they loaded the last sarin warhead into the pickup and packed into the cab, shouting, "Go, professor! Take us back to Turkey!"

Mancini gunned the Ford F-250 through the gate and cut the lights. "Turkey, here we come," he muttered.

"Piece of cake."

They rendezvoused with the Mercedes Sprinter hidden in the concrete culvert where Hassan was waiting nervously, distributed the canisters between the two vehicles, and headed back toward the highway. Almost immediately they ran into problems. The combat between the Assad forces and the jihadists had resulted in impassable roads, which they bypassed by going off-road and driving across the flat plain—more difficult for the Sprinter than for the F-250.

Crocker told Akil, now at the wheel of the Ford, to slow down and maintain a speed of thirty-five.

Assad's guys were pissed off, so they'd shot up some flares, which took away the SEALs' cover. Now, to make things worse, attack helicopters were up in the air patrolling—at least one SA 342 Gazelle and a couple of Russian-manufactured Mil Mi-24s.

"So much for what Katie said about there being no helicopters at the air base," Crocker commented.

"Who's Katie?" Akil asked.

"Katie, the analyst at Ankara Station. The Asian chick."

"She cute?"

"Just keep your eyes on where you're going."

One of the 24s bore down on them. Before its .50 cal guns opened up, Akil hung a sharp right on a little dirt path with homes strung along it. In the process he nearly flipped the truck.

"Easy, cowboy!"

"I'm trying to keep us from getting lit up."

Crocker turned to see whether the Sprinter was still behind them. Couldn't see it through the swirling dust.

"Slow down!"

He heard the .50 cal on the helo open fire.

"Breaker. Breaker, Deadwood here. You okay?"

A few tense seconds passed before Davis answered. "We're in the high grass about sixty feet to your right."

Another pass from the helo and more fire. The Sprinter found a parallel road.

"You clear, Breaker? Report. Report!"

"All good. Over."

Based on the light issuing from their windows, the modest homes they whipped past were occupied. A sniper in one of the houses fired a shot that whizzed past Hassan's shoulder and ripped into the dash.

Crocker picked up the 416 and returned fire. He was so focused on the windows of the houses, searching for other snipers, that he forgot the Mi-24, which had veered off in search of other targets.

"Pedal to the metal," Crocker shouted.

"Make up your friggin' mind," Akil growled back.

"Stay on this road," Hassan shouted. "It will take us straight into Idlib."

They entered through streets piled with trash and rubble. It seemed unlikely that people still lived here, but lights shone from some of the damaged structures and they heard the occasional crack of small-arms fire in the distance.

Crocker stuck his head out the window and saw the Sprinter. "Nice work, Manny," Crocker said into his head mic. "See the bird? You good?"

Mancini, who was driving the Sprinter, responded, "Yeah, Deadwood, high and tight. The bird has flown west. What's the thinking at this point? You looking for real estate?"

"You see something you like, you let me know. I got cash."

"I like the collapsed-roof thing with the jihadist graffiti sprayed all over it."

A very pregnant dog wandered in front of the truck and stopped. Akil had to honk repeatedly to get it to move.

"You guys trying to wake the dead?" Mancini asked through the earbuds.

"No, we're trying to get your mother to move," Akil responded.

"Up yours with a rhino horn, douchebag."

"The good news is that we have the sarin, and aside from a couple of cuts and bruises, everyone's intact," Crocker reported.

"I question, boss, whether Romeo is completely intact," Davis said.

"More together than *you'll* ever be, surfer dude pothead," Akil shot back.

"Focus, guys," Crocker said. "We're still in Syria. Looks like we've lost our escort and probably have little chance of finding him. We've also got about an hour before the sun starts to rise."

"Rising sun means Syrian helicopters, and helos mean rockets," Mancini said.

"Thanks, grasshopper."

"So what's the thinking, boss man?"

Crocker turned to a shell-shocked Hassan in the front seat and asked him a series of questions about the streets ahead. Then he got back on his headset and said, "Hassan knows a completely bombed-out, deserted part of the city where we can hide till nightfall."

"Sounds like our kind of joint," said Akil.

"No electricity, no toilets, no running water," Mancini responded. "The Idlib Hilton. Lead the way."

CHAPTER ELEVEN

The greatest difficulties lie where we are not looking for them.
　　　　　　　　　　　　　—Johann Wolfgang von Goethe

THAT WAS almost too easy, Crocker thought as they entered what once must have been an upscale part of town, now completely destroyed. The Syrian air force had leveled everything. They traveled a half-dozen blocks beside a little park with shattered, dying eucalyptus trees without seeing one light or any evidence of life besides an occasional rodent. There were signs of phosphorus bomb damage on practically every building.

Too fucking easy, Crocker thought. He had expected more resistance from the Syrians at the air base. Then remembered that Assad's men were busy chasing ISIS jihadists. *Our timing was perfect, for once.*

Hassan pointed to some wreckage ahead on the right. "Turn in there," he instructed. "It used to be a primary school. I had a girlfriend who taught there."

"You had a girlfriend?" Akil asked. "I thought you were into guys." But Hassan wasn't laughing.

The three-story modern structure looked as if it had been abandoned for months. Bombs had landed on the roof, collapsing the middle of the building so that the resulting wreckage formed a giant V.

"Welcome to paradise," Akil announced as he emerged from the cab of the Ford, farted loudly, and stretched.

"First let's find a place to hide the trucks," Crocker said. "Then I want you and Suarez to do a quick recon of what's left of the building."

"We looking for ghosts?" Akil was in a jaunty mood.

"Ghosts, rats, busted gas lines."

"Roger that."

"Davis, you establish comms with Ankara Station. Let 'em know that we've got the sarin and we're planning to stay here until it gets dark."

"Awesome."

They found a garage in back that was big enough to accommodate both trucks and made them impossible to spot from above. Several of the washrooms on the first floor still had a trickle of running water—dirty and undrinkable, but enough to rinse their faces. Crocker, Mancini, and Davis pushed the trash out of a classroom with a view of the street.

"We'll assemble here," Crocker announced. "Soon as Akil and Suarez get back we'll set up a sentry schedule and the rest of you bums can catch some z's. I'll take the first watch."

No vehicles had passed along the street so far, which was what they'd hoped for. Since all the structures around them lay in ruins, there seemed no reason for anyone to enter the neighborhood. The buildings had already been looted.

When Ankara Station asked the name of the street and the building number, Crocker went looking for Hassan. He found him standing in a stairway, talking on his cell phone, which he found odd.

"Who are you talking to?" he asked.

"I was trying to reach a friend," answered Hassan.

"Probably not a good idea to use it. If the Syrians are looking for us, which I assume they are, they could be using scanners to pick up cell-phone signals."

"I'll power it down."

"Do it now. Thanks."

He thought of taking the phone away from him, but decided against it. The kid had been useful and cooperative.

Akil and Suarez's recon of floors one, two, and three yielded nothing surprising. The classrooms and offices they had been able to reach had already been stripped of valuables—desks, computers, calculators, books, toilet fixtures, and maps. They were about to wind up their search when Suarez noticed what looked like fresh wax drippings leading toward the basement.

Cautiously and quietly, they descended and entered a dark hallway that led to storage rooms, a laundry, and an electrical room. Here, too, doors had been ripped off their hinges and everything of value taken. Akil spotted water on the floor of the last storage area ahead. Strung from one wall to the other was a line containing items of women's laundry, including two black bras.

In the far corner, behind a large heating unit, they found mattresses, blankets, and two trembling women. One held a pair of scissors, the other a small kitchen knife.

"We're not going to hurt you. We're not going to touch you," Akil repeated over and over in Arabic.

The women didn't believe him at first. But when the one with the long dark hair and amber-colored eyes asked where he was from and he told her that he and his colleague were humanitarian workers from Canada, she started to relax.

Her name was Amira, she said, and explained that the school had been destroyed with the rest of the neighborhood five months ago. She and her friend Natalie had both been teachers at the school. Along with many others, they tried to flee the country, but because they were young unmarried women, they had been picked up by pro-Assad forces and raped.

After about three weeks of abuse, they managed to escape. Hiding during the day and traveling at night, they had returned to the school. They'd now been in the basement for a month and a half, surviving on emergency supplies the looters hadn't managed to find.

Akil told them that he and the men he was with were leaving for Turkey after sundown. When he asked the women if they would like to travel with them, they looked at each other and nodded.

Amira said that her friend thought she might be pregnant and needed medical attention.

"We'll get that for you in Turkey," offered Akil.

The opening chords of the darkly beautiful "'Round Midnight" by Thelonious Monk played on Crocker's iPod. There was something hauntingly sad about the way the angular chords built to the melody. Crocker had read somewhere that the jazz genius had composed it when he was eighteen years old.

It might have been written for this moment—the broken, abandoned school, his men snoring gently behind him, the light from the sun slanting through the wreckage. Kids had played here. The rooms were once filled with laughter and young, eager faces. It bothered him that one man—one tyrant and his supporters—had been allowed to wreak so much damage. How did the world allow this?

Birds chirped, unaware of the human madness around them. A breeze rattled aluminum roofing that had once covered the entrance to the playground.

Where are the children now? he wondered, aware of an engine chugging in the distance. As it slowly drew closer, Crocker shouldered his HK416 and decided to take a look.

Standing at the far end of the third floor where the roof was still more or less intact, he peered out the shattered windows and saw an old Corolla sedan approaching tentatively, stopping every ten feet as though the people in it were looking for a specific address. Nothing about it appeared alarming, but still he kept it fixed in the crosshairs of the EOTech 553 gunsight.

As the Corolla drew within thirty feet of the school, a curious thing happened. Hassan emerged from the building and waved it down. Crocker watched as the Corolla stopped and Hassan ran to the back door, opened it, and helped a very pregnant young woman out. They embraced. Then a young man emerged from the driver's side and kissed them both.

What the hell is this? A family reunion?

Crocker watched as the driver hurried to the back of the car, popped open the trunk, and handed the pregnant woman a suitcase. Then he returned to the Corolla, waved to Hassan and the woman, and started to back the car down the street.

Who's she? Crocker asked himself. *Is she the person Hassan was talking to on the phone?*

His thinking was interrupted by the whoosh of an approaching RPG. The Corolla was twenty feet from where it had left her when it hit the car from behind and exploded, destroying the car and throwing Hassan and the pregnant woman to the ground.

The pregnant woman screamed repeatedly in Arabic. The men

downstairs stirred and reached for their weapons. Crocker flew down the concrete steps two at a time, his 416 ready.

What the hell is going on?

He found Hassan and the pregnant woman lying on the pavement, hugging each other and trembling. He helped her up first. She was bleeding from a cut to her forehead and was blubbering hysterically, pointing at the burning car and saying, *"K…K… Khoya…"*

Hassan pointed to a piece of shrapnel embedded in his arm. "Look. Oh God!"

"Get inside!" Crocker shouted. To the woman: "Lean on me. Hurry."

She struggled to walk. *"Khoya! Khoya!* My…brother!"

"Come."

"My brother! My brother!"

He had to pick her up in his arms. With his free left hand he reached out to stop Hassan, who was stumbling toward the burning car in a half crouch. He was holding his ears and appeared disoriented.

"Hassan, get back inside the fucking school! Turn around!"

Hassan pointed toward the car and mumbled something. Then a peal of automatic gunfire came from beyond the car and ricocheted off the pavement around them. Crocker ran the woman to the schoolhouse. He passed Mancini wearing running shorts and cradling an M7A1.

"Incoming. Down the street! Past the burning car!"

"Who are they?"

"Unclear! Get Hassan. Bring him in. He's fucked up."

Mancini grabbed Hassan under one arm and scooped up the suitcase with the other. Hassan struggled, seemingly determined to rescue the man in the burning car even though he was surely burnt to a crisp by now.

Akil ran out to help wrestle a very resistant Hassan inside. Crocker left Suarez to watch him and the pregnant woman, then returned with Davis to try to deal with the attack from the end of the block.

"Who the hell are they?" asked Davis, slamming a mag into his automatic rifle.

"Unclear."

"How many?"

"Unclear again."

What they didn't need was a big commotion, which could bring Assad army reinforcements and air support. They were completely vulnerable and didn't even know their way out.

"You two stay here and defend," Crocker said to Mancini and Davis, who returned fire from the front of an adjacent structure that appeared to have been a church of some sort. "Akil and I are going to try to flank them from the right."

"What about Hassan?"

"Suarez is guarding him and trying to calm him down."

He signaled Akil to follow him to an alley that ran behind the buildings. Much of it was blocked with rubble and garbage like broken bicycles and furniture, making it impossible for a vehicle to pass. They squeezed through, Akil in Marine Corps shorts and a white Hooters tank top, Crocker in his usual black tee and pants.

None of the men had shaved in the past several days, so they didn't stand out. Nothing to mark them as Westerners, or trained operators. Even their weapons weren't that unusual. HK416s with attached grenade launchers, SIG Sauer P226 handguns, SOG knives, an RPG-7 with an assortment of warheads that Crocker carried in pouches on his black combat vest.

The firing on their left was close. Sounded like mostly small-arms stuff, with the occasional boom of a grenade. Seeing a badly damaged apartment tower ahead and to the right, Crocker signaled that this was their objective. He veered right, breaking a sweat, hopped a low concrete wall, pushed past a bloodstained mattress, and entered the back stairway. The trapped, stale air tasted like bitter coffee.

He pointed upward. At four o'clock, the stairway was completely blocked by a collapsed wall, so he turned left into a hallway and then into a large apartment that had been completely burned out. Ran in a crouch to the front windows, past the burnt remains of sofas and rugs, a child's crib, a cracked flat-screen hanging precariously from the wall. Akil followed.

Below and slightly left sat a jeep and a Toyota pickup with a nasty-looking .50 cal machine gun mounted in its bed. Several men with beards were crouched around the front of the jeep, firing automatic weapons. The jeep flew a yellow flag with the green logo of an arm raising an assault rifle and over it in Kufic script "Party of God."

"Hezbollah," Akil whispered.

Crocker hated those fuckers, having tangled with them before in Lebanon. He was aware that the Iran-backed Hezbollah militia had come to Assad's aid in the south and east. At least they weren't encountering Assad's army. Not this time.

The pickup was in the process of turning and backing up so that the .50 cal would have a clean shot down the street at the school.

Crocker pointed to the .50 cal and raised the RPG-7 to his shoulder. Then he pointed at Akil and signaled for him to deploy downstairs. Akil nodded and hightailed it, clutching his 416 and pushing a grenade into the M320 launcher on its lower rail.

Crocker knew he'd have only one shot before he gave away their position, so he loaded in a 40mm PG-7VR rocket, aimed carefully, and fired. The round glanced off the roof of the truck and hit the guy manning the .50 cal square in the back. The following explosion had the red aura of a direct hit.

Goner!

The hajis below turned and directed their fire at his window. With bullets tearing up the concrete and brick around him, Crocker quickly reloaded with an OG-7V fragmentation charge and fired again. This round hit the back of the jeep, causing it to lift off its rear axle and flip over. The resulting shrapnel downed most of the terrorists around it like a set of bowling pins.

He wanted this over as soon as possible, so he ran down the stairway as fast as his legs could take him. Through the drifting smoke he found Akil on the street, mopping up.

Pop-pop-pop!

A shot to the head finished off one Hezbollah terrorist. Two in the chest silenced another.

"Nice shot from the window," Akil said poking him in the chest with his elbow.

"Like picking off ducks in a pond."

Crocker was fired up to the max, wanting to get out of Idlib as soon as possible. Back at the school, he saw Davis on the radio talking to Ankara Station, his hair matted across his forehead, his eyes bloodshot, his frustration growing.

Because the weather had cleared and Assad's air force maintained complete control of the airspace, it was deemed impossible to rescue Black Cell and the sarin canisters by helicopter without taking a tremendous risk. A downed U.S. or NATO helo in Syrian territory wasn't something the White House appeared willing to tolerate. Still, the military maintained that they were looking for a safe LZ while they waited for approvals.

"Where does that leave us, sir?" Davis asked into the transmitter.

"Up the creek without a paddle," groaned Mancini, who sat near the window reassembling his M7A1 assault gun.

"We'll inform you of new developments," Grissom answered over the radio. "You'll do the same. Over and out."

Crocker didn't like the situation at all. It seemed to him that every minute they remained at the school, their risk of being discovered—either by another Hezbollah patrol wondering what happened to their colleagues or other Assad fighters—increased. FIBUA (fighting in built-up areas) was a hairy proposition and one they weren't equipped for.

"What did Ankara say about moving?" Crocker asked.

"They want us to stay put until dark," answered Davis.

Not happening, Crocker said to himself as a column of black smoke continued to rise from the burning vehicles on the street.

It wasn't clear whether Hassan's pregnant girlfriend, Jamila, had inadvertently tipped off the Hezbollah fighters or they had tracked Hassan's cell phone. All that mattered was that someone had made their current location. And they were sitting ducks.

"Romeo, what are you looking at?" Crocker asked into his head mic.

"Yo, Deadwood. Nothing moving," Akil replied from his lookout spot on the third floor. "Clear as far as I can see. Over."

"Keep looking. Over and out."

Suarez offered MREs to the schoolteachers huddled in the corner. The meals consisted of bean-and-cheese burritos, cheese spread, crackers, powdered Gatorade, a HOOAH! bar, utensils, an accessory pack containing sugar-free chewing gum, a waterproof matchbook, and seasonings, all individually sealed in plastic, and a water-activated exothermic heater made of finely powdered iron, magnesium, and salt. When mixed with a small amount of water, the solution reached a quick boil that produced readily usable heat.

Before Suarez had a chance to show them how to use it, the women had ripped into the burritos and HOOAH! bars. The latter were an apple-cinnamon variant of Clif energy bars. The food seemed to calm their nerves.

Crocker, meanwhile, had medical duties to attend to, examining the cut on Jamila's forehead, which was superficial, then cleaning and bandaging it. She had droopy dark eyes, a round, pale face, and shoulder-length straight dark hair. He poured her a cup of water from one of the Camelbaks. As she drank, she clutched her abdomen and moaned.

"What's going on down there?" Crocker asked gently, checking her pulse, which was more rapid than normal. Little beads of perspiration appeared on her forehead. Her temperature was above normal, too. She didn't answer, and continued to chew her top lip and hold her stomach. He saw a large wet area near the bottom of her long dark skirt.

Suspecting that she was on the verge of going into labor, he asked, "Your water broke, didn't it? How long ago?"

He saw a tear slide down her face and land in her lap. He used a wad of clean gauze to dab her eyes.

"I'll help you, but I need you to tell me what's going on," he said gently. "You understand English, don't you?"

She nodded without looking up.

"When did it break?"

"In…the car," she muttered with a strong accent.

"I need to touch your stomach. Is that okay?"

She nodded again.

He felt along it, carefully. The muscles were hard and the fetus had dropped, indicating that she was already in the early stages of labor.

"It's all good," he said. "The pain has just started?"

"Yes."

"Where do you feel it?"

"It starts here, in the lower back, and moves to the front."

"How long does it last?"

"Maybe twenty seconds."

"The pains occur at regular intervals?"

"Yes."

"How far apart?"

"Maybe five minutes. Maybe more."

"Okay. Drink, relax. We'll take care of everything."

Before he could make a decision, he had Hassan to attend to, carefully extracting the shrapnel from his forearm, disinfecting the wound and bandaging it. He wanted to scold him for the added complication, but what was the point?

"You're fine," Crocker said, "but your girlfriend is going into labor."

The young man immediately tensed up again. "Not now. No!"

"She'll be fine, Hassan. But I need you to think. Is there a hospital or clinic nearby?"

"No, nothing."

"You sure about that?"

"Yes. Yes."

He heard combat in the distance, which added to his sense of urgency. Akil, from the third-floor lookout, reported that the fighting seemed to be happening south of them. He also reported the presence of helicopters.

"Romeo, I need you down here," Crocker said into the head mic. "I'm sending Manny up to relieve you."

"Semper gumby, boss." Always flexible.

Crocker asked Amira to sit with Jamila, give her water, and measure the time between contractions. Then he had Davis and Suarez load the trucks while he huddled with Hassan and Akil and looked at the Garmin GPS and available maps. They were of limited utility.

Not wanting to get into a debate with Grissom and waste more time, he called Janice, who was still in Yayladaği, on the secure satphone.

"I need you to do something for me and not tell Ankara," said Crocker. "If you're uncomfortable with that, let me know now."

"Fine," she answered. "What do you want?"

He gave her their current location, then said, "We're looking for a place to hide for the next four or five hours until it turns dark—hopefully away from the city, which seems to be where most of the action is. Preferably north or northwest."

"Got it."

Janice came back five minutes later with the location of an abandoned chicken farm twenty-five kilometers west of Idlib, off Highway 60.

"That work?" she asked.

"I think so."

"I don't need to remind you that you should approach it with caution, but I will."

"Thanks."

"Let me know if you need an alternative."

"I will."

"Crocker, NSA and TA (threat assessment) are reporting a lot of rebel and government activity around Idlib, so watch the roads," she added.

"We will, Janice."

"One more thing: this call didn't take place."

"No, it didn't. I owe you one."

The problem would be getting to the farm undetected during daylight. He was sure that Ankara Station would strenuously advise against it. Given the fact that he would be delivering a baby soon and didn't want to do it in a compromised location, he decided to risk moving. The other members of Black Cell agreed.

Hassan was the only one who objected. Crocker asked him to cooperate and stay calm, but the kid continued to act like a nervous father-to-be.

They set out at normal speed—Crocker, Akil, Hassan, and Suarez in the lead truck, and Jamila, the two schoolteachers, Mancini, and Davis in the Mercedes Sprinter—navigating bomb craters and local roads piled with rubble.

The small groups of armed men they passed didn't seem to pay much notice. They looked young, hollow-eyed and exhausted.

"SFA rebels," Hassan pronounced, "waiting for the next bombing run or counterattack."

Up ahead they spotted a column of smoke rising from the middle of a row of houses. Gathered around were a small group of angry people chanting in Arabic, "The people want to execute you, Bashar! The people want to topple your regime!"

A beat-up white-and-red civil defense truck blocked the road. A man Hassan identified by his white helmet as an unpaid volunteer explained that the regime was dropping barrel bombs out of low-flying jets. Their job as civil defense workers, he said, was to uncover the bodies and get the wounded to a house that served as a clinic.

Crocker decided to give them the balance of the medical supplies they were still carrying. The grateful men thanked them with several *Allahu akbars*, and they continued.

Another five minutes of passing through narrow streets, and a wider road with a public park appeared ahead, with a large soccer stadium on the right. "The turnoff should be a couple of klicks from here, on the left," Akil said.

Davis through the comms reported that Jamila's contractions were now three minutes apart.

"Good," Crocker responded. "We still have time."

"Problem," grunted Akil, pointing to a roundabout that marked the intersection with a road that circled the outskirts of the city.

Through the windshield Crocker saw a roadblock. One of the jeeps that formed it flew the Free Syrian Army's green, white, black, and red "independence" flag—the official flag of Syria before the Ba'athist coup of 1963 that had brought the Assad family to power.

Crocker said, "Slow down. Tell them we're looking for Captain Zeid. They might be able to help us."

Just in case, he held his 416 in his lap and told the men in the Sprinter to lock and load.

Akil spoke in Arabic to a young fighter with a peroxided Mohawk. He looked like a skateboarder, and had an Element brand sticker affixed to the stock of his AK-47.

"Who are you?" the kid asked, the AK balanced on his right hip so it pointed skyward.

"Humanitarian workers from Canada, carrying a pregnant woman and some wounded civilians back to Turkey," Akil responded. "We're looking for Captain Zeid, who is supposed to escort us back to the border."

"You know Captain Zeid?" the skinny man asked.

"Yeah. He's been helping us."

"No more, brother, because he's dead. Killed in a gunfight with some Assad thugs last night."

"Sorry to hear that."

"Yeah, man, tragic. Like everything else."

Akil glanced back at Crocker, who gestured that he wanted to keep moving.

"You know anyone else who might be willing to escort us?" Akil asked.

"Not today, brother. We're on alert. Assad's got his killers out. Some crazy ISIS motherfuckers hit the Abu al-Duhur air base last night. They're looking for them." He pointed to the slogan on the Element sticker and said in halting English, "Make it count."

"You, too, brother."

Past the roadblock, they found a dirt road on the left that led them to a clump of trees with a small house and a string of chicken coops behind it, along with the nauseating odor of chicken feces and putrefying birds.

"This must be the place," Akil announced as he tied a scarf over his nose.

"It's disgusting," said Hassan.

"Nobody's gonna look for us here," Akil responded.

Just to make sure, Crocker got out with Suarez to recce it. They found no one.

The smell was a powerful deterrent. So was the completely ransacked state of the coops, main house, and outbuildings. They chose a barn with a partially intact roof to hide the trucks, then camped out in the farmhouse and quickly established sat-phone contact with Ankara Station.

Nothing had changed. Decision makers in D.C. were still dragging their feet. They wanted Black Cell to remain at the school until they could be rescued. There was logic to their argument. Black Cell had recovered the sarin; they were now safely in FSA-controlled territory. Aside from the threat of being discovered by Assad's air force, they seemed relatively safe.

But Crocker's instincts told him that D.C. and Ankara weren't taking into account the wildly unpredictable situation on the ground. Boundaries and alliances were shifting constantly. No one, except ISIS, seemed particularly interested in holding territory, since most of it had been destroyed and looted, and most of the residents had fled.

"Tell 'em, boss," Mancini argued. "Explain the situation. Maybe they'll send a helo now that we've got a pregnant woman."

When Crocker got on the sat-phone and told Grissom that they had moved from the school to a chicken farm outside the city and were carrying a woman who was going into labor, the station chief became apoplectic.

"Screw you, Crocker. If you can't obey orders and keep us informed, we can't help you."

"Sorry you feel that way, but I have to trust my own judgment."

"Your judgment sucks, Crocker. A pregnant woman? Who do you think you are, Mother Fucking Teresa?"

"It was unavoidable. But I have no time to explain."

Anders, when he got on the line, was slightly more understanding. "Be sensible, for Christ's sake. Leave the woman if she's an impediment. Don't move again until it turns dark. And before you move, check with us."

"Okay. What's the status of the air rescue?"

"Nothing's happening, Crocker, until it turns dark."

"That's not what I'm asking. I'm asking if it's been approved."

"Approval is still pending. HQ continues to consider all circumstances and contingencies. I'll inform them now of your new location, see if that changes anything. We'll let you know when and if we get the okay. Stay safe."

"We'll try."

He took a deep breath and sucked it up. Dissatisfaction from HQ, Anders, and even the White House was something he'd dealt with before. He knew how this worked. If the mission turned out to be a success and he delivered the sarin, he'd get scolded and given a slap on the wrist. But if the mission went south, he'd be seriously screwed. Possibly court-martialed and dismissed from the service.

He couldn't worry about that now. There were practicalities to deal with, including the fact that Jamila's contractions were growing more frequent and intense.

Hassan was practically hysterical when he found Crocker on the front porch. "We need to leave immediately and get Jamila to a hospital in Turkey."

"What about the clinic they were taking the wounded to in Idlib?" asked Crocker.

"It's even more disgusting than this. Don't you think I thought of that? Are you serious? Why are we staying here? Why are we waiting?"

"We're not waiting, Hassan, so calm the fuck down. You brought us this situation, and we're going to find a way to deal with it."

"How? How?"

"How do you think?" Crocker retorted, checking his watch again. "Deliver the baby."

"Here, in this disgusting place? Are you crazy? Jamila will die. The baby will die, too. And both their deaths will be your fault!"

Crocker reached out and grabbed him by the shoulders. "Listen to me," he said evenly and with authority, even though he wanted to slap him. "You're going to be a father soon. You need to start acting like one."

"What does that mean?"

"It means you need to help your girlfriend by calming her down and acting positive, even if you're scared to death."

Hassan looked like he was about to cry. "How can I look at her, when she will see the truth in my eyes? The midwife who examined her yesterday said that the baby had not turned. It isn't in the right position. She said she needs a surgeon or an obstetrician."

That brought a new wrinkle to the situation.

"Now do you understand? That's why we have to find one in Turkey."

"Great idea, but not happening," Crocker said, trying to remember what he had learned about different birthing methods. "Did the midwife say what position the fetus is in?"

"No, of course not. Why would she tell me that? I'm not a doctor. You're not, either. That's why we have to leave now! What's preventing us? Why are you being so stubborn?"

"Because there's no time, Hassan. The baby's in distress, and so is your girlfriend."

"But the baby's in the wrong position! Didn't you just hear me? It won't come out!"

"It has to," answered Crocker, "and it will."

CHAPTER TWELVE

Death, taxes, and childbirth. There's never any convenient
time for any of them.
—Margaret Mitchell

MORTAR ROUNDS started to fall in the vicinity as Crocker and his men improvised a clean bed out of sheets and an inflatable mattress on a table in what used to be the dining room. One of the two schoolteachers, the shorter woman with a bowl of straight black hair who hadn't said a word so far—Natalie—volunteered to act as Crocker's assistant. She and Suarez boiled water and sterilized the rudimentary tools in the emergency medical kit as Amira held Jamila's hand and Hassan wrung his hands and paced.

"You think you can handle being in the room?" Crocker asked him as a helicopter passed overhead.

He nodded, then whispered, "I want you to know that Jamila's a very wonderful person and has suffered so much already. Her mother is dead, her father was arrested, she hasn't heard from her brothers since they joined the resistance."

"Duly noted."

Crocker had delivered babies before—once to a feverish young woman in a barn in Honduras, another time twins to an injured woman in Iraq.

Upon examination, he discovered that this was going to be his first breech birth. What that meant was that instead of the normal head-first presentation, this baby was presenting itself bottom first, with his or her legs extended at the knees.

"You seen anything like this before?" whispered Suarez, who had some corpsman training.

"No, but there's always a first time."

A shell exploded outside, shaking the remaining tiles on the roof. One of them crashed two feet away from the table where Jamila sat. Amira held up a towel to shield Jamila's face.

"We're fine," Crocker said. "Suarez, find Davis and ask him to check if there are any more loose tiles over this room."

"Aye aye."

If Jamila were in a hospital, chances are the baby would be de-livered via cesarean section. But not having a properly equipped operating room with ultrasound and heart monitors, Crocker didn't want to risk excessive bleeding and infection, so he planned to try to perform a vaginal breech birth, which was problematic but the only real option he had.

The contractions were coming closer together and were more intense—every minute now, and a minute in duration. Jamila was in serious discomfort, with especially strong pains in her back. Crocker was reluctant to administer morphine, because he thought it might numb the fetus and affect its heart.

"Okay," he said, as he exposed her lower back and prepared to inject the sterile water from his kit just below the skin of her lum-bosacral region. "This is going to sting for a minute, but it won't put you out or damage the baby in any way." The way it worked was simple. The sudden burst of intense pain from the injection closed off transmission of the sensation produced by the contractions.

Jamila let out a scream and did the paced breathing Amira had been teaching her. The pain in her back abated. So far, so good.

Crocker had been concentrating so hard he hadn't realized that the artillery and rockets were falling with more frequency.

Suarez, who had noticed, now whispered in his ear, "It could be the lead-up to some kind of ground attack on a nearby target."

"You mean the artillery?"

"Yeah, boss."

"We've got to finish this first."

"How about we move the canisters to the Ford and do the delivery in the back of the van?"

Crocker examined Jamila's cervix again. It was open ten centimeters and the mucus plug had released, which meant that cervical dilation was complete. Aware that it would be hard enough to manage a difficult breech birth in a stationary location and almost impossible in a moving van, he whispered back, "The baby's coming. No time."

His first goal was to turn the fetus by manipulating its body through the mother's abdomen. He had Jamila lie down on her back on the mattress with her feet on the table and her knees apart. Then he and Suarez pressed and applied pressure. They weren't successful. The baby was so big there was very little room inside the vaginal canal for it to be maneuvered. And Crocker didn't want to keep trying because of the stress they were putting on the baby's heart.

"Now what?" Suarez asked.

The baby's butt was showing through the cervical opening. Crocker said, "I'll hold on to the butt while you try to twist the fetus to the right."

"How do I do that?"

"Grab it near the chest. Firmly, and turn gently."

Slowly they applied pressure and managed to turn the fetus slightly, so that its right side faced Jamila's back. Then they watched as her pelvic floor muscles helped complete the process.

"Nice."

"What happened?" Jamila asked through gritted teeth.

"It's all good. We'll have the baby out soon."

Crocker saw that the new position of the fetus would allow the baby to come out one hip at a time. Since its bottom was the same size as its head and the mother's pelvis was relatively large, labor could begin.

The big danger they faced now was injury to the baby's brain or skull due to a rapid passage of the head through the birth canal. With the fetus positioned the way it was, it was impossible to determine the angle of its head. All Crocker could do was hope that the head wasn't in the "star-gazing" position, looking straight up, with the back of the head resting against the back of the neck.

The other serious danger was that the umbilical cord would prolapse, diminishing or cutting off the flow of blood to the baby's brain.

Amira and Hassan whispered encouragement into Jamila's ears while Suarez mopped the sweat from Crocker's brow.

He glanced at his watch: 1855 hours. The sun was starting to set outside as artillery continued to shake the house.

What Crocker hoped to accomplish was a smooth, quick delivery so the baby wasn't hung up in any way that might put undue pressure on its heart.

He took a deep breath. As he did, an explosion shook the farmhouse, causing Hassan and Natalie to gasp and Jamila to tighten up.

Crocker reached for his head mic and whispered, "Breaker, how close was that?"

"A hundred and fifty feet," Davis reported. "Maybe less."

"Do you have any idea what they're shooting at? You see fighters or bunkers?"

"Negative to all three."

They waited. When no more mortars fell in the next two minutes, Jamila relaxed.

Crocker said, "All right. Let's get this kid out."

She nodded bravely as he pulled on a fresh pair of nitrile gloves. Years ago, during his corpsman training in Yokohama, he had watched a video on something called the Mauriceau-Smellie-Veit maneuver. He tried to recall it now, rehearsing the steps in his head. When he felt confident that he could pull it off, he turned to Suarez and said, "When I give the signal to Jamila to push, I want you to apply subrapubic pressure to the uterus."

"How do I do that?"

"Press down on the pubic bone here, thus opening the vagina."

He showed him where to position his hands, then took a deep breath, waited for her cervix to spasm, then asked her calmly, "Jamile, you ready to push?"

She nodded.

He turned to Suarez and asked, "You clear about what to do?"

He nodded, too.

"All right. On three."

He counted out loud.

Suarez pressed, Jamila screamed, and Hassan, Amira, and Natalie furiously massaged her back and whispered encouragement. Crocker inserted his gloved left hand, reached his index finger upward, and inserted it into the baby's mouth. Gently pressing on the kid's maxilla to bring the neck to moderate flexion, he rested his left palm on the baby's chest, reached his right hand around until he held the shoulders in his right palm, and pulled down and out.

The baby's hips and shoulders slipped out easily, but the head became stuck, causing Jamila to start to panic.

"Relax, Jamila," Crocker whispered reassuringly, "We're almost there."

He took a deep breath and felt with his left hand to make sure the umbilical cord wasn't interfering with the baby's neck. Then he turned to Suarez and whispered, "Push again, with conviction."

With his left index finger in the baby's mouth, he slowly maneuvered the chin through the cervix opening and guided the head out. It emerged with a pop, followed by a full-throated cry from the baby boy.

"Oh my God!" Hassan shouted. "Is it okay?"

"You've got a beautiful baby boy!"

Jamila started to bounce her butt up and down on the mattress with joy. "Oh my God! I can't believe it! Praise God!"

"Hold on a minute. Stay still."

Crocker handed the baby to Suarez, then calmly tied and cut the umbilical cord and removed the placenta. The baby wailed.

"Strong lungs."

As Crocker cleaned Jamila up, Suarez wiped down the baby and handed it to its mother. Shouts of exultation followed and ricocheted off the walls. For a few moments the war was completely forgotten. Even for Crocker, who dealt with the minor bleeding, which was normal, and went outside to get some fresh air.

As he stood in the doorway watching the sun start to drop toward the horizon, he sighed deeply and his hands started to shake. Seventeen years ago he had sat in a delivery room in Alexandria, Virginia, and watched the birth of his daughter, Jenny. It seemed like another lifetime now. In a day or two—he couldn't remember the specific day—she'd receive her diploma and graduate from high school.

He wanted to be there but wouldn't. Instead, he'd probably be facing another unknown challenge. Protecting and aiding the innocent was his disease, his compulsion, and through the grace of God the only thing that satisfied the hunger in his soul.

"I don't understand how the world can just watch this," the suddenly talkative Natalie declared, emerging to stand beside him. "Syrians are good people. No one is with us. No one! Why is that?"

Crocker nodded. "It's terrible, I know. We're doing what we can."

"No. Not enough."

She was right. Despite Natalie's distress and the mortars thudding in the distance, he looked out at the sun descending over broken chicken coops filled with putrefying chickens and felt a rare moment of peace. All he wanted now was a beer or a shot of scotch, a comfortable chair, and a place to put his feet up. But those small pleasures would have to wait.

Turning to Natalie, he said, "Do me a favor and find Suarez. Tell him I want him to fix a place for the mother and baby in the pickup."

"I can do that."

"By the way, what did they name the baby?"

"Tariq Yusef Mohammed Sadir, after his maternal grandfather."

"Tariq Yusef Mohammed Sadir. Let's hope he has a better future."

He didn't have time to speculate on what that might be. Seeing Davis on the porch keeping watch, he asked, "Anything new from Ankara?"

Davis wore the coiled, expectant look of a soldier waiting for the next battle to start. "Negative, boss. Nothing's changed. They're still waiting for approval of the LZ site."

He checked his watch: 1938. A helicopter buzzed high in the purplish-black sky. Looked like a little Polish-made Mi-2 with rockets mounted along the sides. As it headed south he heard firing in the distance, then saw a cloud of black smoke, indicating that the helo had been hit by antiaircraft fire. It was unreal, like watching a movie. The resulting explosion reverberated through the house.

Crocker turned to Davis and said, "Tell the guys to prepare to move out."

"Just prepare, or really go?"

"We're leaving."

"Without approval?"

"With it or without it. The situation here isn't good."

"Even without it, I have to tell Ankara something."

"Tell 'em a helicopter was just shot down in the area and we're hearing an uptick in fighting. So we're moving north through what we hope is FSA-controlled territory. We'll apprise them of our new position when we arrive."

"Sounds good but kind of vague."

"That's on purpose."

As Crocker paused to take one last look at the ragged landscape, one of Al Swearengen's best lines came to mind. "Pain or damage don't end the world, or despair, or fucking beatings. The world ends when you're dead. Until then, you got more punishment in store. Stand like a man, and give some back."

For a brief moment he was tired of fighting. All he had to do now was deliver the people and cargo in his charge to safety.

CHAPTER THIRTEEN

If there is no struggle, there is no progress.
—Frederick Douglass

AT 2023 they set out, headlights extinguished, on Highway 60 with their cargo of sarin and refugees. Miles Davis's *Sketches of Spain* played on Crocker's iPod as they rolled down a long straightaway past fields of new wheat. It was a warm, still night with dramatic clouds that reminded him of the J. M. W. Turner paintings he had once seen in the National Gallery in London. He wanted to chill to the dark lyricism of the music and Davis's haunting flugelhorn solo, but his brain wouldn't let him.

The Garmin GPS said they were only fifty-eight miles from the border. At home, fifty-eight miles was a trip to Costco and back, but now they were in northwest Syria, where new horrors seemed to lurk around every corner.

He shut his eyes as the minutes and miles slid past. He was half conscious, lying on his back in a swimming pool, when Hassan grabbed his shoulder.

"Look, Mr. Wallace. Look!" He was pointing toward multiple lights maybe a quarter of a mile ahead.

What now?

"Trouble. Look! There!"

"I see."

It was unclear who was ahead and what the lights belonged to—more vehicles, probably. Crocker grabbed the 416 off the floor, rebombed a mag, slammed it in, killed the music, and leaned forward.

"It appears to be another roadblock," Hassan said anxiously. "Maybe FSA, maybe Islamists."

Even if they were FSA, Crocker wasn't sure they could be trusted—not with his cargo of sarin and young women. He needed time to think. Donning a pair of NVGs, he spotted a path in the field to his right and said to Akil, "Turn off here and kill the engine."

They sat on a dirt path with green wheat swaying on both sides, crickets chirping, and the crescent moon playing hide and seek behind the clouds. Percussive bursts of rocket or artillery fire thundered behind them. Altogether, a strange, ominous symphony of sorts.

"I think it's ISIS with its rockets again," Hassan said nervously, biting his nails and looking behind them. "It could be them both ahead and behind."

"Or could be Assad's forces counterattacking," responded Akil. "Impossible to tell."

Crocker wasn't as concerned about who was behind them as about what lay ahead. "Deadwood, Breaker here," he heard through the earbuds. "What's the plan?"

"Headlights!" Hassan shouted, pointing at the side mirror. "More headlights coming in back!"

Sure enough, yellow headlights shone on the road far behind

them, creeping closer. The lights in front hadn't moved and only seemed brighter.

Crocker felt the tension in the cab inflate like a balloon.

"Deadwood? You read me?"

"I'm thinking. Manny, look through the Steiners and see if you can make out the number of vehicles behind us," he said through the head mic.

Half a minute later Mancini reported, "Looks like a lone wolf."

"What kind?"

"Maybe a pickup. Hard to tell from this distance."

What they sat on now was more a path than a road, so he had no confidence that it led anywhere. He was also worried that the taller Sprinter's roof was visible from the road.

Leaning over the front seat toward Akil, he said, "Let's move forward, headlights off, and find a better place to turn off."

"What happens if we don't find one?"

"We initiate Plan B."

"What's that?"

"Don't know yet."

Crocker communicated the only plan he had so far to Mancini at the Sprinter's wheel behind them. As soon as it moved out of the way, Akil backed the truck up, swung onto the highway, and gunned the engine.

These weren't ideal fighting conditions—three women, a baby, eight canisters of sarin, five SEALs with limited armaments. But Crocker had decided that they weren't stopping anymore, for anyone.

The roadblock loomed two hundred yards ahead. Even though they were driving with their lights doused, chances are they'd been spotted already. Akil and Hassan kept craning their necks left and right, but saw no turnoff.

"We're trapped!" Hassan exclaimed.

"Quiet!"

"Where are the American helicopters? Why haven't they come to get us?"

"Shut the fuck up."

"What do we do now?" Akil asked.

"Slow down, but don't stop."

"Why?"

"Because I'm getting out."

"Why?"

"I'm gonna run ahead. When you get close, flash the headlights and slow down. Whatever happens, don't let those bastards in the trucks."

"That's a stupid idea," commented Hassan.

"Nobody asked you, Hassan."

Hassan muttered something under his breath. They were close enough now to see one of the trucks ahead flying a black-and-white ISIS flag.

"Nasty-ass jihadists," announced Akil.

"This is bad. A very terrible situation," Hassan warned. "We should get out here and run!"

"Keep your head down."

"Maybe it's your buddy al-Kazaz," said Akil. "You still got that letter?"

"Forget the letter."

Sarin and young attractive women would be too much temptation to desperate men. Crocker looked through the NVGs but couldn't find any parked motorcycles. Just SUVs and trucks—one a flatbed with a weapons system mounted on it.

"Even if it's al-Kazaz, we can't let him inside the trucks."

"Copy."

"Breaker, Romeo, Manny, Rojas, ready weapons," Crocker said into the mic. "No one gets in the vehicles. No inspection; no bartering. We're going to slow down, tell them we're ferrying injured civilians, and blast by. We're not letting them in. Repeat. Keep them away from the trucks."

"Copy, Deadwood."

"Roger."

"Here we go. Over."

Crocker readied the 416 in his lap, securing the AAC M4-2000 suppressor and slipping an M576 buckshot grenade into the M320 grenade launcher attached to the rails. He grabbed two more M576s and three high-explosive M441 grenades and stuffed them in the pouches of his combat vest; chambered a round in the SIG Sauer 226 and stuck it in the waistband of his pants; made sure the NVGs were snug around his head and his Dragon Skin armor was strapped on tight. No time even for a quick prayer.

"Ready?" Akil asked.

"Ready. Pull close to the shoulder at that bend up there and slow down."

Akil braked and Crocker opened the back door, jumped out, rolled into the high grass, and sprung to his feet like the athlete he was. Immediately he broke into a sprint through the grass, pulling ahead of the Sprinter and pickup. Building up speed, he was within one hundred feet of what he made out to be two white Broncos and a Mercedes flatbed truck with what looked like a Russian-made ZU-23-2 antiaircraft gun on it blocking the road ahead. He hadn't seen a ZU-23-2 since Somalia, back in the nineties, when they were chasing drug-crazed warlords through the streets of Mogadishu.

Noisy fucking weapon, and nasty.

One of the Broncos had its headlights illuminated and engine running. Six bearded men stood in front of the vehicles, holding weapons and wearing assorted camouflage and traditional garb, all with armored vests. They were gesturing at the oncoming vehicles to stop.

Crocker, breathing hard, barked into the head mic: "The two guys on the right are mine. Breaker and Rojas, you take the dudes on the left."

"Happily."

"Deadwood, check out the twin 23mms on the truck," Mancini said.

"Should be in a museum, huh?"

"If they work, they can rip shit up."

"Copy," responded Akil. "Don't want that piece of shit pointed at me."

"Ain't happening," Crocker said. "I've got it covered."

"Okay, Warrant Manslaughter."

"I have a real bad feeling about this," Hassan moaned to Akil at the wheel of the pickup.

"Keep your head under the dash before they blow it off."

"What happens if they hit one of the canisters?"

"We die," Akil responded.

Davis through the earbuds: "Deadwood?"

"Soon as the bastards level their weapons, open fire."

As Crocker ran, the tall grass sliced his arms and face. He glanced over his shoulder to check if the jeep was still following them. It was. Another complication. One he couldn't deal with now.

"Romeo, ease down on the brakes, but don't stop under any conditions," he said through the mic to Akil.

"Even if Angelina Jolie jumps in front of us naked?"

"Even if she does a booty dance in your face."

The jihadists ahead stood in the path of the lead pickup, waving wildly and shouting warnings. One fired volleys from an AK into the sky. Crocker was bearing down on them in the grass on the right, running in a half crouch, the muscles in his calves and legs burning, breathing hard.

Fifty feet, forty, thirty, twenty, ten. His right foot reached ahead, hit the side of a slight depression, slipped, and turned. He lost his balance and fell hard onto the right side of his chest, knocking the air out of his lungs. He saw stars, felt pain near his ribs, and struggled to stay conscious, feeling for his weapon, willing himself up.

Meanwhile, Akil was reaching out the F-250 window, pointing to the blue cross on the hood and shouting in Arabic, "Medical emergency! Doctors Without Borders! We have wounded civilians. We're Canadians. Brakes don't work! We can't stop!"

Crocker pulled himself to his knees, his head still throbbing. Through the grass he saw one of the jihadists jump onto the pickup's running board and heard him scream through the window, "You stop, infidel! Stop or I shoot!"

"I can't, brother. The brakes don't work!"

Akil and the jihadist struggled through the window. Two shots went off in succession. The pickup veered left and crashed into the side of one of the Broncos. Immediately the confused jihadists leveled their weapons. Crocker knelt in the grass beside the front wheel of the pickup and opened fire.

He launched the M576 first, then raked right with the 416. Keeping in mind that the targets were wearing armored vests, he aimed for their legs, then finished them off with head shots, a tight burst at each. As soon as they went down, he looked for his next target.

One-two-left-right. Through his EOTech sight he saw a jihadist in the back of the flatbed start to swing the ZU-23-2 into position, and caught him with a salvo that practically took off his head.

The flashes through the NVGs blurring his vision, he shoved an M441 round into the M320 launcher, aimed at the flatbed, and fired at the hood. *BLAM!* The front of the vehicle exploded into flames.

Davis and Suarez directed their fire left. Screams, smoke, confusion, cascading bodies. The encounter was pretty much over before it started, except for one jihadist who tried to launch himself through the Ford's passenger-side window. He managed to reach in and grab Hassan by the hair.

Crocker ran up and shouted, "I got him. Back away from the Bronco, then accelerate!"

He smacked the jihadist in the back of the head with the butt of his 416 so that the side of his head smashed into the front post near the window. Then jumped, held on with his right hand, and thrust his SOG knife into his throat with his left. He pulled open the door, grabbed the jihadist by his beard, and threw him off.

"Watch out, boss!"

The jihadist's body smacked the side of the Bronco as they swerved around it. The F-250's door swung open and hit it, too, sending up a stream of sparks, blowing out the window, and almost taking Crocker's right leg off. He pulled it back just in time. Hassan screamed. The baby started wailing.

Total chaos. Akil fishtailed the truck left and right, trying to control it, and throwing Crocker all over the backseat.

"What the hell are you doing?"

"Having fun! Hoo-yah!"

Akil gunned the F-250 down a straightaway, smoke spilling from beneath the hood, then skidded around the next turn.

"Easy!" Crocker shouted, holding on and looking back. He could see that the Sprinter couldn't keep up. "Ease the fuck up."

Hassan was screaming and holding his hands over his eyes. "I'm injured! I'm bleeding!"

Crocker learned over, pulled away his hands, and saw a long scratch across his left cheek, maybe a few millimeters deep. There was just a trickle of blood. He slapped a hand over Hassan's mouth and said, "Pull yourself together! You're fine."

The young man was practically hyperventilating, and his eyes were popping out of his head.

Crocker spoke into the head mic, "Everyone okay? What's everyone's status? Rojas, Breaker, Manny? Report."

"Rocking and rolling, but intact," Mancini responded.

"Shit my pants," joked Davis.

"Praise my Lord and Savior, Jesus Christ," responded Suarez.

"Nicked in the shoulder," said Akil from the front seat.

"What now, Deadwood?" Mancini asked.

"Keep burning out."

He leaned over the seat and saw lots of blood around Akil's shoulder. Looked like a bullet had passed through the fleshy part up top. He reached into his med kit, found a black tactical tourniquet, wrapped it as high around the shoulder as he could, and pulled it tight.

"Damage assessment to the vehicles?" he asked into the mic.

"We took a couple rounds in the hood and one through the windshield. Lucky shot."

"Sarin intact?"

"Seems to be, yeah."

"The women?"

"A little shaken but all good."

The front right bumper of the Ford F-250 was a crumpled mess, and smoke continued to pour from beneath the hood.

"Engine's heating up," Akil reported.

Through the cacophony Crocker made out little Tariq crying and his mother quieting him, which brought him a moment of joy—quickly interrupted by Davis's voice through the earbuds.

"That asshole is still behind us and bearing down."

"How the fuck did he get through the roadblock?"

"Maybe he's one of them," Davis answered.

"It's only one man. You sure?"

"Only one head up."

Crocker had forgotten all about the vehicle tailing them. He craned his neck out the shattered side window to take a look and made out a Mitsubishi J21C jeep with a single driver behind the wheel closing, flashing its headlights and honking.

First he wanted to take a quick look at Akil's shoulder to see if the tourniquet was working.

He said, "Hassan, take the wheel."

"But—"

"Take the fucking wheel and maintain current speed!"

Hassan grumbled something as he grabbed the steering wheel. Akil slid closer to him, then they squeezed past each other and changed places, Akil holding his left shoulder.

Crocker shone a light on it and leaned forward to look.

"Bad?" Akil asked.

"Hold the flashlight and keep quiet."

"As long as my dick is still working."

Crocker cut away the wet T-shirt, cleaned the wound with an alcohol prep, applied some local anesthetic, smeared in some QuikClot, and covered it with a Battle Wrap compression bandage.

Blood was spattered all over the driver's seat and window. He didn't know if it was Akil's or the jihadist's, or both.

"Ugly mofo," Akil said, "with stinking breath."

"Lean back. Drink some water. How do you feel?"

"Like I want to kick ass."

Crocker grinned, slapped him gently on the side of the head. "You're just as fucked up as you were before."

"Lousy doc. I ought to sue."

"For what? Listening to your BS?"

Through the earbuds he heard: "Deadwood, the jeep in back is within fifty feet of us."

"Slow down," Crocker ordered.

"Can you repeat that?"

"Ease up on the accelerator. Slow down."

"Ill-advised, boss," Mancini responded. "Could be a suicide bomber."

"Could be. But I don't think so."

"Not a chance we should take."

Mancini had a point. Crocker into the head mic: "Manny, you still got those portable StunRays?"

"Affirmative."

"They functional?"

"The lithium batteries are pretty hardy, so should be. Want me to test them?"

"No time. What's the range on those suckers?"

"They incapacitate at up to one hundred fifty feet."

"All right. Slow down, then direct 'em behind you and blind the fucker!"

"Like that idea. Will do. Over."

Crocker craned his neck out the window and looked back as the

Mitsubishi pulled within sixty feet of the Sprinter. Suarez, Davis, and Mancini each held one of the XL-2000 handhelds out the window and switched them on at the same time. The intense light turned the road and jeep completely white.

It nearly blinded Crocker, too. He steadied his 416 against the rear windowsill and tried to fix a bead on the driver, just in case.

Whoever it was seemed to be losing control of the jeep, swerving left, then right. The Mitsubishi hit the right shoulder, dipped into a ditch, hit the ground grille-first, and flipped over. One complete turn, then another, and then it stopped roof-down in some shrubs.

"Stop!" Crocker shouted. Akil slammed on the brakes, and Crocker jumped out and ran back, weapon ready. He was joined by Suarez cradling an M5. Together they examined the overturned vehicle through their NVGs but couldn't find the driver. Suarez pointed into the weeds ahead. Through the smoke Crocker saw a large figure lying on his belly and groaning. He had been thrown and landed chest-first. They couldn't see his face.

"*Yadahu! Yadahu!*" (Hands!), Crocker shouted in Arabic. "Let me see your hands."

The guy wasn't moving. Still, Crocker remained cautious. "He reaches for anything, waste him."

Both of the big man's arms were trapped underneath him and he wasn't moving. Suarez stepped over him to get a look at his face.

He leaned closer and exclaimed, "Boss! Boss, look. I think it's Babas!"

"Babas? You mean Zeid's friend?"

"I think so, yeah. Check it out."

Crocker knelt down to get a good look and recognized the thick brow and long nose. Also saw that the man's spine had snapped near his neck.

"Shit," Crocker said with a groan. "He's toast."

They listened to him breathe his last. Watched his body tremble and relax.

Suarez: "What do you think he wanted?"

"Unclear, poor guy," Crocker answered, shouldering the 416. "Let's check the jeep."

Nothing except a loaded AK on the floor, a Glock 9mm in the glove compartment, and an old copy of *Penthouse* stuffed under the seat, along with a half-eaten falafel. The vehicle itself was unsalvageable, with a broken rear axle.

Suarez: "I think he was trying to help us, boss."

"Could be. Yeah. If he was...damn shame."

The light Suarez was holding washed across Crocker's head. "Hey, boss. What happened to your face?"

Crocker ran his hand along it, finding shallow slashes and coagulating blood. "Grass back there sliced me good. Let's go."

Davis, in the Sprinter, was on the phone. Seeing Crocker, he put his hand over the receiver and said, "Ankara's sats picked up our GPS signal, and they're mad as hell. Want to know why we're moving and where."

"Have they cleared air rescue?"

"Negative. But they informed me that they tried to put up a Predator but were overruled by HQ because of the heavy Syrian air force activity."

"So nothing's new."

"What do you want me to say?"

"Tell 'em they're fucking useless, and we don't need their help!"

CHAPTER FOURTEEN

If you come to a fork in the road, take it.
—Yogi Berra

THERE WAS no room in the trucks for Babas, so they buried him as well as they could, uttered a prayer, took his weapons, and proceeded. A Syrian helicopter passed low overhead. Nerves were fraying. Hassan and the women were almost delirious with fright. Crocker asked Suarez to sit with the latter and try to keep them calm, and instructed Hassan and Mancini to keep driving in the direction of the border. He kept an eye out for headlights, roadblocks, and anything in the air.

He used gauze and peroxide to wipe the blood off his face and arms. Stung like hell, especially along the side of his mouth. His watch showed that it was approaching midnight. The handheld Garmin GPS indicated that they were less than twenty miles from the border.

All they needed now was a little luck.

Just when it looked like the road ahead was clear, they heard the roar of jet afterburners as three MiG-21s tore past at low altitude. A panicked Hassan almost steered the F-250 off the road.

"What was that?"

"Ignore everything else and drive."

A minute later the landscape ahead lit up with multiple large explosions. Then the road itself jumped as if it was trying to shake something off.

"You think they saw us?" asked Hassan.

"Likely," replied Akil.

"Pull off," ordered Crocker. "Hide the trucks."

"Here? Again?" Akil said.

"Yeah, again."

"Where?" Hassan asked. "I can't see anything."

"We'll find a spot."

"Deadwood, it's Breaker," heard Crocker through the earbuds. "Ankara reports that Assad's jets are pounding an FSA convoy ahead."

"Great."

"What do we do now?" Hassan asked.

"Stop asking questions, and keep your eyes on the road."

They watched the MiG-21s climb high into the clouds, then dive for another pass. The land ahead lit up again and shook.

Akil pointed to the Ford's heat gauge and said, "We've got another problem, boss. This baby's overheating."

Crocker leaned forward and saw the thermostat had reached the danger zone.

"What should I do?" Hassan asked.

Crocker saw a dirt road ahead that snaked into some hills. He pointed to it. "Turn off there. Pull into that clump of trees and stop."

"Then what?"

"Then we try to fix this shitbox."

Mancini, who knew vehicles and engines, did a quick inspection under the hood and came back with bad news. It wasn't a hose he could patch. Instead, a round had torn into the radiator and done extensive damage.

"Give me a solution."

"All the fluid has leaked out," Mancini replied. "I might be able to rig something around the radiator, don't know what. But it's gonna take time."

Crocker didn't like the idea of sitting there with the MiGs so close and Assad's units maybe moving into the area for some kind of mop-up operation.

"Guys, we're gonna have to pile everyone and everything into the Sprinter."

"Don't know if we'll fit," said Davis.

"Either that or we leave you here and come back for you tomorrow."

"Very funny, boss."

"I'm not kidding."

"Screw that."

"Then let's start unloading."

The men were sweating hard, stripped to their waists, arranging and rearranging, taking special precautions with the sarin and the baby. It reminded Crocker of packing the family station wagon for a vacation when he was a kid.

Eight canisters, a baby, three women, Akil, and Davis all crammed in back. Jamila held little Tariq like he was the most precious thing in the world.

We'll find a way, thought Crocker.

Suarez siphoned out the remaining diesel fuel. He even took the spare tire, just in case. Then squeezed himself into the cargo bay against the door.

Mancini, Hassan, and Crocker sat shoulder to shoulder in the cab, Mancini at the wheel. No room to scratch an itch.

"Hey, Akil, how are you doing?" Crocker asked into the head mic.

"Bleeding's stopped. I might live."

"Good. Keep drinking water."

"Tell Manny he drives like shit."

"Manny, Akil says you drive like shit."

"Tell Akil to stop whining like a little girl."

The badly potholed road they were on didn't appear on any of the GPS or sat maps Ankara Station had provided.

"You want me to call Ankara and ask if they can pull up something better, or send us some better sat imaging?" Davis asked through the earbuds as they approached a moderately steep hill.

"First let's see if this baby can handle the weight."

The 161-horsepower engine whined and struggled. They chugged uphill at twenty-five miles an hour sounding like a tugboat. Passing over the crest and into a little valley Crocker spotted a farmhouse with a bombed-in roof to the right. A wooden shed with a faint yellow light in the window stood near a patch of willow trees.

More bombs exploded to the northwest. Crocker said, "Stop, Manny. Pull over."

Then he grabbed Hassan's wrist. "Let's take a look."

"Why me?"

"I need your language skills. Akil's hurt."

"But—"

"Davis, you come too. I'll hold your hand."

Crocker was already outside, weapon ready and in a crouch, holding Hassan by the arm with his free hand.

"What're we looking for?" Davis asked.

"Help, a road map, directions, a fucking helicopter. You back us up."

He and Hassan ran hunched over and came up under the window. Inside they saw a skinny old man with a dog, listening to an old cassette tape player and darning a pair of socks. Strains of "Hey Jude" by the Beatles passed through the weathered wooden slats. Crocker flashed back to his high school girlfriend Kelly, who learned the song on the guitar and sang in a whispery, sweet voice. She had the prettiest mouth he'd ever seen and green eyes.

He signaled to Davis to kneel to the right of the door, then handed him his 416 and hid the 226 in the back waistband of his pants so he wouldn't look too intimidating, even though he was stripped to the waist and covered with dirt and sweat. He knocked twice, then backed up and knelt on the ground so that if anyone fired through the door, he wouldn't get hit in the chest.

Someone inside groaned something.

"What did he say?" Crocker whispered.

"He says he's an old man," Hassan whispered back. "We can go in."

Crocker stood, turned the knob, and stepped inside.

The little room smelled of old leather and BO. The gray-bearded man looked up as if ready to accept anything. "Welcome," he said in Arabic. "I won't ask questions. If you have any food, I'll be very grateful. Otherwise, take what you want. There's hardly anything left."

Crocker turned back to tell Davis to bring the last couple of MREs from the van while Hassan explained that they were humanitarian workers carrying wounded refugees to Turkey. Highway 60 was under attack and they needed to find an alternative route.

The old man had heard the explosions, even though he was deaf in one ear. All he had left was his dog and a couple of tapes for his cassette player. He showed how he had jerry-rigged the radio to work on AA batteries.

When Crocker handed him the MREs he smiled, revealing only two remaining front teeth. "Rest here for the night," the old man said. "We can talk about the women in our lives and listen to music."

The old man offered to brew coffee on a burner made from an ashtray filled with some kind of anise-flavored liquor. He showed them how he collected the melted wax from his candles and reused it, inserting strips of fabric to serve as wicks.

"You're a generous man," Crocker said in Arabic. "But we're in a hurry to get back to Turkey. Can you show us the way?"

"Of course," the old man said as he drew a map on the back of an old piece of paper. "I was hoping you could stay a while. Because the only thing I haven't been able to solve is the loneliness." He showed them that if they followed the road they were on it would link with another and then a third that would take them to the Turkish border town of Kilis.

Crocker patted the dog's head. "You've got him."

"My friend Arak is even older and more feeble than I am. Maybe before we die things will change again, and people will come back."

"I hope so."

"How long will it take us to reach Kilis, approximately?" Hassan asked.

The man considered and held up a crooked finger. "Maybe one hour."

Mancini drove while Crocker sat with his 416 ready by the passenger window and Hassan slept between them with his head back and his mouth wide open.

"Big day for the young man," Mancini commented.

"Yeah."

Davis reported that baby and mother were resting peacefully in back. Akil was running a fever.

"Give him a couple Advils from the medical pack."

"Roger."

The Sprinter engine labored hard as they climbed slowly through winding hills. Olive and fig groves glistened in the moonlight. A breeze carried the scent of rosemary. The dull thud of explosions continued in the distance to their right.

As they chugged along at thirty miles an hour, Mancini said, "This land was controlled by the Macedonians, then the Romans, the Ottomans, and ceded to the French after World War I."

"All that nonsense, and it probably hasn't changed much."

Mancini changed the subject. "You hear about the blonde who put lipstick on her forehead so she could make up her mind?"

Sometimes the problems came so fast and from so many directions that all you could do was laugh.

"I like that one, Manny."

He looked at the fuel gauge, which showed they were down to less than a quarter of a tank.

"Why do blondes wear underwear?" Mancini asked, rubbing the tribal tattoo on his neck.

"Why?"

"To keep their ankles warm."

"Really?"

"What do you call the skeleton in the closet with blond hair?"

"Give up."

"Last year's hide-and-seek winner."

Crocker liked that one. His back burned, his face and arms itched from the scratches, and his whole right side ached, but none of that mattered. He was looking for the last turnoff, which the old man said would be past two burned-out tanks and a barn on the left.

He and Mancini had been working together for nearly ten years now. They'd witnessed almost every kind of tragedy imaginable—from drownings to bombings, plane crashes, and beheadings. They'd shared a lot of good times, too—hot-air balloon racing in New Mexico, surfing in Hawaii, climbing Mount Kilimanjaro, marlin fishing off the coast of Chile. They'd seen colleagues marry, have children, and watched them die. Even though they weren't close friends off-duty, Crocker thought of him as his brother. He couldn't imagine going on a mission without him.

Seeing Mancini yawn, Crocker asked, "You want to rest while I take over?"

"No, boss. As long as you stay awake and talk to me, I'm good."

"Pretty land."

"Yeah, reminds me a little of Tuscany."

"Good wine and pretty women."

Mancini shook his head and smiled.

"What?" Crocker asked.

"Remember the time you, me, and Ritchie grabbed that Libyan terrorist and his girlfriend outside of Assisi?"

"Yeah. We had to drive to Milan dressed as priests."

"That was Ritchie's idea," Mancini said.

"Pissed the Italian authorities off. Fucking Ritchie."

"I miss him."

"Yeah. Me, too."

An hour and a half later, Crocker spotted yellow-and-orange signs warning that Syrian customs stood ten kilometers ahead. The lack of roadblocks had induced a state of complacency that was quickly replaced by concern.

What if the Syrians try to stop us? We don't know which rebel faction controls the border. If they're Assad's people, we could be screwed.

His anxiety grew as they drew closer. Red-and-yellow warning lights flashed ahead.

"What do you think?" Mancini asked, the bold colors washing over his face. "You want to turn off the road and find a way around it?"

Crocker looked at the fuel gauge, which was already in the red. "Don't want to get stuck here. No. Fuck it."

"Should we stop and contact Ankara?"

"What are they gonna do?" asked Crocker, craning his neck left and right, looking for an alternate route.

"I don't know. Call ahead, maybe. Tell us who controls the border."

"They've been useless so far," Crocker responded. "Let's pull closer and take a look."

They approached within two hundred feet of the border. Mancini paused outside a boarded-up store while Crocker checked out the facility through the Steiners. Saw that the barriers were up in both directions and no one appeared to be manning the checkpoint.

"Looks unoccupied," he said, relieved. "We should be good."

They readied their weapons just in case, then passed an old man sweeping the little guard shack, and a sleeping dog. Neither looked up.

"Sweet."

"Now what?"

"Look for an IHOP and order a big breakfast."

"Pancakes, eggs, bacon, coffee."

SEAL TEAM SIX: HUNT THE FOX

The Turkish side was quiet, too. A couple of young soldiers with M1s looked at the blue cross on the hood of the van and nodded.

They stopped in a parking lot past the blue-and-white customs building and called Janice on the satellite phone.

She answered on the sixth ring from Yayladaği. "Who's this?"

"It's Crocker. We made it."

"You're back in Turkey?"

"Yeah. Just arrived. Where's the closest IHOP?"

"Excellent. Fantastic news. Where are you?" Janice asked.

"The town's called Karbeyaz," Crocker answered, reading the name off a sign and mispronouncing it. Somehow they had missed the turnoff to Kilis.

"That's northeast of here. Hold on. I'm going to go get Colonel Oz."

Ten minutes later she was back on the line. "Where precisely are you now?"

"We're parked in a lot just past the Turkish checkpoint."

"You're in possession of the sarin?"

"Yeah, we've got it, a newly delivered baby, a mother, and an injured colleague who needs medical attention."

"How did that happen?"

"Which, the baby or the injured colleague?"

"The baby."

"It's a long story. How should we proceed from here?"

"Continue a couple kilometers on the same road," Janice instructed. "You'll see a refugee camp on the right with a big AFAD sign."

"What's AFAD stand for?" asked Crocker.

"Turkish Disaster and Emergency Management Directorate. Pull up to the front gate and ask for Captain Nasar. He's with the Askeri Inzibat—the Turkish military police."

"He knows we're coming?"

"Yes, Colonel Oz just informed him. He's awake and expecting you."

"Cool."

"There's a clinic there and a contingent of guards and soldiers. They'll take care of you—feed you, tend to your wounds, whatever you need. Oz and I are on our way. We should be there in about two hours."

"Thanks."

"You're welcome. Sorry about your colleague."

"Nothing serious. He'll be fine."

CHAPTER FIFTEEN

*"To mystify, mislead, and surprise the enemy," is one of the
first principles in war.*

—Sun Tzu

ONCE ARRIVED at the AFAD camp, Crocker left Suarez guarding the Sprinter and made sure the women and baby were taken care of and his men were shown to the visitors' tent, where they could wash up and rest. Then he escorted Akil to the clinic, which was housed in an old train station. In the entryway he stopped to receive grateful hugs from Amira and Natalie, who were being shown to an empty room with beds.

A male nurse cleaned the wound on Akil's shoulder and summoned a doctor to stitch it up. While they waited, Crocker put his feet up on a chair and fell asleep. He dreamt he was back in the Himalayas sharing a tent with his old friend and climber Edyta Potocka. As a kerosene lamp burned in the corner, she ran a hand over his chest and sang a Polish lullaby.

Oh, sleep, my darling,
If you'd like a star from the sky I'll give you one.

All children, even the bad ones,
Are already asleep,
Only you are not.

So sweet he wanted to cry.

Didn't she die in an avalanche? Crocker wondered.

She seemed happy and vital now, kissing his face, snuggling up against him and laughing. Snow fell outside the tent, and the wind howled like a wolf, but he felt warm and safe. Then, realizing someone was calling his name, he opened his eyes into the fluorescent light and blinked.

"Crocker. Crocker, sorry to bother you," a woman's voice entreated.

She looked down at him with brown eyes, not light-blue ones like Edyta's. Mancini stood by her side.

What is he doing here?

"Crocker?"

"Go away."

"We can't. Wake up."

It took him a couple of seconds to realize that she was Janice, the CIA analyst he had first met in Istanbul. He looked at his watch: 0726. That couldn't be right. "Is it really after seven?"

"Something like that," Janice answered. "Crocker, we have a serious problem."

He'd slept almost three hours in the waiting room, totally unaware of where he was or of the passage of time.

"Where're the rest of the men?" he asked Mancini as he sat up.

"They're in the visitors' tent."

"Good. Very good. So what's up?" He wiped the spittle off the side of his mouth and adjusted the light-green medical robe the nurse had given him when he arrived. Saw the long scabs on his arms from last night, and remembered that they were safe inside Turkey. *By the grace of God.*

"It's a very serious situation," Janice said.

"What?"

"The sarin canisters are missing."

"What did you say?" Crocker asked, not sure he had heard correctly.

"The canisters have been taken."

"Taken? What are you talking about?"

"According to Mancini, you arrived with eight canisters of sarin."

"That's correct."

"Well…they're missing," Janice stated.

"From the van? From the Sprinter?"

"Yes, from the Sprinter."

"How the hell did that happen? Who took them?"

"Unclear."

"You mean they're not in the van?"

"They're not in the camp."

"Holy shit!" He jumped to his feet, ignoring the soreness that ran from his neck to his ankles. "Where's Suarez? He was guarding them."

"Suarez was shot," Mancini said. "Two bullets in the back."

"Oh, fuck. Bad?"

"Yeah."

He ran out with them to look. Turkish EMS officials were wheeling a stretcher to a red-and-white ambulance with blue flashing lights. Suarez, immobile, lay on his back with an oxygen mask over his face.

Crocker was torn between going with him and staying. "Where are they taking him?" he asked one of the EMS workers.

"To…hospital," the man answered in broken English.

"From the local hospital he'll likely be medevaced to one of our NATO facilities," Janice added. "Depends on his condition."

"Who shot him? How the hell did this happen?"

He had too many burning questions to be able to leave the camp. As soon as the ambulance left he returned to the Sprinter, where Mancini and Janice were standing. Saw a pool of Suarez's blood on the pavement and four Turkish soldiers guarding the back of the vehicle. The mattress Jamila and Tariq had rested on had been pulled out. Inside, all that remained were discarded wrappers, MREs, and a few boxes of medical supplies.

"Did anyone see what happened?" Crocker asked.

"Most of the Turkish guards were sleeping over there," Janice said, pointing to a large camouflaged tent fifty feet away. "One of them says he heard an engine."

"What kind of engine?"

"A truck engine."

"He hear shots?"

"He claims he didn't. Maybe the weapons the attackers used were suppressed."

"The Turks didn't have anyone guarding the gate?"

"They did, in fact. Both of them were shot and killed."

Crocker turned to his left and saw for the first time that the gate wasn't really a secure gate, only an opening in the fence with a barrier and sandbag-covered guard station.

"Did anyone see the vehicle?" Crocker asked.

"The lighting wasn't good. It was a little after five a.m. All this individual saw was the back of a truck. Maybe a two-and-a-half-ton. Maybe a black Volvo. Maybe a dark-green Mercedes."

"So they knew we had arrived. Someone informed them."

"Who?" Janice asked.

"The attackers."

"Or they watched us enter," Mancini added.

"Video surveillance?" Crocker asked, his brain spinning wildly.

"There's a camera at the gate, but it isn't working."

"Is Colonel Oz aware of all this?"

"He and Captain Nasar are on the phone with Ankara now."

"Who's Captain Nasar?"

"The camp commander."

Crocker now remembered him greeting them when they arrived. "Why didn't anyone wake me up before?" he asked, his anger and alarm rising.

"The Turks were handling it," Janice explained. "There was a lot of confusion."

"Where are Akil and Davis?"

"Davis was with me in the visitors' tent," Mancini answered. "I thought Akil was with you in the clinic."

"He was. That's right."

The enormity of the disaster took time to process. *What the hell happened? Who did it? How did they know we were here and had the sarin?*

Zeid and Babas were dead, so it couldn't have been them. Dozens of questions ran through his mind.

Anders and Grissom were irate when Crocker spoke to them on a phone in Captain Nasar's office.

"Jesus Christ, Crocker. How the hell could you allow something like this to happen?" Grissom asked.

He had no answer, only confusion and rage.

"All of us risked our lives to bring out the sarin," he said, mustering all his reserves of self-control. "So the idea that anyone *allowed this to happen* is highly insulting."

"Insulting, did you say?"

Crocker bit down hard on his anger, but still some slipped through. "Yes, insulting. You heard me right!"

He went on to explain that since the camp was guarded by Turkish soldiers, he had assumed it was safe. As an extra precaution he had left one of his men to guard the truck. Apparently his assumption had been wrong, and for that he took full responsibility. He was as shocked and angry as Grissom and Anders. While he felt terrible about the missing sarin, he was equally concerned about Suarez, and immediately started to second-guess his decision to leave him alone with the truck.

"This is an unmitigated disaster!" Grissom shouted through the phone. "Do you know what that sarin can do if it's released in Istanbul or Ankara, or both? We're looking at mass murder on an unthinkable scale, Crocker!"

"I'm well aware of that."

"You didn't finish the job, man! You screwed up."

Crocker had to fight hard to keep from losing it. "I told you before, I take full responsibility. But as bad as this is, and as pissed off as we are now, we need to focus on recovering the sarin."

"Not you, Crocker," Grissom responded. "Hell no. I want you and your men the hell out of Turkey. Drive immediately to Ankara, get on a plane, and get out ASAP. You've done enough damage already."

Crocker's mind was still partially focused on Suarez and the horrible possibility that he might have lost another team member.

"Don't you have anything to say?" Grissom screamed through the phone. Crocker heard Anders in the background telling him to calm down.

"I understand your anger," responded Crocker, "but I think you're making a mistake."

"You've got balls, Crocker, but no fucking sense."

"We're not running out of here with our tails between our legs, sir. That's not happening."

"You'd better, before the Turks arrest you and hold you for questioning."

Crocker hadn't even thought of that. "I seriously doubt they'll do that, but I'll take that risk."

"Nobody gives a rat's ass what you think!" Grissom shouted. "Just do as you're told, and do it now!"

Crocker took a deep breath. Through the window he saw Colonel Oz standing in the cement courtyard outside with Akil, Mancini, and Janice pointing past the gate and looking highly agitated.

Maybe Grissom's right.

"Sir, we brought the sarin into Turkey," he said into the phone, "and now we're going to help the Turks recover it."

"How?"

"I can't answer that now."

"Of course you can't, because you're out of your depth. And you're not going to accomplish a goddamn thing, because you'll be behind bars in a Turkish prison. Like *Midnight Fucking Express*, but worse."

Crocker hung up the phone and tried to compose himself. Going to prison wasn't a concern. Recovering the sarin was. They had to act quickly, and they needed a plan.

As soon as he stepped outside Janice separated herself from the group near the gate and hurried toward him, her hair flying and her fists clenched.

"Have you seen Hassan?" Janice asked.

"Hassan?"

"The engineering student. Have you seen him?"

"Not since we arrived this morning. Why?"

"When's the last time you saw him?" she asked with desperation in her voice. "Do you remember?"

"He was walking with Jamila and Tariq over to the clinic," Crocker said, gesturing behind him. "Why?"

"Did you see him go inside?"

"No, I didn't see him enter the clinic. No. Have you talked to Jamila? She should be able to answer that."

Janice nodded and looked at the ground deep in thought.

"Something happen to Hassan?" Crocker asked. "What's going on?"

"He's missing."

"What do you mean, missing?" asked Crocker.

"He's not in the camp."

"What?" It made no sense.

"We've questioned everyone. Oz had his men search the camp. Nobody can find him."

It seemed incredible.

"What about Jamila and their son?" Crocker asked, as he tried to grasp the implications.

"They're still here," Janice answered. "Everyone else has been accounted for."

It was hard to believe that Hassan would have exited the camp voluntarily and left his girlfriend and son behind.

"Maybe he was kidnapped," Crocker conjectured out loud.

"Why?" Janice asked. "Why in the world would the hijackers want Hassan? Why would they bother to take him? Why?"

Hoping to find answers, Crocker ran to speak to Jamila. He found her sitting in a sun-filled room in the clinic, nursing Tariq. She seemed as confounded as he was, but strangely calm, given the fact that the father of her son had suddenly disappeared.

"I'm worried about him," she said, shaking her head. "I can't find an explanation. Hassan was happy the last time I saw him. He kissed me and Tariq good night and told me he loved me. It was the first time he ever said those words. Then, next thing I hear, he's left the camp without telling me."

He noted sadness in her voice, but no fear or anxiety, which was odd. "When's the last time you saw him?" Crocker asked.

"It was about thirty minutes after we arrived. Sometime after four. We were here in this room, Tariq and I. Hassan kissed us goodbye and left."

"Did he say where he was going?"

"He said he was sleeping in the visitors' tent with your men. Tariq and I remained here in the clinic with Natalie and Amira. If something was wrong, he didn't tell me."

Strange.

"Did he mention anything about wanting to meet someone— anyone—here in Karbeyaz?"

"No."

"Does he have relatives here? Friends?"

"Not that I know of."

"Did he say anything about expecting someone to visit him?"

She shook her head as Tariq pulled back from her nipple and yawned. Jamila quickly covered herself, and Crocker looked away.

Very fucking strange.

She held a crying Tariq to her chest and patted his back.

"Did he mention anything he was worried about?"

"No," she answered. "But Hassan and I don't have such a close relationship where he tells me everything. He keeps a lot to himself. Maybe he's worried about the responsibility of being a father, and went away to think about that."

Curious answer.

"You think that could be the reason he left the camp?" Crocker asked.

Tariq burped loudly.

"It's the only one I can think of," she whispered, laying the baby down on the bed.

"So you think Hassan left because he's not sure he wants the responsibility of being a father?"

She nodded. "I hope not, for our son's sake."

When Crocker related what he had heard from Jamila to Colonel Oz, the colonel seemed highly skeptical. "This man leaves because he doesn't want to be a father, and the WMDs are taken at the same time? I don't believe in such a large coincidence. Forget that theory. It's bullshit!"

Crocker had his own doubts. There were contradictions in Jamila's story. She'd said the last thing Hassan had told her was that he loved her. Then she'd suggested that he might have left the camp to get away from her and their son.

"Why would the same person who warned us about the existence of the sarin and led us to it, at some personal risk, participate in hijacking it when it arrived in Turkey?" he wondered out loud.

Human motivations were often gray and murky.

Oz ran a hand over his smooth head and looked directly into Crocker's eyes. "I don't know the answer to this question, but we'll find out. We have to. My country is now in tremendous danger."

The question Crocker had posed to Colonel Oz burned in his brain as he and Janice huddled with the rest of the SEALs and the two schoolteachers in the lobby of the clinic, discussing what everyone had seen or heard that morning. Meanwhile, Colonel Oz went with his men to account for every single refugee in the camp to try to ascertain whether any of them had participated in the theft.

What should have been a happy morning had turned into a nightmare. Amira and Natalie were frightened and had little to say. In fact, Natalie completely shut down again. Amira explained that the women had been offered beds in the clinic housed in the old train station. They fell asleep immediately, heard nothing, didn't see Hassan after they left the lobby, and were unaware that anything had happened until they were awakened by camp commander Nasar, who they claimed had treated them harshly. Now they worried that they would somehow be held responsible and forced to return to Syria.

"Why do you say that?" Crocker asked gently.

Amira covered her eyes with her hands. She had worn the same black stretch pants and a dark-red tunic since the first time they'd met. "Because the Turks are angry, and they're men."

He wanted to tell her that she was wrong, but he stopped himself, remembering what the two schoolteachers had gone through in Syria.

"Not to worry," he said. "My men and I will make sure you're treated well and never forced to return."

"Thank you," Amira replied, lowering her eyes. "You've been very kind…so far."

Next he went to the visitors' tent and asked each man to describe what he had seen or heard since their arrival.

"I slept in the clinic on a cot," Akil said. "I don't remember seeing Hassan after I left the truck. I went out like a light and didn't hear or see shit. Don't even remember dreaming."

"I carried all the comms out of the van and set them in the corner of this tent," Davis remembered. "I wanted to Skype with my wife and tell her I was safe but was too tired to even think. And I was scheduled to relieve Suarez at 0730, so I wanted to catch some z's. Don't remember seeing Hassan at all. I was awakened by shouts from the Turkish guards at around 0700 and saw them trying to revive Suarez. I looked for you, boss, but didn't know where you were. That's all…"

"Davis and I helped the women out of the van," said Mancini. "Jamila and Hassan seemed to be squabbling about something. I couldn't understand what they were saying, but they both looked unhappy. I saw him checking his phone, which I thought was odd. Then one of Nasar's men escorted Davis and me to the white visitors' tent. I threw my gear in, and went outside to the latrine to wash up. When I came back, Hassan was sitting by the cot beside the door. I asked him if anything was wrong. He shook his head. I lay down and fell asleep."

Hassan's backpack, with a Spiderman pin attached, still lay by the cot. They searched it: a change of clothes, dirty underwear, toothbrush, toilet paper, and three thousand pounds in Syrian currency, which was worth about twenty U.S. dollars.

"Travels light," said Davis.

Akil: "Not even a pack of rubbers."

Interesting that Hassan was arguing with Jamila when they exited the truck, then went to the clinic a few minutes later, kissed her, told her he loved her for the first time, and disappeared.

Crocker sorted through the information in his head, thinking that he had to talk to Jamila again, when the light on the sat-phone lit up. On the other end of the line he heard the voice of his commander, Captain Alan Sutter, calling from ST-6 headquarters in Virginia.

"Crocker, you okay?" he asked in the raspy Kentucky drawl that evoked horse farms and bourbon.

"Been a whole lot better, sir. I'm here with my team trying to make heads or tails of a very troublesome and confusing situation."

"I imagine you were halfway home in your head when it happened."

"I was asleep, sir," said Crocker. "Dead to the world. Most of us were."

"How's Suarez?" Sutter asked.

"Not so good, from what I've heard, but still alive. He was taken to a local hospital. Soon as I sort things out here, I'll follow up."

"Wait....Good news. Just got word from Ankara that his condition has stabilized."

Crocker felt relieved. "That means they've stanched the internal bleeding. That's good."

"He's being medevaced to the NATO hospital in Diyarbakır."

"When?"

"Soon. Hold on." Sutter came back twenty seconds later and said, "Look, Grissom wants you out of the country. He's pretty adamant about that. Anders seems too overcome by events to express an opinion."

Crocker said, "I believe it's a mistake to run away now. We've got a very dangerous situation here, and we need to help the Turks figure it out."

"I knew you'd say that. And I know that if I tell you to take your tail straight to the airport you'll find a way to stick around."

"Sir—"

"Do what you gotta do, Crocker. But keep in mind that you're the one who's going to have to justify this at some point. This goes further south and guys like Grissom will feast on your throat."

Crocker swallowed hard. "I know how it works."

"Remember, he's the chief and he's under fire, so don't expect him to be supportive."

"I won't."

"Stay alert, be smart, don't get led by emotion."

"Sound advice, sir."

"Godspeed."

CHAPTER SIXTEEN

The truth does not change according to our ability to
stomach it emotionally.

—Flannery O'Connor

CROCKER FELT as though everything he had ever accomplished was slipping down the drain and the earth itself was shifting under his feet. On his way back to the clinic to talk again with Jamila, Captain Nasar—a tall man with a gray handlebar mustache—intercepted him and said, "Colonel Oz is waiting for you by the gate. He wants you to bring one of your men and go with him."

Crocker looked down and saw that he was still wearing the medical robe over his black pants. "Where?"

Nasar shook his head.

"Did he say why?"

"No, but he asked you to hurry."

If Akil hadn't still been recovering from the wound to his shoulder, he would have chosen him, because even though he didn't speak Turkish, he had a good understanding of people from this corner of the world.

He asked Mancini to accompany him instead, borrowed a black

tee from him that he pulled over his head, and told Davis to monitor developments at the camp as best he could. Should he learn anything new from Jamila, he should communicate it to Captain Nasar, who seemed to be a smart guy.

"Inform me, too. I'll carry my burner."

"Where are you going?"

Crocker shrugged. "No idea. But I'll let you know when we get there."

Two Turkish-made Cobra light-armored vehicles waited outside the gate. Most of the U.S. Cobras Crocker had seen were equipped with overhead Rafael Spike antitank missile systems. The Turks had armed theirs with Nexter 20mm M621 cannons with day and thermal imaging sights instead. Otherwise they had the same compact profile, with all-welded steel hulls and wide, fully opening side and rear doors that facilitated rapid crew entry and exit.

The two SEALs were directed into the rear of the second vehicle by a Turkish commando who looked like a ninja in his black uniform, black helmet, and black face mask.

"Batman," Mancini muttered under his breath as he climbed in after Crocker.

The air inside was already cranked up, chilling the sweat on Crocker's arms and neck. They sat opposite the ninja and four similarly outfitted soldiers on one of the rear benches. Almost immediately the driver powered up the turbo diesel V8 engine, put the auto transmission in Drive, and they took off at high speed following the Cobra ahead. Through the glazed side window Crocker saw that they were climbing into mist-covered hills.

"Any clue about our destination?" whispered Mancini.

"South Beach, I hope, for a couple cold Coronas at the Love Hate Lounge."

"Any idea what this is about?"

"I thought you liked surprises."

"Not when the guys taking me there are wearing face masks and armed with M5s."

Crocker grinned. He was trying to remain calm and centered. One way or another he and his men were going to recover the sarin.

"The next surprise can't be any bigger than the last one," Mancini muttered.

"Yeah."

His brain was burning. *Had elements of ISIS or AQ followed them from Syria? Did they radio ahead to their colleagues in Turkey, who then raided the camp? Did they kill Hassan and dump his body? Did Hassan play some part in the plot?* This seemed like a stretch, given how studious and physically cowardly he had appeared to be, but anything was possible.

The Cobras were hauling ass now, climbing into mountains. Feeling tired and empty, and somewhat discouraged, he fought the negative thoughts that floated into his head. *Shit happens. I've dealt with it before. Even major fuckups.*

He remembered one of his first missions with ST-6, when they had gone into Croatia in search of an HVT, a high-value target, during the Bosnian War. They were looking for a Serbian financier, drug and arms trafficker, and human rights abuser—a nasty guy who was said to keep a collection of human thumbs. They received intel that he was living in a villa on the island of Lokrum in the Adriatic Sea, just off the coast near Dubrovnik. Picturesque as hell.

Crocker and three other SEALs had swum in and raided the place at night, literally separating the guy from his girlfriend and carting him off. When they got back to the navy frigate they had launched from, they found out they'd nabbed the guy's brother, a former professional tennis player and restaurateur. The government had had to pay him major bucks to keep his mouth shut.

He drifted off and woke to the sound of urgent Turkish voices over the radio. The Cobra slowed down. According to his Suunto, almost an hour had passed. Mancini sat holding his arms across his chest, eyes shut.

He shook his buddy awake as the commandos across from them lowered the visors on their helmets and readied their weapons.

"Something's about to go down," Crocker whispered.

"Yeah? What?"

Mancini sat up, blinked, and looked around. Immediately alert, he reached for his weapon only to realize he was unarmed. They both were.

The vehicle had stopped on an inclined gravel road. Not much to see out the side window except for a huge mound of gray gravel mixed with dirt. The back door flew open and the commandos hustled out. The ninja who had escorted them in indicated to Mancini and Crocker to stay inside.

The big doors shut behind them and they waited. They didn't hear gunfire and couldn't see the Turk commandos until two of them opened the back and waved them out.

"Now what?" Mancini asked.

"Showtime."

The commandos pushed the SEALs up the incline and followed. Boots crunched against gravel. They passed the lead Cobra with one soldier inside talking excitedly on the radio, his boots up on the dash. Climbed another ten feet and smelled the sea in the distance.

From the summit Crocker spotted a large gravel quarry to their right, partially filled with still blue water. Reflected clouds floated across the surface, dreamlike.

He didn't see the commandos at first, then heard Oz's voice, rough and urgent. The Turks were standing on the continuation of the gravel road that curled along the other side of the gravel-and-dirt mound and wound downward. They had surrounded a parked Mercedes 2.5-ton truck—a deuce and a half. Dark blue, maybe ten years old, with a worn canvas cover over the back.

Oz saw Crocker and waved him forward. Other soldiers wearing light-blue plastic gloves were examining the inside of the cab and cargo area.

"This is the truck they used," Oz pronounced. "It was abandoned here."

"You sure?" Crocker asked, looking around and seeing not a house or a structure. It was a good place to hide a truck or do an exchange.

"Yes. This is it."

"You find anything inside?"

"Not yet, but we're looking."

"How did you locate it?" Crocker asked, calculating that it had probably taken the hijackers about an hour to get here. That meant they had at least an hour and a half lead on them. Maybe more.

Oz pointed proudly to the sky. "Air surveillance." The engine of the small spotter aircraft buzzed in the distance.

"Clever, Colonel. I assume they're looking for the next one now? The second vehicle?"

"Or the third. Yes."

Mancini whispered into Crocker's ear, "Boss, this is a damn mess from a forensics perspective. Look." He pointed to the soldiers inside the trucks who were touching every surface, smudging possible fingerprints, dragging their boots over the seats and across the cargo bed.

"You absolutely certain this is the truck?" Crocker asked.

"Yes," Oz answered, puffing out his chest. "Why else would it sit here abandoned, with the keys still in the ignition?" He reached into his pocket and proudly held up a single key in a plastic bag.

"You find any witnesses? Anyone who saw anything?"

"No. No one. They're too smart."

"Who?"

"ISIS."

"How do you know that?"

Oz grinned and pointed to his head. "We have information."

"What information?"

One of the commandos handed Oz a Motorola radio, and he started speaking into it excitedly.

From the bluff where they stood, the SEALs could see the coast about a half mile away through the mist, which was starting to burn off. Mancini pointed to a relatively busy four-lane highway that snaked along the rocky shore.

The sarin was probably far away by now, hidden somewhere or on its way to its destination. Crocker felt the same way he did when he saw the World Trade Center towers tumble to the ground—devastated and filled with rage.

Oz continued barking into a handheld radio. A half minute later, when he pulled it away from his ear, Crocker pointed to the highway and asked, "What's that?"

"The O-52 motorway. Of course, we've blocked it and are in the process of blocking all other roads. We're inspecting everything. We'll have the sarin back soon."

Crocker wished he felt as confident, but "in process" didn't sound good. "What about the coast?" Crocker asked.

Oz frowned before he answered. "It's very rocky here. Very difficult currents. I don't think so, because it would be hard to load anything there. But I'll send up some helicopters to look."

It wasn't the answer Crocker wanted to hear. "Good idea," he responded. "Maybe you should deploy some launches, too."

"We're taking care of everything." Oz seemed to be getting annoyed.

"And check all local airports."

He could tell by Oz's expression that he hadn't thought of that. In drastic, chaotic situations like these it was hard to stay sober and think straight.

CHAPTER SEVENTEEN

You don't have to be naked to be sexy.
—Nicole Kidman

NINETY MINUTES later Crocker stood beside Oz as his men inspected a long line of trucks at a roadblock outside the city of İskenderun on the Mediterranean coast, thinking that this was necessary but probably wouldn't yield squat. Whoever had stolen the sarin was too smart to transport it in a truck on a major highway. The hijackers had probably moved fast, via local roads, and had most likely passed the WMDs to the next stage, or end user, hours ago. Oz had assured him that every avenue east, north, and south, and all local airports, were now being carefully monitored.

Mancini remained as anxious as Crocker, constantly offering suggestions and warnings. Now he was telling Crocker about the ancient cave city of Cappadocio, north of where they stood now, and explaining that it was a perfect place to hide the canisters.

"Mention it to Oz," Crocker said, nodding toward the Turkish colonel, who stood ten feet away talking into a cell phone and looking overwhelmed and angry.

Crocker kept eyeing the coast. Helicopters and surveillance aircraft were up and boat crews were on their way, according to the colonel, but he saw no sign of them.

Almost four hours after the sarin was taken, all they had found so far was a 2.5-ton Mercedes truck stolen the night before from a construction company in Adana, farther west and north. There was no evidence that linked it to the sarin except for descriptions from the guards at the AFAD camp of a similar-looking truck driving away.

Crocker was growing increasingly anxious. Hoping for some good news, he called Davis on his burner cell.

"Anything new there?"

"Not really, no. According to Captain Nasar everyone in the camp has been accounted for. So the only one missing is Hassan."

"Any word from or about him?"

"No."

"You talk to Jamila?"

"Yeah. She was nice, but kind of evasive."

"In what way?" Crocker asked.

"When I asked her about the argument she and Hassan had as they were getting out of the van, the one Mancini overheard, she denied it. Said maybe she was complaining about her back, which has been sore since the birth of the baby."

Whether they were arguing or not didn't seem like a big deal to Crocker. "Anything more from Ankara?"

"No."

"Any word from the hijackers?"

"Not according to Nasar. He's been real helpful. Has a brother who works with the police department in Seattle."

"Good," Crocker said. He had something else on his mind. "I want you to call Captain Sutter back at HQ. Tell him that with Suarez in the hospital and Akil nicked up, we might need more men. Tell him we can use Cal and Tré if they can get out here quickly."

Cal was the sniper assigned to Black Cell who had been injured in the helo crash that had killed Ritchie four and a half months ago. Dante Tremaine was an African American former marine, University of Nevada basketball player, and explosives expert who had worked with Black Cell a year ago in Venezuela. Everyone on the teams called him Tré, as in the three-point shot in basketball, which had been his specialty. He was a tough young operator and a fun guy to be around.

"Will do," replied Davis.

"Tell Sutter my gut tells me that whoever took the sarin is going to use it quickly. These guys, whoever they are, seem smart and well organized. I sense that they have a plan and specific target in mind." In the past Sutter hadn't put a lot of stock in Crocker's instincts, but they were all he had so far.

"We should make sure we have air, sea, and land assets on alert," Crocker added.

"I'll tell him."

"When you're done with Sutter, ask Nasar if you can borrow a vehicle so you and Akil can drive here and meet us. Bring our weapons and gear with you. Do you know what happened to them?" Crocker asked.

"The Turkish guards confiscated everything after the theft."

"Tell Nasar we need them back. Explain that we're working with Oz and trying to recover the sarin."

"Nasar's cool. I don't think he'll be a problem."

"Good."

"Hey, one more thing, boss. When I was talking to Jamila, I mentioned that Hassan had been introduced to you by his uncle, Mr. Talab, and his half sister, Fatima."

"That's correct."

"She claimed she knows all of Hassan's extended family and has never heard of an uncle Talab, and she was, like, totally adamant that Hassan doesn't have a half sister."

"No, half sister, stepsister, or adopted sister named Fatima?"

"No, none of the above."

"Interesting," said Crocker.

"I thought so, too."

The longer they waited, the more the consequences of the situation beat down on him, until his head, neck, shoulders, back, and legs hurt. It was impossible to stand and watch the black-uniformed Turkish commandos running back and forth at the roadblock, barking orders as they choked on diesel exhaust from the dozens of backed-up trucks while he knew some dastardly plan was unfolding somewhere else.

Mancini, who had pitched in to help with the inspections, looked equally impatient and grim. He stood beside Colonel Oz, who was now screaming at some young officer about the kebab sandwiches he had ordered for his men and looking as if he was about to wring the young man's neck. They'd been here three hours now, and all the while the hijackers were probably gaining ground. The only good news was that Akil, Davis, and Janice were on their way.

Feeling that he had to do something, Crocker excused himself and called Anders in Ankara on one of his burner cell phones. The CIA officer sounded harried and exhausted.

"Crocker, you're still in-country? Where are you now?"

"With Oz, inspecting trucks on the O-52 motorway a few klicks north of İskenderun."

"Where's that?" Anders asked.

"Hatay province. East and south of you."

"I'm up to my frigging eyeballs here. How can I help you?"

"How well do you know Mr. Talab?" Crocker asked.

"What kind of question is that?"

"How well do you know him?"

"Talab? Personally, not well. But he's been a trusted Agency source for years. Why?"

"What about that Fatima chick? His aide."

"The very fine looking woman he had with him? All I know is what I saw. Why?"

"They both claimed to be related to Hassan, right?"

"Did they?" asked Anders. "Why's that important?"

"When we met Talab at the hotel, he said Hassan was his nephew. And while we were waiting for the order to launch in Yayladaği, Fatima told me she was his half sister."

"So?"

"So Hassan's girlfriend, Jamila, just told Davis that she knows all the members of his family and that Hassan isn't related to either of them."

"The girlfriend, the one who just had the baby?" asked Anders.

"Yeah."

"You believe her?"

"No reason not to."

"Maybe Talab and Fatima were speaking loosely," Anders offered. "You know, 'family' can be a loose term here. Maybe they were trying to impress on us how close they are to Hassan so we'd trust him."

"Yeah, they wanted us to trust him. You have any idea where Talab and Fatima are now?" Crocker asked.

"Last I heard, Talab was in Damascus taking care of family business. Fatima, I don't know. Maybe she went with him. I'd take her with me, wouldn't you?"

"Probably. But that's irrelevant."

"What are you trying to say, Crocker?" Anders asked. "Seems to me you're reaching for something. It's very likely that Hassan is a victim here. Anyway, I've got to go."

"Just a second," Crocker said. "You basing that on anything—that part about Hassan being a victim?"

"Yes." Anders whispered something to someone on the other end before continuing. "NSA has picked up something online from some ISIS AQ-affiliated jihadist who calls himself the Fox."

Anders and Janice had mentioned him before, during the first meeting at the Sultanhan Hotel. "This Fox guy mention Hassan specifically?" asked Crocker.

"No, no. Everything he says is in code, very difficult to decipher. But he does talk about an upcoming big strike and kidnapping the enemy."

"Anything else?"

"Maybe you should let us do the analysis and targeting, and focus on working with Colonel Oz to recover the sarin."

Crocker couldn't hold back this time. "Fuck you, Anders."

"Crocker, look…I didn't mean to insult you. We're all stretched to the max. I'm glad you're still here. We might need your services. Stay ready and alert."

"I will."

A swath of deep magenta leaked across the darkening sky as the black Range Rover passed between the faux-marble columns that marked the entrance to the port of Kuşadası, Turkey, and stopped.

Two multitiered cruise ships rose ahead on the right, both impressively lit with hundreds of deck lights that gave the impression they were massive wedding cakes.

The female passenger on the Rover's backseat said a quick prayer and waited for the door to open. She was dressed to attract attention and ready to play her part. She adjusted her wide-brimmed white hat, clutched her light-green Bottega Veneta crocodile shoulder bag, and stepped out.

The warm evening air rushed to greet her, ruffling her long dark hair and passing through the thin silk suit and blouse to caress her skin. Behind her two men unloaded two large trunks and several suitcases. Local porters rushed forward with metal carts and offered their assistance.

The tourist city of Kuşadası hummed behind her, a maze of tourist stalls, cafés, air-conditioned malls, and sleek high-rise hotels. Most people staying there were drawn by the ruins of the once-powerful Greek and later Roman city of Ephesus, nine miles away. But none of that seemed to interest her, neither the history, nor the commerce, nor the delicious local Muscat wine served chilled in the cafés.

Steely-eyed and sober, she strode toward the modest modern glass terminal with a Welcome to Turkey banner across the front. Slightly behind her followed her dashing associate, Stavros Petras, in a white shirt and expensive-looking black suit.

Before they reached the terminal door a uniformed concierge emerged and greeted her with a toothy smile. He wore a light-blue vest with a Disney insignia on the pocket and spoke with a slight Spanish accent. His words were tightly scripted. "Good evening, Mrs. Girard. My name is Marco. It's my pleasure to serve as your concierge and welcome you to your Disney cruise. That's our ship, the *Disney Magic*, straight ahead." He pointed over his shoulder to the closest and largest of the two ships. Handsome, and a massive 984 feet long, with eleven passenger decks and a capacity of 950 crew members and 2,713 passengers.

She quickly took in the details—the Mickey Mouse–ear logos on the twin black-and-red funnels, the bright-yellow lifeboats, and the figure of Goofy wearing overalls and hanging from his suspenders at the stern. The sight gave her an impression of fun, wealth, and class.

"I'm here to make everything as enjoyable for you as possible. Check-in will take a few minutes," Marco said. "Please follow me."

She smiled. "You're so kind."

They entered a relatively empty high-ceilinged space, her white patent-leather Louboutin heels clicking against the tile floor. In the corner a uniformed Turkish customs official sat up, his German shepherd held by a metal leash. Two other bored-looking customs agents stood behind a long counter. One of them, an older man with short gray hair, extinguished the cigarette he was smoking as Mrs. Girard, Petras, and Marco approached.

Since they were the only two passengers joining the Mediterranean cruise at Kuşadası, security was light.

Marco stopped at the counter, turned to her, and smiled. "I'm going to need to show them your passports and tickets. I believe your destination is Barcelona. Is that correct, Mrs. Girard?"

"Yes, Barcelona. I'm staying there two nights, then taking the train to Paris for the fall fashion shows."

"You'll be traveling alone?"

"No. It's myself and my assistant, Mr. Petras. We're booked in separate cabins."

"Of course."

She handed over the tickets and her stolen French passport with the photo expertly attached and appropriate entry and exit stamps. Petras's passport, also stolen, was Greek.

"Thank you, Mrs. Girard. You're in one of our deluxe oceanview staterooms, which features a bedroom with a queen-sized bed, a living room, two bathrooms, a wet bar, and a private veranda."

"Excellent."

"Your associate, Mr. Petras, has one of our junior staterooms on the deck below. We arrive in Barcelona next Saturday morning, so you'll be with us for eight wonder-filled nights. I'll stop by your cabin and fill you in on all the ship's services and amenities after you get settled."

Local porters arrived pushing two carts loaded with her trunks and other luggage, which meant the moment of truth was near. She felt sweat trickling between her breasts and running down her upper thighs, but she managed to appear perfectly composed and calm.

She had been told that luggage moving through the port wasn't X-rayed, nor was the port equipped with visual scanners or chemical sniffers. All the officials there used were low-frequency handheld metal wands. As a precaution, the trunks were made of a metal fabric that would shield their interiors from electromagnetic signals in the 800 megahertz to 2.4 gigahertz range. They were also padlocked. Should the officials demand to inspect them she would say she had no keys because the trunks contained valuable jewelry. They had been sealed and locked by a French bonding agency, which would open them only when they arrived in Paris. However, the inspector seemed more interested in the presence of narcotics, pulling the dog closer to the trunks and suitcases.

She removed her suit jacket and draped it over her left arm. The thin silk tank top underneath clung to her bare breasts. The eyes of the luggage inspector and two Turkish customs agents standing behind the counter were drawn to them as if by some secret force.

"Beautiful dog," she said to the inspector. "What's his name?"

"Rocky."

"Hi, Rocky."

As the officers behind the counter examined her passport, Marco nodded toward the luggage and said, "I assume you want those taken directly to your suite."

"Yes," she answered. "Please handle them carefully."

"Of course."

"Any additional fees, please charge them to my husband's credit card. Mr. Girard—you should have it on record."

"Yes," he said, adjusting his shirt collar and trying not to stare at her chest.

Before handing back her passport, the gray-haired customs agent spoke. "I'm required to ask you this question, Mrs. Girard. Are you…are you carrying illegal narcotics? Hashish, heroin, opium?"

"No, I am not."

He looked at the officer with the dog, who nodded, then said, "You're cleared to board. The last thing we ask is that you remove any metal items in your purse, including your cell phone, and step through the metal detector."

"Fine."

"I'll give you these Spanish customs declarations now, Mrs. Girard, and wish you an enjoyable trip. Everything will have to be declared and inspected when you reach Barcelona."

"I'm aware of that. Thank you."

She and Petras passed through the metal detector without incident and followed Marco down the corridor that led to a covered walkway and into the main atrium of the ship. Standing near a life-sized statue of Mickey Mouse, she removed the iPhone from her purse—a phone recently lifted from an Aussie tourist—and texted *"Tout bien. A bord."* (All's well. On board.)

Akil, in the backseat, was trying his best to lighten the mood, exchanging hazing stories with Mancini—the time they'd bound a teammate's wrists and ankles with gaffer's tape and tossed him into the ocean, the times they'd shaved off teammates' eyebrows and pubic hair before their weddings, and so on—but Crocker wasn't in the mood. He didn't find humor in the stories, or the dick wagging, or the fact that the four SEALs and Janice were all unarmed and in a Suburban, driving down a highway in the middle of the night, an hour into a seven-hour drive to Ankara.

Why Ankara? For a personal dressing-down, a spanking, at a time like this? Screw that.

If he thought standing with Oz and his men on the O-52 inspecting trucks seemed senseless and frustrating, this was ten times worse. Eight canisters of sarin were lost somewhere in Turkey, and where were they? Made no fucking sense. Maybe it was time to finally call it quits. Maybe he'd be given no choice. If he got canned, at least Holly would be happy.

Remembering her, he reached for his burner cell, considered calling Virginia, then returned the phone to his pocket. It had only one bar of reception. Besides, this wasn't the time or the place. Despite the absurdity of their situation, he had standards to maintain as the team leader.

He didn't feel like one now. He felt himself slipping back into bad times and places. Like the time he'd left the dying mother as she was begging for him to stay, and she died the next day when the cabin she was in was hit by lightning and caught fire, and she burned to death. And the ugly arguments he'd had with his first wife, Jenny's mother, before their marriage broke up. He remembered one horrible night in Panama City, when he'd returned from a two-week training assignment near the Caribbean coast and she'd intimated that she'd been spending time at the officers' club, drinking in the company of a young navy commander. He was furious, of course, but didn't know whether to believe her or not. When she was drunk and angry, she said incredibly nasty personal things that he would never have taken from anyone else.

That night in the entrance to their bungalow, with two-year-old Jenny sleeping in the back bedroom, she'd accused him of being boring and lacking ambition. Said he didn't measure up to the young commander who was going places and with whom she might or might not have been sleeping. The belittling comparison to the commander had infuriated him more than the possible infidelity. He'd shouldered his duffel and turned back at the door, saying, "I'll be back when you're sober."

She'd countered, "If you leave now, I'll consider that a sign that you know you're pathetic and don't measure up. And I'll call him. I'll call him over and let him fuck me."

He'd stopped and looked back at her leaning in the doorway, her hair crazy, her eyes bloodshot, the smell of Jim Beam on her breath, wondering how the sweet thing he'd loved so much had turned into this.

She leaned toward him and snarled, "If you were a real man, you'd hit me."

The blood rushed to his head as he cocked his right fist. Then a voice in his head told him to stop. He looked at her one last time, leaning in the doorway, and left.

Separation and divorce followed. Sometimes it seemed that no matter how hard you tried, things went bad. Love affairs ended. Marriages turned bitter. Teammates got injured and died.

Janice and Davis were now debating the existence of ghosts. Davis claimed he could sense their presence and believed in the continuance of spirit after death. It was an interesting theory and one that Crocker had considered. But it gave him no solace now, in this dark night, trapped as he was in his own distress.

No matter how much he loved, worked, and accomplished, it felt as though he always came up short.

He looked out the window as Davis and the others debated the abilities of psychics and whether or not some people could really communicate with the dead.

Whatever anguish, pain, or doubt he faced, he wouldn't feel sorry for himself. He'd battle, take his bruises, pick himself up, and try again. And in quiet times like this one, ask for answers. Now, as he looked at the crescent moon, one came. A voice in his head that sounded like his grandfather said, "Give more."

Give more, he thought. *I will.*

CHAPTER EIGHTEEN

No fox is foxier than man!
—Mehmet Murat Ildan

WEARING AN elegant royal-blue Versace draped cocktail dress with a low V neckline and an asymmetrical deep V back, Mrs. Girard entered the exclusive Palo dining room on Deck 10 looking like a movie star. Because she was a new passenger, and a woman staying in a deluxe oceanview stateroom, she was immediately shown to the captain's table.

Captain Ian Hutley wasn't feeling well, and had chosen to eat in his office. In his place sat First Officer Sven Kalberg, a good-looking man of fifty with wavy blond hair and a sparkling white uniform. The flirtation between the two of them began the moment she sat down by his side.

"You're happy with your accommodations, Mrs. Girard?" he asked, clearly admiring her smooth skin, high cheekbones, and hourglass figure.

She sipped the cold yogurt-and-leek vichyssoise variation that had been set in front of her, dabbed her lips with her napkin, and answered, "Oh, yes. The ship is so massive. It's very impressive."

He smiled into her eyes and saw the possibility of an on-sea romance, which excited him further. Even though he was married with a young son, he considered it one of the perks of the job.

"Mrs. Girard, after dinner allow me to take you on a tour of the ship."

"How sweet of you. I'd be delighted," she answered, batting her dark lashes and leaving her lips slightly open. "Can we start at the bridge? I've always dreamed of what it must be like to stand at the top of a ship like this with your hands on the wheel."

His smile took on the aspect of a leer. "Yes. We'll start at the bridge if you like, and go as far as you like."

She squeezed his wrist and whispered, "I can't wait."

Eight decks below, forty-year-old Scott Russert looked at the clock, turned to his wife, Karen, who was lying on the queen-sized bed beside him, and said, "You hear this nonsense?" referring to the loud EDM emanating from the cabin next door. "It's bloody one o'clock."

She lifted a finger to her lips and pointed to their twin sons—Randy and Russell, both red-haired like their father—sleeping peacefully on a sofa bed that almost touched theirs. They were in the next-to-last cabin on Deck 2, which sat at the end of a long narrow corridor beyond the images of Dumbo and other assorted Disney characters painted on the light-blue walls.

Scott had won the trip as part of a raffle to benefit Dogs for the Disabled, a British charity. Three and a half months ago he had stopped at a car park near Frimley after doing his sales calls for Medical Value Company, UK. He'd filled the Nissan Qashqai with gas and bought a chocolate bar and a bottle of water from the female clerk. As she rang him up, she tried to sell him a five-pound ticket to a raffle. She asked so sweetly and seemed so nice that he said yes. Then lost the ticket and forgot all about it until the phone rang one Saturday night as they were cleaning up after dinner. The England versus Ecuador World Cup preliminary match was about to begin on the telly.

"Sorry to bother you, sir. But are you Scott Russert of twenty-two Coronation Place in Putney?"

"That's me, love. Who's this?"

"Rachel at the Value Store on the M3."

He couldn't recall a Rachel. "Who?"

"Mr. Russert, several months ago you stopped in here and bought a raffle ticket for a Dogs for the Disabled benefit. Do you remember?"

"Vaguely."

"Well, congratulations, Mr. Scott Russert. You're the lucky winner!"

Scott, a light sleeper, didn't feel lucky now. Ever since the ship had docked at Civitavecchia, near Rome, they'd endured four nights of loud music and Middle Eastern–looking men coming and going from the room next door.

He wanted to sleep, relax, and enjoy the ship's many amenities with his family—the theaters with live shows and movies, the AquaDunk thrill slide, Goofy's Pool, the Oceaneer Club, and the full array of pubs and restaurants with an endless supply of food and drink.

Now he'd reached his limit. As he reached for the phone to call Security, the music suddenly stopped and he heard what sounded like chanting.

"What the bloody hell are they doing now?" he asked in a whisper.

"Sounds like they're praying," Karen answered. "Close your eyes, Scotty. Go to sleep."

The chanting stopped, and he heard the door open and men leaving. "Rude wankers," he muttered as he lowered his head to the pillow.

Speed, aggression, surprise were their watchwords as the twelve men spread throughout the ship. They moved according to a carefully rehearsed plan, four to take the security station that controlled the hundreds of video monitors, four to the engine room, four to the bridge. They carried grenades, gaffer's tape, mags, ski masks, and fake beards in their pockets, and in the waistbands of their pants Vertex Standard VX-354 walkie-talkies with coverage of 350,000 square feet and a UV signal that could travel thirty stories through concrete and metal. They held suppressed automatic weapons under their long coats, the serial and model numbers scratched out.

No insignia, IDs, or uniforms. Nothing that could identify them in any way. They looked more like trained special operators than standard-issue terrorists. All were athletic, lean, and strong. Petras, in the lead, was hoping that the gentle rolling of the ship, the calm night, and the unreal beauty of the Aegean had lulled the ship's security officers into a state of complacency.

He signaled the other three to wait behind him as he knocked on the door of the Security Office on Deck 4.

A man inside asked, "Who is it?"

"Johnny."

As soon as the door opened, Petras and the others pushed their way in. He grabbed the man at the door by the throat so he couldn't scream, pushed him against the wall, and shot him in the head. Three of the six officers on duty were asleep before one wall of monitors. The remaining two were so out of it, it took them a few seconds to realize what was happening and reach for their weapons. That was all the time the attackers needed.

A dozen shots, and half a minute later the terrorists were fully in charge of the Security Office. Already almost a third of the ship's thirty-man security team had been taken out. Petras raised his left thumb to his three associates, left immediately, and climbed eight flights of stairs to the bridge. Once there and barely breathing hard, he texted Mrs. Girard.

She was standing with her hands on the ship's wheel with First Officer Kalberg pressing into her from behind when the phone in her purse pinged. Turning toward him, she whispered, "I have to return to my cabin to make a call, but would like to see you later."

"That sounds lovely. When?"

"Say fifteen minutes?"

"We can meet at the Keys piano bar on Deck 3, or I can come to your cabin."

"I think my cabin will be more private. It's 832."

"I'll be there in fifteen minutes," First Officer Kalberg said, leering at her breasts.

"I'll be waiting."

As he watched her walk away, fantasies unfolded in his head. He had no idea that her real purpose in leaving was to hold open the secure bridge door for Petras and the four terrorists waiting in the hallway.

They entered forcefully, fake beards, masks, and black head-scarves in place. Kalberg saw them coming like a scene out of a horror movie. Before he could open his mouth to shout, a bullet entered his brain and his world turned dark.

The shots they fired were silenced, but when Kalberg spun and crashed against a radar console, one of the two security guards on duty whirled around, saw the masked men, and drew his Glock. The former Scottish Special Air Service operative managed to wound one of the terrorists in the foot before he was cut down in a hail of bullets.

The attackers continued to spray rounds everywhere, tearing up equipment, shattering one of the forward windows, catching the navigation officer in the throat. Bullets hit the first ship security officer in the groin near his femoral artery; multiple rounds ripped into the second security officer's heart.

Blood and glass everywhere, the air clogged with cordite and smoke, Petras screamed, "Everyone down on the floor! Down on the floor! Hands over your heads!"

Those who didn't comply immediately were shot. The rest of the crew members hit the floor facedown—two in the cockpit area, another two at the navigation station in the middle of the bridge, the last four near the computer monitors that measured air quality, electricity usage, radio signals, and so on. The two ship security men lay dead as the navigation and first security officers bled out. The remaining officers were seized with a combination of panic, horror, and disbelief.

At this moment Captain Ian Hutley stumbled out of his office, his tunic unbuttoned, his eyes bleary, and a TASER clutched in his right hand.

"What the hell is this?" he shouted, tasing the first armed man he saw. The probe flew twelve feet, pierced the terrorist's nylon face mask, and entered the skin under his left eye, penetrating a quarter inch and releasing 50,000 volts of energy at 7 watts. The jolt shot through his system like lightning, causing the terrorist to scream and fall to his right, his head smashing against one of the instrument panels and his fully automatic AKM spinning in the air and crashing onto the deck. As he bled from his nose, his colleagues attacked the captain with their fists and rifles, smashing his teeth and destroying his right knee.

Then two of them dragged him to the ship's PA station, sat him in the leather chair, and showed him the typed-out statement, which he seemed too stunned to read. One of the men pushed it into his bloody face.

"You read! Read now! Tell all passengers to stay in cabins."

"I can't fucking *see* it without my glasses!"

"You read, or I shoot you in the head."

While this was taking place, Petras hurried to the cockpit and pushed a large red button that sent an electric signal to slow the liner. Then he turned a dial that lowered the speed from eight and a half to six knots. Because the ship was moving relatively slowly through the gentle Aegean Sea, only two of its five generators were engaged, each producing 20,000 pounds of horsepower.

Next he flipped a series of switches that shut off the ship's fire, man overboard, abandon ship, and security alarms.

Petras knew that the ship's planned destination for 0730 that morning was Mykonos, Greece. On one of the full-color computer screens in front of him, he saw that they were currently ten nautical miles off the coast of the island of Samos, famed since the time of the Peloponnesian War between Sparta and Athens for its muscat grapes.

Before he disabled the ship's cell-phone repeater, he called a man on a launch waiting near the coast.

"Sinbad, this is Stavros."

"Yes."

"We won the tournament. The trophy is all ours."

This was only partially true, because when the master mariner in the engine room tried to communicate with the bridge to ask why they were changing speeds and why he couldn't activate any of the primary and secondary communication systems, he alerted the engineers on duty. Following security procedures, the nine men locked themselves in a secure room from which they immediately issued VHF voice, and DSC and Inmarsat distress signals. The DSC (digital selective calling) signal was programmed with the ship's MMSI (Maritime Mobile Service Identity) and GPS coordinates.

Within seconds both DSC and Inmarsat distress signals coded 39 (maritime emergency) were received by the Turkish Coast Guard Command (Sahil Güvenlik Komutanlığı) in Kuşadası, which alerted its two patrol boats on duty in the Aegean. Crews on the coast guard patrol boats scrambled. Courses were reprogrammed and throttles pulled back.

The closest Turkish patrol boat was within five and three-quarter miles of the liner when a forty-foot launch pulled alongside the *Disney Magic*. Terrorists inside the ship swung open the starboard cargo door and used pulleys to load the launch's cargo of sarin canisters and additional weapons onboard. They worked quickly and expertly, as though they had rehearsed this procedure many times.

Petras, on the deck of the *Magic*, whistled to indicate that the cargo was safely aboard. Then he helped lower a set of aluminum stairs so that Mrs. Girard could climb down into the launch. Jeans, a T-shirt, and sneakers had replaced her gown and heels.

As she prepared to climb over the railing and leave the ship, she turned to Petras and said, "As soon as we reach land we'll issue the proclamation."

"Good work."

"You, too. For Syria," she shouted above the launch's engine.

"For Syria. *Allahu akbar!*"

Crocker and company were speeding up the six-lane O-21, halfway to Ankara, when the light on the sat-phone lit up. Mancini was at the wheel, with Akil asleep beside him. Janice snored gently from the back row. Davis, on the middle bench next to Crocker, answered.

He recognized Anders speaking urgently on the other end. "Davis? Where are you?"

"Sir, we just turned onto the Tarsus–Ankara freeway."

"Put Crocker on the line. I need to talk to him immediately. It's important."

"Yes, sir."

He nudged the team leader's shoulder, but the half-conscious Crocker didn't respond. Stan Getz's version of "Corcovado" lilted through his earbuds, luring him toward a dreamland of tropical foliage and turquoise seas. Ahead he glimpsed a barefoot young woman in a red sarong.

"Boss."

Crocker partially opened his left eye and waved Davis away. "I'm trying to get some rest."

"It's Anders. He says it's important."

She was brown-skinned and stunning. He didn't want to let go of the dream. "Tell him we'll be there after sunup. We'll drive straight to the embassy."

"He needs to talk to you now," said Davis.

"Why?" he asked, coming out of his fog and wondering what the deputy director of operations wanted. He took the receiver from Davis. "Sir?"

"Crocker, where are you?"

"We're driving. Maybe...another three hundred miles from Ankara. Should be there by around 0700."

All he saw out the window was a flat dark landscape—no structures, no signs.

Anders said, "Text me your GPS coordinates immediately."

"Why do you need our exact location? What's up?"

"The next field or rest stop you come to, pull over and text me your coordinates. A TAF helicopter is on its way. I'll be on it. When you see it, flash your emergency lights and prepare to board."

"Yes, sir. What's going on?"

"You'll soon find out."

The line went dead. As his mind revved up to process the conversation, Crocker handed the receiver back to Davis.

"What's the story?"

"I think they located the sarin," Crocker said.

Scott Russert was on his knees, tying his son's sneakers and hoping to beat the early line for breakfast at the Lumiere's dining area on Deck 3 when he heard three loud, sharp blasts over the ship's alarm system. His entire body tensed and his blood pressure shot up.

"What's that?" his wife asked as she emerged from the bathroom, drying her hair with a towel.

He was about to reach for the brown binder on the desk that outlined all the ship's signals and emergency codes when Captain Hutley's voice came over the PA system. He sounded tense and unsteady. "Ladies and gentlemen, we're currently experiencing a security situation that requires all passengers and nonessential crew to remain in their cabins until further notice. Anyone out on the decks, in the hallways, dining rooms, or other public areas, will be subject to grave danger."

He repeated the message, then signed off.

In the pregnant silence that followed, Scott's wife stared at him from across the cabin, her cheeks turning deep pink and her hands trembling. "Does that mean what I think it means, Scotty?"

"No, darling. Don't go there."

"Is something wrong, Daddy?" son Randy asked, picking up on his parents' sudden anxiety.

"Does that mean we can't go to breakfast now?" asked Russell.

Scott, who had trained himself to focus on practical solutions to immediate problems, started to calculate what they had in the room to feed the boys and keep them occupied until the "security situation" was resolved: a box of animal crackers, several fresh oranges, water, coffee, tea, a flat-screen TV and DVR loaded with dozens of Disney movies and TV specials.

He didn't notice his wife and two sons surrounding him until he felt Karen's fingers digging into his arm.

"Oh, Scott!" Her whole body was shaking.

"Daddy."

"Yes."

They held on to him as though he were their strength and only possible salvation from whatever danger lurked outside.

"Daddy, can we still get pancakes?"

"Does that mean the ship's going to crash?"

"The ship's okay, boys," Scott said. "We're fine."

Someone cried out something from a room down the hall. As he listened for sounds of violence, he felt the ship slowly turning to starboard, and assumed they were returning to Turkey. Scott considered it a good sign. They'd re-dock at Kuşadası, officials would address the problem, and they'd soon be under way again.

He thought of their home back in Putney as the alarm blasted again and Captain Hutley repeated his message for the third time. After the message finished, Scott listened carefully for any sound from the cabin next door. It remained quiet.

In some deep chamber of his mind he started to put two and two together. He looked at Karen, who was wiping tears from her eyes before mouthing "Pirates?"

He shook his head, reached out, wrapped his arms around his wife and sons, and squeezed all of them together. "No, love. Don't think like that. We're headed back to Turkey. We're together. We're a family. The intrepid Russerts. We'll be fine."

"Will we, Dad?" Randy pleaded.

"Yes. I promise."

The SEALs parked the Suburban in the empty parking lot of what appeared to be an abandoned factory just off the O-21 and waited for the French-made, twin-engine AS532 Cougar helicopter to circle and land. Red lights washed over the surrounding buildings and freeway, and then the landing light came on and turned the asphalt bright white.

Crocker felt adrenaline coursing through his veins as he climbed onboard and strapped himself into a seat between a security man in civilian clothes clutching an M5 and a grim-faced Grissom. The helo lifted off and banked to the right. Anders reached over the seat behind him and handed Crocker a single piece of paper.

As he read the hijackers' statement in the dim overhead light, his blood started to heat up. Terrorists had seized control of the *Disney Magic*. They were threatening to release sarin and kill all the passengers unless the U.S. president publicly pledged to withdraw all American troops from the Middle East immediately and deposit two billion dollars in various Cypriote and Dubai bank accounts. The terms had to be accepted within twenty-four hours. The document had been issued at 0700 hours on the eighteenth of June and was signed "The Fox—ISIS."

Unacceptable. Not fucking happening.

Crocker turned to Anders and shouted over the engine noise, "How many passengers?"

"Some 2,687. Another 857 crew members."

Jesus.

"How many hijackers?"

"Unclear."

"Who's the Fox?"

"Don't know. But analysts at HQ are narrowing the list of candidates."

"Where's the ship now?"

"It's been turned around and is heading east."

"It's clear the terrorists are in charge?"

"Yes."

"And the sarin is aboard?"

"We believe so, yes."

CHAPTER NINETEEN

Chaos is a friend of mine.

—Bob Dylan

CHAOS REIGNED at MiT headquarters near the port of Kuşadası—Anders, Grissom, Janice, Crocker, Colonel Oz, the commander of the local Turkish coast guard station Captain Shamaz and two of his officers all crowded into one stifling command center, staring at radar screens and satellite images on computers while talking into cell phones in English and Turkish. Anxiety radiated from all of them.

It was a terrible atmosphere for clear analytical thinking.

Crocker's head pounded from the confusion and the heat. Events were unfolding so rapidly. Rumors, shards of information, and possible opportunities ricocheted through the room like stray rounds.

A group of Turks perused passenger lists faxed from Disney headquarters in Florida, looking for the names of known Islamic terrorists.

Unlikely they're using their real names. He understood the need in crises like this to want to do something, but he also knew the danger of wasting precious time.

As Crocker was downing a bottle of water, he was summoned into a corner where Anders, Janice, and Grissom were all huddled as if for a two-minute drill.

"Here's the latest from HQ," Anders announced, sweat beading on his brow and upper lip, his voice breaking up. "The *Disney Magic* is moving at eighteen knots, three-quarters speed, east southeast. According to the latest computer models, it's headed back into the Mediterranean in the direction of Cyprus, and beyond that possibly the Syrian coast."

"Why is that important?" Grissom grumbled, his jaw tensed, his blue eyes narrowed into slits.

"For various reasons," Janice interjected, her white blouse wet with perspiration, strands of hair plastered to her forehead and neck.

"Let me finish," said Anders, raising his voice. He cleared his throat and spoke with confidence this time. "The president's in the White House situation room with his national security advisors—DCI, NSC, Defense, Homeland Security."

Grissom cut him off again. "We know the players."

"They've decided it's impossible to concede in any way to the terrorists' demands. Any sort of statement from the president or attempt at negotiation is off the table."

Grissom: "I'm not surprised."

Janice: "Me either."

"So the question is: Are the terrorists willing and able to carry out their threat and kill all crew and passengers?" Anders continued.

"I believe so," Grissom groaned.

"The conclusion arrived at by the president and his top advisors is yes."

Janice nodded. "Totally agree. We have to operate on that assumption."

"I agree. But are we sure they have the sarin?"

Janice added, "They said so in their statement."

"That doesn't prove anything."

"I know, but…"

"No one else has located it," Grissom continued as if he were the one in charge. "We have to assume it's somewhere and it was taken for a purpose. I think we can conclude the purpose is goddamn clear now. Agree?"

Anders nodded. "We have to assume the terrorists have the sarin onboard, and if not, some other means of destroying the ship."

Crocker stood quietly and listened as his mind raced ahead, riffling through the hundreds of ship takedown exercises he'd participated in and the half-dozen actual ones he'd pulled off.

Anders looked at his watch, which read 7:14 p.m. "That gives us approximately eleven and a half hours to organize, plan, and launch some kind of rescue—which appears to be the only option we have left."

Janice nodded. "Agreed."

All the real ops Crocker had done involved freighters or oil tankers. None were on passenger liners with so many lives at stake.

"If we can pull off a rescue attempt in this small window of time, the question then is, Do they really have the ability to deploy the sarin?" asked Anders.

Grissom thrust out his chin and answered, "All they have to do is hook it up to the ship's ventilation system. Take 'em five minutes if they know what they're doing."

"How long will it take to deploy?"

"Seconds, probably," Janice observed.

"Damn right," Grissom said. "We have to assume seconds. If they have it attached to some kind of mobile digital device, all they have to do is push a button."

"So how do we get our operatives onboard without losing the element of surprise?" asked Anders.

"Good question."

"Real good question."

All eyes turned to Crocker.

"What do you think?" Anders asked. "You think you and your men can fast-rope onto the deck from helicopters?"

Crocker shook his head. "Not without being seen and heard. Not happening."

Janice agreed. "You're the expert."

Anders scratched the side of his face. "There's another problem. According to BBC Weather, if the *Disney Magic* continues on its route southeast, it's going to run into a major storm that's sweeping out of the Caucasus."

"When?" Crocker asked, glancing again at his watch.

Anders answered, "Sometime before midnight."

"How long is it likely to last?"

"It's a big storm. Projected to continue into the morning."

Grissom slapped his hand against the wall and said, "That's terrible news."

Anders nodded. "Yeah. Makes this real problematic."

"Kind of rules out using helicopters, don't you think?" asked Janice, looking at Crocker.

Grissom: "Or any other kind of rescue."

"How about we block the ship somehow? Trap it, so it can't go anywhere," Janice suggested.

"Then the jihadists kill everyone aboard," countered Grissom.

Anders turned to Crocker and almost pleaded, "What do you think? There must be something…"

Crocker remained calm. His mind quickly sorted through possible scenarios, none of which so far seemed appropriate. "I think that my men and I are going to have to board that ship before the deadline, but fast-roping onto the deck is not an option."

Grissom: "Then what the hell is?"

"First I'm going to need a detailed plan of the ship. Then I'm going to need to talk to an engineer from Disney who knows how the vessel's ventilation system operates and where the terrorists are most likely to have hooked up the sarin."

Anders turned to Janice and said, "Call HQ and tell them to get us an expert from Disney. Get him or her up on Skype. Now!"

She hurried off as Crocker continued thinking out loud. "This person…this engineer needs to tell us the best way to quickly shut down the system in a way that can't be overridden."

"Check." Anders wrote furiously on a yellow legal pad.

"We're going to need to move lightning fast. The terrorists release the sarin or detonate any sort of bomb and the mission goes completely south."

"Understood. We'll get that for you. But you haven't answered the important question."

Grissom: "Yeah, Crocker, how the hell are you going to get on the ship?"

"The only way we can in this situation."

"What's that?"

"From cigarette boats dropped in the water."

"You're kidding, right?" asked Grissom.

"No. We've done it before."

"Where?" Grissom asked, hands on his hips, chest jutting out aggressively. "And where the hell are we going to find cigarette boats?"

Crocker turned to Anders and asked, "Any aircraft carriers in the vicinity with SEAL rescue teams attached?"

"I'll find out."

"I'm going to need six more SEALs. Guys who are experienced jumpers and swimmers, and have practiced underways."

"Underways?" Anders asked.

"That's what we call them. You'd better write all this down."

Anders did, quickly. "Go ahead. What else?"

"We're gonna need at least three cigarette boats on wooden pallets equipped with Vetus HD silencers. Three experienced steer-and-throttle men. Three telescopic poles equipped with cave-in ladders. And two planes—one to drop the boats and another that we can parachute from into the water."

"Seas might be extremely rough."

"We should expect to lose some men, but we'll manage," continued Crocker. "We'll also need to get to the carrier or base that we're going to deploy from. Once at the exfil point, I'll need to huddle with the other six SEALs. All of us are going to need the complete package of weapons and gear—NVGs, comms, explosives, tear-gas grenades, percussion grenades, smoke grenades, et cetera, all waterproofed or in waterproof weapons bags."

"Check."

Grissom's demeanor brightened. He said, "I'll call the Station and have them put us in direct contact with Special Operations Command in Tampa."

"Good," answered Anders. "Focus first on the carrier with the appropriate resources—SEALs, cigarette boats, pallets, jump platforms."

"Will do."

As Grissom strode outside with his cell phone, Janice hurried back with news that HQ had already located an engineer who had worked on the design of the *Disney Magic* and knew the vessel inside and out.

"Excellent," Anders said. "When can he talk?"

"He's standing by now, ready to Skype."

Anders looked at Crocker. "Chief Warrant, you're driving this mission. What do you want to do first?"

Crocker considered quickly, then answered, "Ask Oz for a private room with a computer, then summon the rest of my men. I want them to hear this."

"Okay. Will do."

Scott Russert looked at the glowing green LED number on the nightstand, which read 9:53 p.m. He and his family had watched the movies *Aladdin, The Lion King, Beauty and the Beast,* and *Sleeping Beauty,* played four games of Parcheesi, eaten most of the fruit, candy, and animal crackers, and consumed all the bottled water. They were exhausted and ravenous as a result of the relentless anxiety.

They had heard nothing further—no messages or announcements—since the warning from Captain Hutley that morning. Neither Scott's nor Karen's cell phone could pick up a signal, and the TV transmitter on the flat-screen wasn't working.

The stateroom where they had laughed, played, planned activities, and sung silly songs together had become a prison cell. All he could tell from looking out the portholes, which were located about five feet above water level on the port side, was that the ship had turned around and was moving rapidly.

Karen lay on the bed suffering from heart palpitations and their sons were antsy and hungry. When he tried calling room service on the blue courtesy phone by the bed, no one answered.

"I'm hungry, Daddy," Randy said. He was the more inquisitive and vocal of their two sons. "Can we try to see if Lumiere's is open?"

"It isn't, son."

"How do you know?"

"Because the captain said all the dining rooms are closed."

"But how can we know for sure, if we don't try?"

"You have to trust me, son. The captain made an announcement."

"Did he say when the dining rooms will open?"

"No."

"Are we just going to sit here and starve?"

"Of course not. Don't talk like that. I'll set up the Wii for you and your brother."

"What about the pizzeria? It's not a dining room. We can have pizza, right Russell?"

Russell chimed in, "Yeah, let's get pizza and Cokes!"

"The pizzeria is closed, too," Scott answered.

"How do you know?"

"Listen, boys. The captain told us to stay in our rooms. We have to do as he says."

Randy thought for a minute and said, "I want to get off this ship."

"We'll do that, son, as soon as we can."

Scott flicked on the flat-screen again, activated Wii tennis, and handed the wands to the boys, who were soon slapping the virtual ball back and forth. Then he sat beside Karen, who looked hot and uncomfortable.

He wanted to help his family get through this and back to their lives in Putney. He wasn't a churchgoing man, but found himself praying. Reciting a Hail Mary in his head, he retreated to the bathroom to get a wet towel for Karen. When he shut off the water, he heard muffled voices in the hallway.

Dear God! What now?

A door shut and a few seconds later he heard a knocking sound and more voices. They were moving closer.

This could go very badly.

Looking at himself in the mirror, he whispered, "Scott, you can do this. Think of your family. Stay calm."

Three knocks sounded on their metal door, sending a jolt of panic down his spine. He waved the boys farther into the room, took three deep breaths, and answered.

Standing on the other side of the door were two crew members in white tunics beside two metal carts piled high with sandwiches and bottles of water. One of them had a large bruise on his face and swollen skin around his right eye. The other had spots of blood on his tunic and a cut across his lip. Standing behind them were two bearded men wearing black masks and holding automatic weapons.

The ferocity in their eyes unnerved him to the point that he wanted to scream or run. He fought to keep it together.

"Sir, sorry for the inconvenience," said the porter with the swollen eye. "We have a limited number of cheese sandwiches and bottles of water. How many are there in your cabin?"

"F-f-four," Scott stammered, holding onto the doorframe for support.

One of the porters handed him four sandwiches wrapped in plastic. The other placed four 16-ounce bottles of Evian on the floor just inside the room.

They had moved fast and were ready to leave.

Scott's legs shook as he blurted out, "My wife isn't feeling well. She suffers from high blood pressure."

The porter with the swollen eye said, "I'm sorry to hear that, sir. Does she have her medicine with her?"

"Uh, well…no. She ran out."

One of the armed men leaned forward and grunted something into the ear of the steward, something Scott couldn't make out.

The steward said, "Tell your wife to drink lots of water and try to rest. We'll see what we can do."

He swallowed the last word: "Okay."

Janice, bleary-eyed, sat before a computer next to Colonel Oz, looking through passport and customs surveillance photos of passengers that had been collected by Interpol from immigration services in Spain, Italy, Malta, Greece, and Turkey. To Janice it seemed like a useless exercise. She had petitioned to go with Anders, Davis, Akil, Mancini, and Crocker when they left forty minutes earlier to fly to the aircraft carrier USS *Dwight D. Eisenhower*, currently positioned southwest of the island of Cyprus. It only added to her discomfort that Oz puffed on one Camel cigarette after another and occasionally glanced down the front of her blouse. With each cigarette he lit, he apologized and said, "For my nerves. I'm sorry."

As much as she wanted to dislike him, she couldn't. He was stressed out, too. None of them had ever faced a crisis of this magnitude.

Smoking, fidgeting, then biting his lip, he announced, "That's all of them. That's all the pictures."

She nodded.

Interpol had told them it wasn't a complete set.

Oz dropped the butt to the floor and lit up another. "We take a few minutes, then try again?"

"Okay."

She stood, stretched her back, and used her cell to check her encrypted e-mail account. Having entered the passwords, she waited for the special program to translate the e-mails into readable English. Her mailbox was almost full, with a hundred new messages sent in the ten minutes since the last time she had checked. She quickly scrolled through subject lines like "Ship course and location," "Estimated fuel consumption," "Estimated number of terrorists required," and "Ports of call and number of passengers onboarding at each."

Janice opened and scanned through a handful. More conjecture about the identity of the Fox and several possible candidates. Consensus seemed to be building around Mohammad Farhad al-Kazaz, the ISIS leader Crocker had met in Syria. He fit all the primary criteria—a known and active ISIS jihadist, considered highly intelligent, with a fervent following and global ambitions.

Colonel Oz had his elbows propped on the desk and his head buried in his hands. "Anything I should know?"

"Just more ideas about the identity of the Fox."

He looked as if he was about to cry. "It's got to be al-Kazaz."

"Why?"

"Because…" His voice trailed off.

She quickly ran through everything she knew about the ISIS leader—born in Syria, fought alongside bin Laden in Tora Bora, around forty years old, had built a base of followers in southwestern Iraq, had become a major player in northern Syria.

"You know what he looks like?" she asked, pocketing her phone and returning to the chair beside Oz.

"Of course."

"Then let's look through the photos again."

He nodded and chicken-pecked the keys to set the sequence in motion.

She had already decided that if the crisis ended in tragedy, she would resign from the Agency and use the hardship money she had saved to start an organic farm in eastern Virginia. Settle down, maybe marry and adopt two needy children.

The photos flew by. The faces all started to look the same. Noses, eyes, mouths, all randomly placed, overlapping one another. She was reminded of some strange iteration of Mr. Potato Head, a toy she had loved as a child.

The sequence arrived at a set of stills taken from a surveillance camera above the customs desk in Kuşadası. In it appeared a tall, fit, good-looking man in a black suit with an attractive woman. She thought the man resembled a model she had seen in a magazine ad for men's suits. The woman also seemed familiar. The sequence moved automatically to the next set.

"Wait," Janice said. "Go back."

She studied the woman's face and tried to place her.

"Can you zoom in closer?"

He did. There was something distinctive about her, the curl of her top lip, the narrowing of her nose at the tip. She tried to imagine her with her hair pulled up. And then it hit her.

"She's Mr. Talab's assistant! I met her with him four days ago at the Sultanhan Hotel in Istanbul."

"This woman?" Oz asked, pointing a thick finger at the screen. "You know this woman? Are you sure about that?"

She looked again. She was certain. "Yes."

"Do you know her last name or relationship to Mr. Talab?"

"She was introduced to us as Mr. Talab's assistant. I believe he called her Fatima. I don't remember her last name."

"She's on the ship?"

"Apparently."

."If it's really her, this might be something."

Mentally, she started to assemble the pieces. Mr. Talab had led them to the sarin and to Hassan, both of whom went missing. His assistant had boarded the ship in Turkey hours before it was hijacked.

It had to be more than a series of coincidences. This seemed like evidence that pointed to people and motives behind the attack. The first person she wanted to tell was Anders, who had been at the meeting in Istanbul. Maybe he would remember Fatima's last name and her connection to Talab.

Anders answered from the command center of the *USS Dwight D. Eisenhower*, in the Mediterranean between the coasts of Cyprus and Turkey. The ship was a nuclear-powered Nimitz-class carrier first launched in 1975, and had since played an important role in numerous military deployments in the Middle East, including the 1990 Gulf War. She was a massive 1,115 feet long, armed with sophisticated radars and electronic jamming systems, Seasparrow antiaircraft and antimissile missiles, RIM-116 Rolling Airframe missiles, and ninety fixed-wing aircraft and helicopters.

"Janice, we're extremely pressed for time here," Anders answered. "What do you have to report?" He was sitting at a conference room table between Crocker and the ship's electronic warfare officer, who had just reported that the AN/SLQ-32 (V)4 electronic warfare system had successfully deployed focused radio waves and laser light to disable the *Disney Magic*'s electronics. It was also collecting incoming and outgoing radio signals and carefully tracking the ship's movement, speed, and fuel consumption.

Janice informed him that Mr. Talab's assistant, Fatima, had boarded the ship at Kuşadası, Turkey, only hours before it was hijacked.

"Who?"

"Mr. Talab's assistant, the woman he brought with him to the meeting at the Sultanhan Hotel."

"Interesting," Anders said, not sure what to make of the information or how it related to the rescue mission that he and the others in the room were a hundred percent focused on. "Report this to Grissom in Ankara. Tell him I suggested that he track down Talab. Let's find out exactly what this means before we jump to any conclusions."

"Okay."

"What about Hassan? Has he been located? Any evidence that he's on the *Magic*, too?"

"As far as I know, he's still unaccounted for. We continue to pore through customs records and passenger lists. At this point our information is incomplete, but Interpol is updating it constantly."

"Good."

The lights in the conference room dimmed and grainy real-time aerial footage of the *Disney Magic* shot from a high-altitude surveillance drone appeared on a screen.

"I've got to go, Janice. But excellent work. Call Grissom. Keep up your pursuit. It's an interesting lead, no question."

"I will, sir."

"Thanks."

The circular room was crowded with Mighty Ike officers who were coming and going, whispering in Admiral Marcelus's ear and leaving reports. The captain sat at the middle of the table in a high-backed executive chair, rubbing his chin and studying the various data—including wind speed and direction measured at various altitudes, the course and speed of the *Disney Magic*, radar readings, and incoming weather patterns—projected on various screens on the walls.

It was a whole lot for Crocker to digest.

One of the *Eisenhower*'s executive officers reported that they had located two cigarette boats in the ship's hold that were currently being loaded onto wooden pallets. Six additional SEALs from Team Ten had been flown in from a base in Crete where they had been practicing amphibious landings with members of British SBS and the Greek First Raider Paratrooper Brigade.

Neither of the cigarette boats was equipped with a Vetus HD silencer. The bigger problem was the turbulent wind conditions. Current readings near the *Magic* showed gusts of up to forty knots (forty-six miles an hour) at three thousand feet, which made any kind of canopy parachute jump impossible. Enhanced satellite weather prediction data indicated the windy and stormy conditions would abate beginning at around 0700—the same time as the terrorists' deadline.

At 0002 hours, time was running out.

In spite of the extremely dangerous conditions, Crocker called Captain Sutter in Virginia Beach to request permission to launch.

Sutter said, "I admire your courage, Crocker, but I can't make that decision."

"Who can?"

"Admiral Evan Thompson of U.S. Special Operations Command in conjunction with the president."

"Put me in touch with him," demanded Crocker.

"I just got off the phone with the admiral, and his answer was a big no. Given current conditions, he doubts that the cigarette boats will ever make it to the ship. His engineers tell him they'll break up as soon as they hit the water."

"Then we'll deploy directly from the *Eisenhower*."

"The cig boats will never make it."

"It's worth a try," Crocker argued. "We're looking at the real possibility of three or four thousand casualties."

"We all realize that," Sutter answered.

"Then what's the alternative?"

"The Turkish president has initiated secret discussions with the terrorists in hopes of talking them down to some kind of reasonable settlement."

"How's that going?"

"Badly."

"That means you've got to let us deploy."

"I can't. The president will never allow it. And Admiral Marcelus won't let you leave his ship."

Crocker hung up, seething with so much frustration he couldn't stand still. He got up, paced behind the table, then told Anders he was heading to the men's room to splash water on his face.

He needed something—a ray of hope, a possibility. In the narrow passageways lined with photos of the ship's officers, he saw Mancini standing with one of the ship operations men, a tall red-bearded fellow in a khaki uniform. They were going over a list of equipment on a clipboard. Weapons, NVGs, comms.

Mancini saw the intensity in Crocker's eyes and asked, "What's wrong? You look like you're about to explode."

"The op's on hold. Looks like a no-go."

"The weather?"

"Yeah, weather sucks big time."

"I was afraid of that."

"Admiral Thompson from SOCOM has decided it's too dangerous to deploy from the air. We can't swim because of the conditions, and we can't get close enough without being detected."

"Mules, man. What do we do?"

"Nothing. Wait. Hope for conditions to improve. But that seems unlikely to happen before the deadline."

"Condition FUBAR." (Fucked up beyond all recognition.)

"You got any crazy ideas?"

Mancini was always good at thinking outside the box. He pulled at his beard, rubbed his huge biceps, then nodded. "Yeah, I might."

Crocker nodded at him. "What?"

"The SEALION II."

"What the fuck's that?"

"It's the high-speed experimental insertion craft developed by NAVSEA Future Concepts."

Crocker remembered seeing one at the Naval Amphibious Base in Virginia. "You mean that long, weird, alligator-looking thing?"

"Yeah, looks like an old Confederate torpedo boat, only a whole lot faster and sleeker."

"Does it work?"

"I hear the fancy electronics suite it carries is filled with kinks, but it's fast as hell, with low visibility and an almost-zero radar profile. I rode in one once. Cool beans. The advantages it has over cigarette boats include superior ballast, strength, and stealth, including much lower noise production."

Leave it to Manny to know the latest shit. But the odds of one being on the *Eisenhower* were about the same as finding a snowball in the Amazon jungle.

"Is the one in Virginia the only one in existence?" Crocker asked, bracing himself for disappointment.

"I think NAVSEA has built four or five. I'll check."

"You find one for us and I'll put you on my Christmas card list."

*　　　*　　　*

At 0035 Crocker was on the phone with Captain Sutter again, informing him that Mancini had located a SEALION II at the U.S. Naval Command Center in Naples, Italy—where it was being tested in ocean conditions—and requesting permission to cram it into a C-130T Hercules and transport it to the *Eisenhower*.

"God bless, Mancini," Sutter responded. "But how long is it going to take to get there?"

"Approximately three and a half hours flying at max speed, which is why they need to leave now," answered Crocker.

"Who's they?"

"The boat, the chief special boat operator, and pilot."

Sutter didn't need more than several seconds to think about it before he answered, "Permission granted."

"A heartfelt thanks, sir."

"That doesn't mean you've got a go to launch. That's the sole prerogative of the White House, but let's see if the SEALION makes it there in time first."

"Sound thinking."

Crocker immediately called Naples and relayed the approval from Sutter, then sat down with Admiral Marcelus and Anders and told them about the plan. They were as excited as he was, but remained leery about the weather.

The SEALION II, like other low-displacement-hull crafts (including cigarette boats) had the capability to navigate the ocean but was designed for littoral (or coastal) waters. High, turbulent seas posed a real danger of capsizing.

Crocker, who was willing to take that risk, next huddled with his men—Mancini, Akil, and Davis, and the six SEALs from Team Ten. The incoming SEALs introduced themselves as Storm (sniper), Revis (logistics), Diego (chief climber), Nash (breacher and explosives), JD (comms), and Duke (weapons). Crocker briefed them on the pending arrival of the SEALION II, the dangerous weather conditions, and the mission to take down the terrorists on the *Disney Magic*. All nine men expressed their readiness and eagerness to go.

Next they moved to a conference room where they studied plans of the cruise ship and consulted with the Disney engineer via Skype. Given the large number of video surveillance cameras on the ship, the distance from the Security Command Center to the bridge, and the very small margin of time they had to work with, it was a mission that required precise planning and perfect execution.

Surprise and speed had to be impeccable.

For the next two hours they developed an elaborate PLO (patrol leader's order), raised questions, voiced concerns and criticisms, then amended the PLO and started again. They tried to cover every possible contingency—lack of interior lighting, booby traps, use of chemical agents, what to do if the terrorists started shooting hostages, how to deal with passengers, and so forth. They talked about the dangers posed by rounds ricocheting off metal walls, pressure waves traveling through narrow hallways as the result of an explosion, and the ways they could expect sound to travel in different compartments of the ship.

Thoroughly briefed and mentally exhausted, they took a break at 0256 to dry-check their weapons and organize first-, second-, and third-line gear. Crocker left Mancini to supervise, and went to the ship's command center, where he learned that the C-130T with the SEALION aboard was scheduled to land in an hour.

Even if they were able to unload the SEALION, fill it with fuel, deploy it in the water, and load on their gear in thirty minutes, they'd be real close to sunrise, which was scheduled to begin at 0548. He learned that Captain Sutter had briefed the White House via encrypted conference software about the nature of the mission, but it still hadn't been officially approved.

The other problem was the distance between the *Eisenhower* and the *Disney Magic*, currently twenty-five nautical miles—as was the case for all other combat ships, per Naval Command orders. At that distance and at the SEALION II's max speed of twenty-five knots, it would take the SEALs approximately an hour to reach the cruise ship.

Crocker explained the situation to Anders and Admiral Marcelus, who called the Naval Command Center in Norfolk and requested permission to move within ten miles of the *Disney Magic*. After strenuous arguments back and forth, permission was granted.

The mission still had a chance.

CHAPTER TWENTY

It is a sin to believe evil of others, but it is seldom a mistake.
—H. L. Mencken

THE DIGITAL display on the console on the bridge of the *Disney Magic* read 0355, and Stavros Petras and his fellow terrorists were getting anxious. The man who had recruited them and planned this mission (code name the Fox) had told them that the United States would quickly accede to their demands and the terrorists would go down in the history of the Middle East as heroes. But with the deadline only three hours away, they were completely cut off from communications from the outside and with each other in different areas of the ship, and had no idea what was happening.

Petras blamed this on the *Magic*'s officers and crew. He was convinced that one of them had flipped a switch or disabled a computer that had shut down all telecommunications, short-wave and medium-wave communications systems, the air conditioning, some lights, and even interfered with their radios. He didn't understand that the real cause of the blackout was a massive bombardment of electromagnetic energy from flux compression generators and other sophisticated electronics on the *Eisenhower* and other U.S. ships as well as malware dispatched by computer experts back at NSA headquarters in Maryland. Petras understood little about electromagnetic pulses and radar jamming. All he knew was that they were literally operating in the dark and on their own. Even though the ship's engines were still working intermittently, he was enraged. So he decided to take matters into his own hands.

Standing on the bridge with three other heavily armed terrorists, he informed the ship's officers that he and his men were going to execute one crew member or passenger every twenty minutes until the lights, computers, radio communications, and air conditioning were fully restored.

"But you don't understand," argued the first engineer, a mustached Bangladeshi named Amitava Sanguri. "We are as powerless as you are in this situation. If I could restore these things, I would. I promise."

"Two minutes until we shoot the first man," Petras announced, pointing at his watch.

"The interference is coming from outside," Amitava continued. "If you want me to, I can explain the electronics."

"Too late," Petras said, grabbing him by the collar.

He turned to one of the other terrorists and said in Arabic, "Two of you take him down to the pool and shoot him in the head. Leave his body in the pool as an example. He'll be the first."

The terrorists led First Engineer Sanguri out, while one of the chief officers protested, "Don't do this. We want to cooperate! The blackout has nothing to do with us!"

Petras pointed at him and screamed, "Shut up! You'll be next!"

*   *   *

Scott Russert was lying awake in bed, clutching his sleeping wife to his chest, when he heard what sounded like automatic weapons fire from one of the decks above, followed by shouts of *Allahu akbar.*

The killing has started, he said to himself. He had expected it. Somehow he knew that more terror was coming.

"God, help us," he prayed out loud. "Deliver us from this, somehow. Me, my wife, our sons, the passengers and crew. God be merciful, please!"

Crocker and the other SEALs watched from inside the flight deck island control tower as the C-130T Hercules approached the *Eisenhower.* With wind speed at forty knots, the captain had increased the speed of the ship by ten knots to reduce yaw motion. He also changed course so the plane could land with the wind on its nose, thus helping it stop.

The ship's deck crew had laid a line of orange phosphorescent tape down the middle of the flight deck to help the pilot of the C-130T avoid hitting the island with his wings. Still, as the turbo-powered plane drew closer, Crocker wasn't sure it would clear the island.

Turning to a lieutenant who was filming the Hercules with a digital video camera, he asked, "C-130s have landed on this deck before, correct?"

"Not on this deck, no, never," the lieutenant answered, "but they've landed on other aircraft decks a handful of times. Kind of problematic, because unlike, say, an F-16, they don't have a hook that can deploy and catch the cable."

"Then how will it stop?"

The lieutenant shrugged and continued filming. The pilot of the C-130T was trying to level the plane in the robust wind, but was experiencing problems. The big aircraft tilted up and down and veered into the path of the island as it approached.

Crew members on deck dashed for cover. Others used flashlights to direct the pilot to climb, circle, and try another approach. But the C-130T kept bearing down.

Crocker held his breath as the pilot leveled the wings at the last second and the big plane touched down, immediately reversed engines, braked, and stopped to loud cheers and applause from the crew on the bridge and the deck.

"Fucking incredible," the lieutenant shouted. Following him out onto the flight deck, Crocker observed that the aircraft's wings had cleared the island by only three feet.

When he got a chance to introduce himself and congratulate the pilot, the Navy Reservist told him he'd been flying C-130s since Vietnam but had never done a landing this dangerous before. Crocker also shook hands with the two Special Warfare Combatant-Craft Crewmen (SWCCs) who had accompanied the SEALION II from Italy. They were the waterborne equivalent of the 160th SOAR helicopter force, with whom he'd often flown.

"Glad you could make it. How was the flight?" Crocker asked one of the SWCCs, as the aircraft's engines powered down.

"I thought we were on a carnival ride. That old dude has got some stones." He was a stocky man with a big nose and a ruddy complexion, and he wore a Special Boat Team 20 (SB20) insignia on the chest pocket of his black flight suit. "Surface Warfare Officer Dan Cowens."

"Welcome, Dan. Chief Warrant Crocker. We better get the SEALION fueled up and in the water. Time is short."

"Let's get to it. Follow me."

Crocker had worked with SB20 before, everywhere from the jungles of Colombia to the coastal waters of Somalia, and knew them to be tough, smart men. Reaching the back of the C-130, he saw the bow of the SEALION II protruding from the door like a spear.

"The craft is so long, we had to improvise and make some modifications," Cowens explained.

"To the SEALION?" Crocker asked, hoping they wouldn't need time to reassemble it.

"No, to the C-130. Had to kick out the cockpit panel and door."

When the rear gate was raised, Crocker saw that the SEALION was an elongated, covered-canoe-type vessel, painted gray. Looked like something borrowed from the set of a sci-fi movie.

The deck crew carefully lifted it out, then wrapped its hull in a MEATS insertion delivery system, which consisted of very strong nylon cables configured as a giant sling. Then a CH-53 Sea Stallion helicopter with the MEATS attached lifted the SEALION off the deck and set it in the water. After crew support technicians and SWCCs had fueled the boat and set the ballast, Crocker and his men started loading in their gear. With everyone's expert cooperation, the entire process took less than fifteen minutes. Now the mission was ready to launch.

Captain Marcelus, his officers, and the crew assembled on the *Eisenhower*'s deck to see them off with three rounds of hoo-ahs and raised thumbs. The copilot checked that the SEALs were buckled in, then the craft's two MTU diesel engines fired up, providing 1,136 shaft horsepower to each of the two Rolls-Royce Kamewa waterjets, and they were off, ripping through the seas at twenty-five-plus knots.

Immediately tension started to build and stomachs did loop-the-loops. The copilot produced a yellow plastic bucket, which quickly saw use. Crocker managed to hold his dinner down by visualizing the mission, step by step. Several times he and the others were tossed violently left or right and the vessel seemed about to capsize, but somehow it righted itself and continued to pull them closer.

Usually during infils, guys relieved stress by taking the piss out of one another. But this time all the operators remained quiet, occupied with their own thoughts. Some listened to music through earbuds; others prayed silently. Crocker focused on his breathing, trying to keep the breaths soft and of equal length—in and out, in and out—in an effort to keep the fear away. Still, errant anxieties drifted into his head: The terrorists would be expecting them. They'd find themselves in a death trap. They would cause the terrorists to release the sarin, resulting in the deaths of everyone on board.

"Six miles to target," SWO Cowens announced. "We've established visuals."

Crocker turned and squinted through the side slit window located just inches above the waterline, but couldn't see anything through the mist and splash.

The ST-10 SEALs on the opposite bench measured every minute, with fear and determination in their eyes. Each man wore a black skin suit with hood, operator gloves, a nylon holster with a SIG Sauer P226, quad-tube NVGs, earbuds and bone phones, and carried either an HK416 or a German-made M7 chambered with 4.6x30mm rounds with their greater ability to penetrate body armor. Most of the men had M203 grenade launchers fixed to the rails; Mancini chose to carry his favorite single-shot, break-action M79. Attached to their black web belts were SOG knives, grenades, pouches with extra ammo, Tuff-Ties, Motorola Saber portable radios, medical supplies, and other gear.

Though they looked like ninjas with their black suits and body armor, what Crocker saw weren't cold-blooded killers but dedicated operators with families, who loved their country. Difficult, high-risk ops like this were what they'd been selected and trained for. If they succeeded and came back alive, they'd be talking about this mission for the rest of their lives.

Scott Russert lay in bed looking at his sleeping sons and wife, thinking that he was responsible for putting them in harm's way and wondering how he could get them off the ship. In the hot, airless room his mind raced through numerous scenarios—including sneaking them onto the main deck and commandeering a lifeboat—and each time ran into the same dead ends, as though trapped in his own mental maze.

The waiting and uncertainty were excruciating. He tried to find something positive to think about, but kept drifting back to the image of the two armed men with black masks standing in the hallway. And every twenty minutes, the blasts of gunfire from the deck above and shouts of *Allahu akbar* sunk his spirits further.

He sensed death creeping closer, and longed for the tranquility of Putney—the Thames River path, the rowing clubs, the cafés, the botanical gardens that were home to kingfishers, bitterns, and swans.

Scott imagined he heard the echo of footsteps from the hallway. Then they became real. They approached. A moment of silence passed before a knock on the door caused his heart to leap into his throat.

Scott carefully lifted Karen's head off his chest, and crossed the cabin on bare feet, clad only in boxers and a T-shirt. He almost fainted at the sight of the three armed, masked men standing in the doorway. Before he could think of anything to say or do, they were dragging him down the hall past images of Daffy Duck and Minnie Mouse that now seemed like gargoyles. He sensed that his life was soon about to end, and he tried to slow down time.

Even the fresh air on Deck 9 seemed indifferent. Half stumbling, half dragged by two of the armed men, he saw the Goofy-themed pool ahead. Yesterday he had been splashing in it with his sons and other happy kids and parents. Now it seemed dull and quiet with only one of the underwater lights on, and the water appeared red. He wondered why—until he saw the floating bodies. Then something in his head shut off and he lost consciousness.

Crocker stood on the bow of the SEALION II holding the long pole aloft and trying to hook onto the rail of the main deck of the *Disney Magic*. A difficult task in any circumstances, it was made more challenging by the rolling, bobbing vessel. The muscles in his arms and shoulders quaking, he focused intently and managed to steady the hook enough to rest it on the rail and pull down, releasing a small caving ladder that unrolled thirty feet to where he stood.

As the lead climber he went up first, two rungs at a time, like a mountain lion. In addition to the other first-line equipment secured to his web belt, he carried a carabiner with four one-inch tubular nylon runners. Reaching the deck, he knelt, did a quick 360 through his NVGs, saw that the coast was clear, secured the ladder to the rail with the carabiner, slung the nylon runners over it, and attached a safety line from the runners to the ladder.

Done!

Now he signaled the rest of the team to board the ship. They hurried up, grenades and anything that could rattle taped to their combat vests. The ten SEALs broke into three groups designated Alpha, Beta, and Delta. Delta, led by Mancini and including Revis, JD, and Diego, headed directly for the Variable Air Volume (VAV) system on Lower Deck D, near the ship's engine. Beta, consisting of Duke and Nash, with Davis in charge, had been tasked with securing the engine room and helping Team Delta clear the lower decks. Crocker directed Team Alpha, which included Akil and Storm, directly to the ship's bridge.

Precisely as planned.

The element of surprise uncompromised, Team Alpha hurried up the metal stairway two steps at a time, Crocker in the lead, finger resting on the safety guard of his suppressed HK416, heart pounding. The electromagnetic energy directed toward the ship interfered with their comms, too, so they were using hand signals—left fist pumped up and down for "hurry," hand around the left eye for "sniper," and so on.

They were halfway to Deck 10 when Crocker felt a hand on his shoulder. He turned back to Akil, who flashed three quick signals in succession—"hostage" (left hand under chin), "enemy" (slapping the right wrist), and "direction" (pointing behind him).

Where?

Mid-deck below, near the pool, he saw three armed terrorists in black, with black beards, dragging a hostage. It was unclear whether the captive was alive or dead until one of the terrorists slapped him hard and the man moaned and waved his hand as though he were drunk, or coming out of a stupor.

Crocker placed his palm on his head, indicating that he wanted the other two SEALs to cover him, then sprung.

Scott was disoriented, but still alive. His head felt swollen and hot, and every muscle in his body was seized with terror. He knew what was about to happen as the terrorists positioned him against the Goofy fountain and stepped back.

What have I done to you? he wanted to ask them, but there was no point now. Instead, he said out loud, "Please, God, watch over my wife and sons." He closed his eyes as the terrorists lifted their AK-47s and waited for the bullets to enter his head and body, hoping it would end quickly and he wouldn't feel much pain.

His body flinched as he heard the shots, which sounded more like spitting than pops. Curiously, he didn't feel anything pierce his skin. Even so, his knees gave way and he started to sink.

Halfway to the deck he was stopped by strong hands that pulled him close and covered his mouth. He heard a voice whisper in English, "Sir, are you a passenger?"

Scott nodded and looked up. He wasn't sure whether he was seeing a demon or a rescuer. It was a heavily armed man all in black, peering at him through elaborate goggles. No eyes, no smile, a serious expression.

"I'm an American," the man whispered. "We're liberating the ship. Hide in there." He pointed toward the shadow behind the Goofy fountain. "Don't move or make a sound until we come back."

It all happened in the blink of an eye. When the man turned and left, Scott saw the three terrorists' legs bent and torsos twisted, bleeding out on the deck. He reached down and pulled a weapon out of one of the dead men's hands. Holding it, he was about to fire it into the inert body when he remembered his rescuer's words and stopped.

His whole frame shaking with relief and fury, he knelt behind the fountain, took a deep breath, and said to himself, *I'm still alive.*

The air hung thick and still in Lower Deck D, because the ventilation system wasn't working. Condensation clung to the metal surfaces and walls. Wondering what had happened to the crew, Mancini carefully led the way into the ship's dark bowels, past the massive electric turbines, when he saw a dim light from a metal catwalk above and to his left, and held up his fist: "Freeze!" The three SEALs responded, lifted their weapons to their shoulders, and knelt. Everything was in shades of green—walls, turbines, electric switches, catwalk, even the dim light. He signaled to Revis and Diego to climb up and determine what it was, while he and JD waited. The two SEALs hurried up the slick metal ladder as Mancini glanced at the laminated chart in his hands, trying to determine the direction to the HVAC (heating, ventilation, and air-conditioning) system, which appeared to be farther aft, past the sixth turbine and on a platform of its own.

He was squirming on his belly to massive Turbine No. 3 when he heard the echoes of suppressed fire—subtle, yet unmistakable. Two quick bursts, three, four, five, then silence. Then the loud sound of metal pounding metal that echoed through the cavernous space, then more silence. Then a loud explosion, then more suppressed fire and silence again.

"What the hell was that?" JD whispered.

Mancini shook his head and whispered into his head mic, "Delta 3, Delta 4, report."

No answer.

"Delta 3, Delta 4, do you read me? Over."

Nothing.

"Delta 3, Delta 4?"

Praying that the comms weren't working, he made a quick calculation. Since the HVAC wasn't functioning, the danger of released sarin quickly spreading throughout the ship had lessened considerably. He handed JD the laminated chart and indicated that he should continue searching for the HVAC while he went back to check on Revis and Diego. JD nodded.

Mancini grabbed hold of the wet metal rail and hoisted his big body up two rungs at a time like an ape. Reaching the catwalk, he hurried along it in a crouch, and stopped when he heard something splatter. A warm, wet liquid hit his neck.

Blood!

Above him he saw an arm and leg hanging over the partial deck, then heard a squeak behind him. Turning, he saw a terrorist aiming an AK at him and pulling the trigger. He hit the metal grid, felt bullets ricocheting around him. Two rounds hit the ceramic discs of the Dragon Skin that covered his back under his black nylon suit.

He flipped over, located the man through his NVGs, and squeezed off a round from his suppressed and specially modified M7A1, hitting him in the face and hands.

The terrorist tried to hang on to the ladder and pull himself up, but Mancini fired a quick round that caused him to twist, fall, and hit the lower deck.

Mancini wiped the terrorist's blood off the goggle lenses with the sleeve of his suit, took two quick breaths to clear his nostrils, and squinted into the vast space behind him and to his right and left. Then, facing the way the young SEALs had gone, he saw the flash of an IR strobe, invisible to the naked eye but easy to make out through NVGs. He signaled back with his.

Revis emerged from the darkness like a black ghost and whispered, "We took out two enemies. You okay?"

"Yeah. Where's Diego?"

"The terrorists were guarding a mechanical room. We took them out and found about a dozen crew members inside."

"Diego's with them now?"

"Affirmative."

"Show me. Maybe one of the crew can lead us to the HVAC."

"We spoke to the chief engineer. He knows where they set up the sarin but says that's not the only problem."

"What is?"

"They've set explosives throughout the ship."

Davis and Team Beta encountered that problem as soon as they entered the interior of Deck 4 and had to climb past a pile of propane tanks. Connected to them were strips of plastic explosive wired to a detonator and a digital timer. The massive explosion and fire they would cause if detonated would block access to the Deck 4 lifeboats. All passengers and crew on Deck 4 and below would be trapped and likely die of smoke inhalation if the sarin didn't get them first.

Fortunately, he had Nash with him, who was the breacher and explosives expert with ST-10. Davis held a red MagLite cell flashlight as Nash removed his NVGs and carefully disabled the detonators and timer. Then they moved down the hallway to the Security Office, pushed open the unlocked door, and dispatched the three terrorists dozing in the dark in front of a bank of blank surveillance monitors.

As one enemy fell to the floor, Davis noticed that the beard he was wearing was ripped partially from his face.

"What the fuck is this?" he asked out loud.

He knew that the plan called for his team to join Delta and clear the lower decks, but there were likely more propane tanks connected to other timing devices on the upper ones that Crocker and Team Alpha might have missed as they hurried to the bridge. So Davis decided to change the plan and clear Decks 5 through 11, first.

It proved to be a critical decision.

Crocker was the first man on Team Alpha to enter the hallway that led to the bridge. Approaching the secure door, he saw a dark trail on the carpeted floor and more dark smudges on the walls. He touched a smear with his operator gloves and held it up to his nose. It was blood.

He tried to push in the door with his shoulder, but it was either locked or bolted shut. A breaching charge would eliminate the element of surprise and give the terrorists time to hit the button that could release the sarin.

He checked his watch as he considered alternatives: 0538, ten minutes before sunrise.

He leaned close to Akil and whispered. "Attach some det cord to the frame and doorknob. Don't set it off until you hear me and Storm come busting through the forward windows."

"Copy."

"Wait for us. You should hear us and their response."

"Fuck, yeah."

He directed Storm, a tall former Sooners tight end, to follow him up to the comms deck. There, with the wind whipping their faces and the sun starting to spread a dim ribbon of light across the horizon, he used his SOG knife to cut through the twelve-foot length of nylon rope he wore attached to his belt, handed half to Storm, and asked in a whisper, "You ever rappel down a building?"

"I've rappelled down a mountain, sir."

"Good. Follow me."

He saw that two panes of glass on the port side forward had already been blasted out. On the safety rail above them he secured both lines with the double figure-eight fisherman's knot he'd learned while scaling Devil's Rock in northern Ontario, then pointed to Storm and down to the bridge.

Storm nodded back.

Weapons resting on their right hips pointed forward, left hands grasping the line, they hopped the rail and started down with their boots against the metal face. Crocker pushed out, eased his grip on the rope so he could lower four more feet, and swung forward through the broken window boots first. As he did, a shard of glass in the frame ripped through his nylon suit and cut into his leg along the outside of his calf. He ignored the pain and flash of heat spreading through his body as in a split second he located targets and a place to land.

Through the NVGs he spotted a man gaffer-taped to a chair and a stunned-looking terrorist standing behind him. He directed fire from his 416 into the terrorist's chest, hit the floor, skidded, landed on his butt, and spun up.

The nerves in his right leg screamed. He ignored them. Located another enemy to his right and directed a burst of fire into his groin. The man screamed and fell back, and almost simultaneously the secure door blasted into the cabin, filling the space with smoke and sucking out the oxygen.

In the midst of hellish confusion and screams in Arabic and English, he gasped for air and looked for targets, who were now harder to distinguish from the crew members because of the smoke, not yet aware that the blast had ripped the 416 out of his hands, and only partially aware of Storm grappling with someone to his left.

Instinctively he reached for his SIG Sauer pistol as Akil charged in, shoved aside a terrorist standing in his way, and in one fluid movement shot him in the face. As the terrorist fell onto Crocker, Crocker saw another, taller one turn to his left, reach for something in his vest pocket, and run in the direction of the captain's quarters. Crocker intuited what he was about to do. Without wanting to expend the half second it would take to find his weapon, he propelled himself up and lunged onto the man's back.

Stavros Petras crashed chest first into an upholstered chair and flipped over with Crocker still holding on to his neck. The fall resulted in Crocker landing on his back on the floor, with Petras's full weight smashing into him, and forcing the air out of Crocker's lungs. He felt a rib snap and saw spinning stars but he refused to let go, putting Petras in a headlock and squeezing with all his strength.

He reached for his SOG knife with his left hand, aware that the terrorist was desperately clawing for something at the front of his shirt. Crocker didn't have another hand with which to stop him. He found his knife, raised it, and thrust it into the back of the terrorist's neck, hoping to sever his spine.

Petras's whole body jerked three times and froze, and an instant later an explosion from Deck 11 threw both men into the air.

CHAPTER TWENTY-ONE

The deed is everything; the glory is naught.
—Johann Wolfgang von Goethe

AS SOON as the waiting firefighting and chemical weapons teams from the *USS Dwight D. Eisenhower* saw the explosion, they sped toward the *Disney Magic*.

Davis and his men had been defusing the explosives on Deck 10 when the propane tanks on Deck 11 went off. Luckily for most passengers and crew, charges on the other decks had already been disabled, and Mancini and Team Delta had unhooked the eight sarin canisters from the ship's inoperative HVAC system. Also fortunate was the fact that there were no passenger cabins on Deck 11, nor were any crew or passengers present in the Deck 11 teen Vibe Club when the explosion went off. The handful of crew huddling in the Wide World of Sports Bar and Palo restaurant escaped with minor burns and bruises.

Firefighters from the *Eisenhower* found Crocker, Akil, and Storm using the ship's fire extinguishers to battle the flames on Deck 11. All three men were only half conscious, bleeding from various cuts and bruises and suffering from smoke inhalation. They had to be over-powered and dragged away.

Crocker came to five minutes later, lying on a deck chair on Deck 4. He squinted up at the man sitting beside him and saw the sun rising over the man's right shoulder. When he sat up abruptly to see whether the ship's superstructure was still intact and the fire was out, all appeared normal except for wisps of light-gray smoke from the upper deck. A sharp pain in his lower chest reminded him of the terrorist landing on him, which had probably resulted in a cracked rib. The suit on his right leg was stuck to his skin and caked with blood.

"Who are you?" Crocker asked, wincing.

"Scott Russert, from Putney, England," answered the man with red hair.

"What are you doing here, Scott?"

"You saved my life, and I don't even know your name."

"Crocker. You here alone?" He saw groups of passengers being escorted down to a lower deck.

"Traveling with my family."

"They're safe, I hope."

"Already been rescued. Waiting for me on one of the patrol boats."

"Shouldn't you be with them?"

"I wanted to thank you first."

"For what?"

"For saving my life when I was about to be shot and tossed in the pool."

Crocker remembered the event; it seemed to have happened a month ago. "Hey," Crocker said. "Glad I could be of service."

Scott's smile revealed a wide space between his front teeth. "You're one of those bloody but unbowed blokes, aren't you?"

"Something like that. But I can't answer that definitively until I've checked on my men."

Of the ten SEALs who had taken down the ship, Crocker had arguably suffered the most damage. Davis and the Team Beta guys on Deck 10 were treated for cuts and bruises, minor burns, and smoke inhalation. Akil had lost a tooth when he crashed through the bridge door. Storm had dislocated a vertebra in his lower back.

The medical staff on the *Eisenhower* stitched together the skin on Crocker's calf and taped his ribs. He still wasn't sure exactly what had gone down on the *Magic* and didn't know the identities of the terrorists who had seized the ship. Figured he'd be briefed on all that when he got back to HQ in Virginia.

Most of the SEALs flew to Naples Naval Station in Italy and from there home to Virginia Beach. Crocker and Mancini detoured to Germany to check on Suarez. Both men needed time to process the psychological whirlwind they'd been through. In Crocker's case, he wanted to get his head right before he returned home and faced Holly. There was always a huge emotional letdown after a mission of this magnitude, and he wanted to be ready.

At the Landstuhl Regional Medical Center, near Ramstein, they were escorted by a male orderly who explained that during a typical day the military hospital served 1,178 meals, administered 1,598 doses of medication, handled 2.3 births, and accommodated twenty-three new patients and nine new acute emergencies. The number of incoming acute cases was more than many civilian hospitals admitted in the space of two months.

"What's the pace like currently?" Crocker asked.

"With combat winding down in Iraq and Afghanistan, it's about a fourth of that," the orderly answered.

"Good."

In the ICU on the third floor they found Suarez flirting with a cute blond nurse with a cross tattooed above her right breast. He was covered with thick white bandages from his neck to his waist.

"Glad to see you with a smile on your face again," Crocker said.

"They're taking good care of me."

"I can see that."

"Heard you guys kicked ass without me," Suarez said.

"We missed you," Crocker said. "Everything happened so fast. It's still a blur."

"He didn't do shit, like usual," Mancini joked.

"Yeah, right. While this guy was jerking off in the engine room, I was killing terrorists."

"Man, I wish I was there," said Suarez.

"Hey," Crocker said, "I meant to ask you, you remember anything from the night you were shot?"

Suarez's expression turned serious. "Not much. I was standing near the cab of the van, talking to Hassan."

"Hassan?"

"Yeah, Hassan."

"What was he saying?"

"Some stuff about his girlfriend. I don't remember anything after that."

"He disappeared with the sarin," Crocker said. "Nobody's seen him since."

"I heard. Yeah. Strange dude."

"Real odd."

* * *

They were resting in their room in the hospital's visitor center, getting ready to go into town for dinner, when the phone rang. It was Jim Anders.

"Crocker, you alone?" Anders asked.

"No. Mancini's with me. Why?"

"How do you guys feel about detouring to Paris?" Anders asked.

"For what purpose?" If this was for a confab of some sort, he'd pass.

"I'll explain when you get here. It's pretty basic. Won't take more than a day or two."

"It's ops-related, right?" asked Crocker.

"Yes. You'll understand why I called you specifically when you get here."

"Okay." It would give him more time to prepare to face Holly.

"I'll have a Gulfstream waiting for you at the airport in an hour," said Anders. "Once you land in Paris, take a cab directly to the InterContinental, on the Right Bank near the Opera House."

"We have time to grab dinner before we leave?"

"As long as you get here before midnight. You'll be traveling undercover, so use your alias passports."

"Got it."

Four hours later he and Mancini were zipping down the Beaux Arts–era boulevards of Paris with the taxi's windows open, both lost in thought. They registered at the InterContinental under their aliases and met Anders in his suite on the ninth floor.

"Glad you're here," he said, ushering them in. Janice was there, too, looking sharp in a dark-blue blouse, along with two officers whom Anders introduced as FBI Special Agents Leslie Farrell and John Wilkens from Overseas Operations.

Anders was all business, showing them to seats around a coffee table in the living room. "We're here to wrap this up," he said, sleeves rolled up.

"What, exactly?" Crocker asked, helping himself to one of the bottles of Perrier on a table in the corner.

"The operation that began in Istanbul," Anders answered.

"I thought that was over."

"Remember Mr. Talab?"

"Sure. I thought he was still in Syria."

"Farrell and Wilkens have been searching for him. And guess where they found him."

"Here?" Mancini asked.

"Good guess," Wilkens said, handing Crocker a black-and-white surveillance photo taken through the back window of a passing Mercedes. "We took these as he was coming out of the Syrian embassy." It showed someone who looked like Talab seated in back, with a short beard and wearing sunglasses.

"You sure this is Talab?" Crocker asked.

Wilkens handed him a stack of eight more surveillance photos of the same man standing and talking to several men and getting into the car. It was Talab.

The gears in Crocker's head started grinding, trying to figure out what was going on. "Why are we going after Talab?" he asked. "I thought he was our friend."

"We thought so, too," Janice said. "But it turns out he's the guy who set the whole thing in motion."

Crocker had been suspicious of the Syrian from the start. "Wait. He's been acting as a kind of double agent?"

"More than that," Janice muttered.

Anders leaned forward and said, "We now believe Talab has been working for President Assad of Syria all along, first as a double agent, fingering people like Jared, and then as the mastermind of the entire sarin-slash-hijacking operation."

Crocker remembered the light resistance they had encountered while stealing the sarin from the Syrian base, and how it had surprised him.

"It's extremely devious, really," Anders continued. "They led us to the sarin, then made it appear that it had been stolen by ISIS terrorists who then went on to hijack the cruise ship. Their larger objective was to alert the United States and the rest of the world to the worldwide threat posed by ISIS—which was easy to do, given recent events in Iraq and Syria—and to shift U.S. and Western sympathies back to President Assad as a more reasonable alternative."

Made sense, in a diabolical way.

"I never liked Talab," Mancini offered.

"You think the Syrians are that clever?" Crocker asked.

"The Assads aren't dummies, which is why they've survived so long."

"So Hassan was involved, too, working for Talab and the Assad regime the whole time?" Crocker asked.

"We believe so, yes."

It felt like a punch to the gut. He'd rescued that little bastard off the street in front of the schoolhouse in Idlib and helped deliver his son. Never for a second had he suspected that Hassan was an agent for Assad.

"You find Hassan?" Crocker asked.

"No. But we will."

"Make sure you do."

They'd been double-crossed to such an extent and had expended so much effort that Anders's cool-headedness bothered him. *Hadn't*

Anders been so sure that Talab was a friend? Wasn't the Agency's trust in him the basis of everything we had to endure inside Syria, and on the Disney Magic?

He wanted to kick the table in front of him, but he held back. Everyone made mistakes. They misread people and situations, and as a result put others in danger. There was no point pointing fingers or complaining now. It was time to put this hydra-headed monster to bed and move on.

Leaning forward, he asked, "Tell me, what do you want us to do?"

At 0812 the next morning Crocker was sitting behind the wheel of a red-white-and-blue American Airlines van parked in front of the Hotel de Suede on Paris's Left Bank, not far from the Les Invalides and beyond that, the Eiffel Tower. Under the blue American Airlines overalls he wore an armored vest, the straps of which were cutting into the skin under his arms.

He and the CIA Ground Branch and former British SAS operative named Sully were acting as though they were there to ferry a flight crew to de Gaulle Airport. They were really waiting for a signal from FBI agents Farrell and Wilkens, who were standing in the alcove of a photographer's studio across the street from the Syrian Embassy at 20 rue Vaneau. A delivery truck with Mancini at the wheel idled in an alley off the cité Vaneau, and a third vehicle waited beyond the embassy on the one-way rue Vaneau.

It was a simple snatch-and-grab. Crocker had executed dozens of them in much more dangerous locales than Paris. Farrell, Wilkens, and their team had been watching Talab for days, tracking his movements, monitoring his security, and establishing the patterns and routes he followed.

As Crocker scanned the street through the windshield, Sully

leaned in the passenger window and said, "The doorman with the stick up his arse is complaining. He wants the room numbers of the crew we're picking up."

"Tell him you don't know room numbers. Give him some names instead. Stonewall the bastard. Buy us another ten minutes."

"I'll do my best."

Crocker and Black Cell had worked with Ground Branch often, but never with Sully, who was new to the unit. He glanced at his watch: 0815. The target was late. Looking right, he heard Sully joking in French with the uniformed head doorman.

The voice of Special Agent Wilkens blasted through his earbuds. "All units, stand by to move. The side gate is opening."

He turned the knob on the Motorola in his pocket that controlled the volume. Two seconds later Wilkens continued: "Observe a black Mercedes 450 limo emerging. Stand by thirty seconds."

Crocker honked twice. Hearing the go signal, Sully slid in.

"Stand by ten seconds while we ID the target," said Wilkens through the earbuds.

"What's going on?" asked Sully.

"Close the door," Crocker ordered.

"All units, target IDed. Go!" Wilkens shouted.

Crocker pulled the black one-hole face mask over his head and hit the gas. A small Fiat sedan was up ahead, between him and the Mercedes limo, but he managed to weave around it. A white sedan beyond the limo did a sharp U-turn, stopped, and blocked the street. A second later a truck sped out of an alley and T-boned the Mercedes.

Bam! Metal into metal, glass flying, sparks. Game on.

In his ear he heard Wilkens screaming, "Teams two and three engage! Go! Go! Go!" The guy sounded like he was losing it.

Crocker screeched to a stop right behind the Mercedes, grabbed the suppressed M7A1 off the floor, and jumped out. A second delivery truck spun out of the alley and blocked the gate to the Syrian embassy so no follow-up vehicle could exit.

Mancini was already out on the street, using a metal bar to smash the window beside the driver. The terrified man came out with his hands on his head. Simultaneously another man exited the passenger door with a Glock in his hand and started shooting wildly. Sully cut him down with a suppressed blast to the chest.

Mancini leaned over the front seat and faced a terrified-looking Talab in back just as Crocker opened the back door and saw the Syrian reaching for something in his briefcase. He held the M7A1 to Talab's temple and shouted, "Stop!"

The Syrian froze. Crocker pulled him out and saw another man crouched on the floor, trying to be invisible. He was a big man with a tattoo of a spider on his neck. When Crocker straightened him up against the side of the Mercedes, he recognized him as the man he had grappled with in the van back in Istanbul.

"Hey, fuckface, remember me?" he asked. Unable to contain his anger, Crocker reared his head back and butted him hard in the face. The big man wobbled and caught himself on the car, blood streaming from his nose down his chin.

Sully pulled Crocker back.

"What was that about?" Sully asked.

"He killed a buddy of mine."

"In that case, you want another go at him?"

"No, that's good. Let's split."

They dragged both men to the back of the van. Once inside they Tuff-Tied their wrists and ankles together and slapped gaffer's tape over their mouths. Ninety-five seconds after the op had started,

Crocker gunned the van around the Mercedes and headed for the Orly military air base on the outskirts of Paris.

Later that night, after a celebratory dinner at the famous La Coupole in Montparnasse, Crocker, Anders, Janice, and Mancini returned to the InterContinental to pack their bags and check out before their midnight flight to Dulles. As they entered the lobby Anders informed Crocker that Talab and the three men with him had been ferried by military helo to the *USS Abraham Lincoln*, stationed in the South Atlantic, where they would be interrogated outside the legal jurisdiction of any country.

"I'd love to hear what you get out of him."

"I'll make sure you do," said Anders.

Maybe he would, maybe he wouldn't. It didn't really matter. Crocker decided that as soon as he got upstairs he was going to call Holly and tell her that he was sure they could get through this rough patch together if they both tried a little harder, which he was one hundred percent willing to do.

As they passed the newsstand in the lobby, Mancini pointed out headlines in French, Spanish, English, and Italian that announced the daring rescue of the *Disney Magic* by "NATO commandos." The attackers, according to the headlines, were "Islamic terrorists."

Curious, thought Crocker. *I wonder if their real affiliation will ever be revealed?*

This wasn't the first example of government misinformation he'd witnessed. Most of the ops he and Black Cell participated in were kept secret and never reached the public.

"You want one as a souvenir?" Mancini asked.

"Not really. Thanks."

He stopped and glanced at his watch, wondering if there was still time to shop for a graduation present for Jenny. Typically, he experienced physical and emotional letdowns after a difficult mission, and he was starting to feel his brain and body relax.

Civilian life was more challenging. He'd keep that in mind and try to be more attentive to Holly when he got home.

He saw Anders, Janice, and Mancini wave from an open elevator. They all looked happy. Charlie Parker's mournful, beautifully shaded version of "Everything Happens to Me" played over the hotel PA system. He waved back as if to say *Don't wait for me*. As the elevator doors closed two women wearing black headscarves ducked in at the last second. There was something vaguely familiar about the way one of them moved. It alarmed him enough that he headed for the stairs to hurry up to the fourth floor, where he and Mancini were rooming.

On his way up, he remembered that his three colleagues were unarmed. So was he, except for the five-inch koppo martial stick Mohammad al-Kazaz had given him. He'd taken it to dinner to show to his friends, and it was now in his right rear pocket.

Crocker pushed through the stairwell door at four, dashed to the elevator, and reached it just as the doors were closing.

"Manny, wait!"

Maybe he was overreacting. Still, he stuck his leg out and squeezed in, bumping into something on the floor. Someone had disabled the lights so it was almost completely dark inside, and he couldn't distinguish anything at first.

He made out the outline of a body at his feet, then heard people grappling in the far right corner. Reaching for the koppo stick in his pocket, he looped his middle and ring fingers through the paracord and stepped forward, slipping on a metal object on the floor and falling against someone's back. It was a big man. Mancini, he thought as he crashed into one of the covered women. Except it wasn't a woman, which Crocker discovered shortly after the person elbowed him in the gut. The pain he felt woke him up completely and unleashed an almost primordial rage that caused him to drive the point of the koppo into his attacker's throat.

When the attacker gasped and raised his hands to his neck, Crocker saw Hassan's beardless face.

"You again," he grunted. Using the high-low principle from hand-to-hand combat, Crocker slammed a knee hard into Hassan's groin, then grabbed his face with his left hand and smashed it, one, two, three times, hard, into the back of the elevator until Hassan lost consciousness. He would have kicked him a couple of times, too, if he wasn't still in danger.

Before he could even take a breath he heard a metal clicking sound to his left. Turning, he saw that a second attacker—who really did appear to be a woman—had just loaded a mag into her pistol. He immediately recognized the eyes and mouth as she pointed it at his chest.

"Fatima."

"Yes, Wallace."

"This my reward?"

She hissed a kind of sneer and squeezed the trigger as Crocker turned sharply right, ducked, and, holding the koppo in a forward saber grip, drove it into her solar plexus. The shots went off so close to his face that they burned the skin on his cheek and numbed his eardrums. He kept charging into her knees until they gave way and she screamed. Grabbing the wrist with the pistol, he slammed it against the side of the elevator twice until it clanked to the floor.

Screaming and flailing like an injured animal, Fatima reached up and raked her long nails across his cheek. She was trying to find his eyes, breathing furiously and struggling with all her might. But he had trapped her in the corner from behind.

For a second he thought of detaining her. Then, remembering the extent of her betrayal and his colleagues on the elevator floor, he took her head in both hands, pulled up, and twisted hard to the right so that her spinal column snapped and she went limp.

"Peace be with you."

Somehow the three Americans in the elevator managed to survive. Crocker didn't know how, because they had all suffered gunshot wounds. The French EMS team had acted quickly and expertly, for which he was enormously grateful, and his colleagues were out of danger.

He left Paris clinging to that knowledge, like a kid holding on to a favorite toy, and proud of the fact that they had completed the mission without losing anyone. He'd learn the details later. Now all he wanted was to get home to Holly and Jenny, decompress, and rest.

Since he'd flown civilian, he landed at Norfolk International Airport at around 1850 local time. He was so tired he couldn't remember which airport the team had left from or where he had parked his truck, so he hired a cab to drive him to the Navy Gateway Inns and Suites, where he and his family were staying temporarily.

Jenny answered the door in shorts and a Virginia Tech T-shirt and immediately threw her arms around him. "Dad, you're home! Yay!"

"Sorry I missed your graduation. I'm so proud of you, sweetheart. How did it go?"

"It was fun. Grandpa came. We missed you."

"I'm sorry. I couldn't help it. I bought you something."

He entered the little red-tiled foyer and set down his bag as familiar smells surrounded him. Jenny followed, looking happy to see him yet somewhat wary, as if she knew to treat him carefully. "What happened to your face?" she asked.

He quickly manufactured a lie. "Oh, I fell off the hotel Stairmaster and scratched myself. Burned it a little, too."

"Gee, Dad."

He'd had the presence of mind to buy her something at the duty-free shop at Charles de Gaulle. He found it now in the side pocket of his bag and handed it to her—a stunning silver Michele Deco Day chronograph dial watch that had been recommended by the young woman at the shop and had set him back almost seven hundred dollars. The look of surprise and joy on her face made it worth the price.

"Wow, Dad. It's so beautiful. Thanks!"

She kissed him again and bounced around in a circle with her arms in the air and her new watch on her wrist. "I feel like a princess."

"It looks great on you. You here alone?"

He watched Jenny's mood change on a dime. She sighed loudly, and reached out and held his forearm. "Dad, Holly left yesterday," she said softly. "There's a note for you on the kitchen counter by the mail. I'm so sorry."

A wave of sadness almost knocked him off his feet. Leaning against the kitchen wall, he read:

"Dear Tom: I've moved in with my friend Lena. I'm sorry things didn't work out between us. I'll always love you, but I can't live with you anymore and be fulfilled and happy. I'll come over Saturday for the rest of my things. Love, Holly."

He felt something give way in his chest, followed by relief mixed with profound hurt and disappointment. He'd opened up his heart to her and loved her, but it wasn't enough.

Jenny squeezed his hand and said, "You're a good man, Dad, and I love you, if that's any comfort."

He put his arm around her shoulder, hugged her, and said, "Of course it is. I love you, too, with all my heart."

As tears gathered in his eyes, he knew that somehow he had to find the strength to soldier on. He didn't know how, but he would. It was what he did best, and what he would always be. A soldier, through and through.

ACKNOWLEDGMENTS

Don and Ralph would like to thank our agent, Heather Mitchell, and the talented professionals at Mulholland Books / Little, Brown who have made this book possible, including Wes Miller, Pamela Brown, Joshua Kendall, Ben Allen, Kapo Ng, Tracy Williams, Chris Jerome, and Morgan Moroney. They would also like to extend a special thanks to their loving and supportive families and friends.

ABOUT THE AUTHORS

DON MANN (CWO3, USN) has for the past thirty years been associated with the U.S. Navy SEALs as a platoon member, assault team member, boat crew leader, and advanced training officer, and more recently as program director preparing civilians to go to BUD/S (SEAL Training). Until 1998 he was on active duty with SEAL Team Six. Since then, he has deployed to the Middle East on numerous occasions in support of the war against terrorism. Many of today's active-duty SEALs on Team Six are the same guys he taught how to shoot, conduct ship and aircraft takedowns, and operate in urban, arctic, desert, river, and jungle warfare, as well as Close Quarters Battle and Military Operations in Urban Terrain. He has suffered two cases of high-altitude pulmonary edema, frostbite, a broken back, and multiple other broken bones in training or service. He has been captured twice during operations and lived to talk about it.

RALPH PEZZULLO is a *New York Times* bestselling author and an award-winning playwright and screenwriter. His books include *Jawbreaker* and *The Walk-In* (with CIA operative Gary Berntsen), *At the Fall of Somoza, Plunging into Haiti* (winner of the Douglas Dillon Award for Distinguished Writing on American Diplomacy), *Most Evil* (with Steve Hodel), *Eve Missing,* and *Blood of My Blood.* His nonfiction book about the shadowy world of private military contracting with former British Special Forces commando Simon Chase, *Zero Footprint,* will be published by Little, Brown next year.

If you have enjoyed *Hunt the Fox*, why not catch up on Thomas Crocker and SEAL Team Six's earlier adventures?

SEAL Team Six: Hunt the Wolf

When the team learn that young girls are going missing all over Europe, they are determined to track down the ruthless men behind the kidnappings. But as they follow the trail from Scandinavia to the Middle East, they find themselves facing a web of terrorist cells with more terrifying ambitions than they could have imagined.

SEAL Team Six: Hunt the Scorpion

A series of attacks all over the globe are linked by a single, deadly intent: someone is gathering everything they need to make a dirty bomb. The terrorists behind it are shadows; their targets unknown. Thomas Crocker and his team need answers. They need to go to the source: to find the material the terrorists are searching for, and stop it falling into the wrong hands.

SEAL Team Six: Hunt the Falcon

The team's number one enemy, Iranian terrorist Farhed Alizadeh, codename 'the Falcon', resurfaces as the mastermind behind a series of attacks on American diplomats across the globe. Crocker and his men are ordered to bring him to justice, and their hunt leads from Bangkok to Caracas, and finally to Iran itself, when the team go in 'full black' to take down their mark.

SEAL Team Six: Hunt the Jackal

When a Senator's wife and teenage daughter are kidnapped, Crocker and SEAL Team Six are sent to the cities of Mexico and the jungles of South America. With drugs, gangs, double-crosses, and plenty of bullets, *Hunt the Jackal* throws the team into a new environment and an unexplored corner of the world.

All available in print and e from Mulholland Books

MULHOLLAND
BOOKS
HODDER